Only One

Barbara Woster

ISBN-13: 978-1732843318
ISBN eBook: 9781732843394

DEDICATION

For my family, without whose love and support,
I could never have written this book. I love you all, very much.

Find more works by this author at www.LiteraryAdventures.net

Author Note: In this book, set in 1799/1800, I mention the practice of the mail-order bride. In truth, this practice started in the 18th Century primarily in the burgeoning western territories. While I always endeavor to incorporate authentic period lifestyles and behaviors, I may on occasion veer off and take liberties in order to construct a creative work of fiction.

PROLOGUE

"Are you going to take all day counting it?"

The man doing the counting stopped and aimed a disgruntled look at the man in the frock coat pacing in front of him animatedly. He didn't know the reaction his displeasure had, for the man hiring him kept the brim of his top hat pulled low over his brow, obscuring his features. A difficult feat for so narrow a hatband. It was a comical distraction watching the man attempt to pull his hat low without it toppling from atop his head, which did make his counting slower. If only this man realized his identity would be revealed momentarily—after he finished counting, that is—he would be less apt to struggle.

The hireling returned to his counting, pondering over this man and others like him—nameless, oftentimes faceless individuals who needed a disagreeable task tended to, but lacked the fortitude to see it done. That was the only difference between him and they—he had the fortitude. One less significant difference was his lack of concern about any of them identifying him, for he never pulled his hat down low, or tried to obscure his features in any way. They could easily describe him to the law if they bothered to look at him, which they never did, unless he made them, which he always did. Still, no one ever looked his way more than once, and never sufficiently to describe him as other than 'horrifying'.

Still, he often wondered whether that moment when they looked him full in the face would offer a satisfactory identification should someone deign to inform police of his illegal activities. Possibly. Would anyone dare turn him in? Never. After all, what would they say? He grinned at that potential conversation.

Constable, I hired a man with skin so scarred it's barely identifiable as a face. Truly horrifying.

What did you hire him for?

What?

You said you hired him...

No, he wasn't concerned in the least, but this man should be. He snapped at the man to allow him to finish his counting, deflecting onto him his own distractions which were the true cause for the time consumption. "Bother me no more, and I will finish sooner."

"Certainly," the procurer of the services replied, pulling his hat lower on his head. "It's just that the longer I stand here, the more likely it is that I'll be recognized."

The man scoffed, both at the arrogance of the man in assuming anyone even cared he was in this part of town; and that he accompanied the comment with another tug on his hat, pulling it so low that it nearly covered his eyes entirely, uncovering a majority of his sandy blonde hair. It was a wonder the man could see at all. His comment however, ceased his counting once more, exasperating him.

"If recognition is such an enormous concern, don't ever approach me during daylight hours. Now, from this second forward, remain silent and I will endeavor to finish in all haste." He bent back to his task. As he counted, his eyes bulged in pleasure, as it always did when he handled such large denominations.

"All here," he breathed. "Any particular day in mind, or would you like me to tend to it at my leisure?"

"Tonight."

"Can't," he said, feeling the money slipping from his grasp that swiftly. "I have a prior engagement that prevents my doing so. Tomorrow night too late, or do you need to take your money elsewhere?"

"Tomorrow night's fine," the man responded, and the hireling felt his feeling of euphoria return. "Just make certain that it looks like an accident."

"I always do."

"And I don't want anyone being able to trace the deaths back to me."

Ah, there it was. That one phrase always uttered, which he used to ensure no one ever told the constable about the disfigured face of a criminal, if any grew a twig of bravery to do so, "The only way that will happen is if I elect to tell someone, or if you do." And there was the look of alarm, which brought the man's face up, his top hat tumbling to the ground. Eyeball-to-eyeball they stood, for just long enough for each to memorize or recognize the other.

It was always the threatening words he spoke, which caused those that would hire him to reveal their identities. *Tell anyone who I am,* that one phrase promised, *and I will silence you as surely I do those men or women whom you hire me to silence.*

"I haven't any intention..."

"Nor do I. Your identity is known only to me," he whispered again, the threat clear. "Tomorrow night will see the deed done. Have a pleasant afternoon, Mr. Middleton. A pleasure doing business with you."

The hireling laughed as the man's eyes bulged at having his name trip off the tongue of an assassin. He reached down and snatched up his hat, jamming it low on his brow again, then turned and disappeared into the shadows, the sound of the scar-faced man's laughter ringing in his ears.

CHAPTER 1

Lara Esterhaus pricked her index finger with the darning needle again, and fought hard against slinging the material across the sitting room. Instead, she laid the aberrant work-in-progress across her lap and stuck the injured digit into her mouth, sucking on it gently.

Why she had to sit three evenings a week to practice a craft that was beyond her was…well, beyond her. She marveled at how she, a woman of intellect, was unable to master something as simple as applying stitches to a satiny fabric without coming close to removing the tip of her finger.

Still, this agreement with her mother was a long-standing one, dating back to when she was only thirteen years of age, and while she regretted ever making the bargain, she would not fail to uphold her end. One would think however, that after a six year battle with needle and thread, she'd have conquered at least a rudimentary ability; however, she had to admit, looking at the few stitches running along the seam that she had, in some small measure, succeeded. They did look sort of uniform, at least to her, even if her finger was full of holes. She pulled the finger from her mouth to examine it; wondering whether pink lemonade would spurt forth if she were to take a drink. Then she glanced down at the material on her lap, allowing her imagination to run free. *If*, she thought, *the lemonade did spurt from my fingers while I was working, it could very well ruin the fabric and bring my lessons for this evening to a halt.* She smiled at the thought, for she knew it was such a silly one. Besides, if she were to ruin the fabric—wittingly or unwittingly— her mother would simply buy her more material and make her start again. She knew she would, because it had happened before—too many times. Of course, not from lemonade spurting from her hole-ridden fingers.

She glanced out the window at the twinkling flame of the street lanterns, which Mr. Solow hadn't gotten around to extinguishing yet, and then at the grandfather clock sitting in the corner of the room. Eleven o'clock in the evening. Where were her parents? They had assured her that the assembly they were attending would only last a couple of hours and they would return forthwith. Thus, to her way of thinking, they should have been home hours ago, unless her father chose this evening for one of his romantic carriage rides, she surmised, grinning. The grin faded. She looked out the window again at the smattering of snow remaining on the ground and shivered. She couldn't feel the cold with the warming brick beneath her feet, but she could certainly sense it. Surely, her father wouldn't take a leisurely buggy ride on such a cold evening. She sighed. She needed to stop fretting over nothing, especially since spontaneity was one of her father's endearing traits.

She picked up the dress on her lap and braced herself for another round of battle, when a knock sounded at the front door, halting her in mid-stitch. She sighed aloud in relief. Whoever the late night visitor was, they had just saved her from adding more holes in her already pain-ridden fingertips.

She laid the gown aside and stood, waiting patiently for Joshua to announce the visitor. That was another thing that she'd promised her mother early on—that she'd at least attempt to behave as a civilized lady, and allow others to tend to their appointed duties. If she had her way, she'd simply answer the door herself, but her mother assured her that ladies simply did no such thing.

It registered a moment later, the lateness of the hour, and that Joshua could very well be abed. That meant she would have no choice but the see who was at the door. She made her way toward the study door, but jumped, startled, when someone knocked. "Come in."

"Good evening, Miss Lara."

"Good evening, Joshua. Don't you ever sleep?"

"There's time to sleep when all in the house are sleeping. For now, I stay awake in the event that I'm needed."

"Oh, Joshua, you know that isn't necessary."

"Apparently it is, as I heard a knock on the front door. Had I been asleep, I would have been remiss in my duties," Joshua said with a grin.

"Point taken, Joshua. You may go and tend to your duties."

"Yes, Miss Lara."

A few moments later, a more subdued Joshua returned, "There's a Mr. Pembroke here to see you. As it is a male caller, I think that I should waken Sasha before showing him in?"

Joshua's decorum was flawless, but Lara didn't miss the hesitation in his voice or the lines creasing his normally smiling face, as someone else may have done. "Is something amiss, Joshua?"

"I wouldn't know that, Miss."

That formal delivery let Lara know that something was indeed amiss; however, Joshua was relaying to her, in his best butler tone, that it was none of his affair and that she should simply let her visitor explain the purpose of his visit.

"Very well, Joshua. Go ahead and waken Sasha. You don't think he's any sort of a threat, do you?"

Joshua's old smile returned, "No, Miss. No serial killer lurking inside this character," he answered, and then turned and shuffled out. Lara smiled in remembrance.

It was an old game they had played beginning when Lara was but a child. Whenever a visitor would come to call, she would pull a reluctant Joshua behind a nearby plant, and then each would try to guess the real person lurking behind the smiling facade. After all, Lara had concluded, no one could maintain an obviously fake smile for as long as their visitors did, so they had to be empty shells holding dastardly fiends. Mad scientists, evil monsters, and serial killers were just a few that she determined occupied the bodies. Furthermore, Lara was convinced that those fiends were just waiting for the right moment to spring forth and attack their small city, beginning with the Esterhaus dwelling.

Joshua often told Lara that she had an over-active imagination, which she wouldn't have, had her father not taught her to read, and then audaciously supplied her with reading material well above her age level. Material, such as *Frankenstein*[a],

---

[a] The original work, written by Mary Shelley in 1817. Published in 1818.

The Mysteries of Udolpho[b], *The Old English Baron*[c], and the works of William Shakespeare provided Lara with fuel for her imaginings.

Of course, that was when she was a child. Lara was all grown up now and realized that the pasted smiles were just society's way of coping with the tedium of everyday living.

Sasha walked in, bleary-eyed, a few minutes later, having not bothered dressing.

"Did Joshua disturb your beauty sleep, Sasha?" Lara grinned at her attendant, who simply stood there rubbing her eyes excessively. Of course, had her parents been there, she would have been the model of etiquette, but Lara never held her to such standards when they were on their own.

"Why did you have him drag me out of bed?" Sasha whined, plopping onto a nearby chair, stretching her long-legs out in front of her. Just as quickly, she pulled in to herself, wrapping her arms in a tight embrace about her waist, "Brrrrr, it's chilly in here. You pulled me from my warm bed to catch cold? And just when I was getting to the good part of the dream where the knight in shining armor rides in and whisks me away on his mighty steed."

"Oh, posh! There is no such critter, and I dragged you out of bed because we have a late night visitor. I obviously need a chaperone, so since you didn't see fit to dress, you might want to, um, cover up a bit and move that chair into a shadowy corner. I'm sorry it's chilled in here. I didn't have Joshua light a fire because I didn't see the need, since it was but me in here at the time."

"Couldn't Joshua have acted as chaperone?"

"Joshua has his own duties to see to, as well you know, Sasha."

"Fine. Well maybe this person can make his visit short, so I can crawl right back beneath my blankets and write this off as a short annoyance. Who would call at such a god-awful hour anyway?" Lara didn't supply an answer, merely staring at her in that fashion which told Sasha she needed to stop whining and see to her instructions. Sasha sighed, sat up, and wrapped her robe

---

[b] Written by Anne Radcliffe and published in 1794.
[c] Written by Clara Reeve and published in 1778.

tighter around her generous cleavage, securing the belt snugly about her little waist. She was thankful that Lara hadn't insisted she return to her room and get dressed, as her robe was far cozier. She scooted the chair as far back into the shadows as possible, and behind a nearby plant. When done, she theatrically called out, "Send in thou late-night caller, for I am ready to remain out of thine sight!"

Lara laughed, "Well, that's a relief!" She shook her head in bemusement and then turned to Joshua, who was watching the antics with fondness, "Please show Mr. Pembroke in—if he's still here," she said, casting a mock stern glance at her attendant.

Joshua opened the door with formality, "Mr. Daniel Pembroke, Miss."

A squat, portly gentleman entered the room, his coat draped over his arm and his hat clenched tightly in his fist.

"Wouldn't you like Joshua to take your hat and coat, Mr. Pembroke?"

"No, no, child. Thank you just the same, but I won't be staying long. I do apologize for the lateness of the hour, but I'm afraid this couldn't wait until a more appropriate time."

As a rule, his reply would be Joshua's cue to depart and supply refreshments for an extended visit, or continue about his other duties. When he didn't leave the room, Laura's brow quirked in question. He gave her a less-than-convincing smile and moved into the shadows to stand next to Sasha. His behavior made her nervous. What was it about this stranger? Did Joshua sense a danger that she had yet to perceive that made him feel the need to provide added security—not for her alone, but Sasha also? She wanted to question him, but now wasn't the time, as her caller had begun to address the reason for his visit.

"Perhaps you'd best take a seat, Miss Esterhaus."

"Very well. Will you sit also?" Lara settled into her father's chair behind his desk and repressed the urge to throw her feet up on the oak surface, especially when she studied her visitor's face more closely. It reminded her of Joshua's countenance when he came into the study to announce Mr. Pembroke's arrival. She cast a glance toward Joshua, who moved further into the shadows.

Something is *bothering him then,* she thought.

She looked more closely at their visitor. Worry lines creased the heavy brow of his face, and he seemed to have difficulty maintaining eye contact with her. Something was definitely wrong.

"I'll stand, thank you just the same." He cleared his throat loudly and twisted his hat in his hand. "I hate to be the bearer of bad news," he said softly, and then stopped, as if uncertain on how to proceed. After a few more minutes of apparent mental battle, he seemed to come to a decision. He straightened his shoulders and finally made eye contact with Lara. "Do you know who I am, Miss Esterhaus?"

"I can't say that I do, Mr. Pembroke."

"No, I guess you wouldn't, since I've only been assigned my duties a week past. I'm the new constable."

Lara sat quietly, fingers of dread tracing up and down her spine. *A dastardly fiend is hidden inside this one,* she thought absurdly. *There must be. His gentle, lilting English accent conflicts with his sloppy appearance. A contradiction like that must mean that he's a dastardly fiend in disguise, and he's come to strike at my heart and soul.* When he next spoke, she wanted to grab her father's sword and run him through, just as his words pierced through her, as powerful as if he'd wielded his own sword.

"There was a dreadful carriage accident this evening. Heavy fog this time of year, and icy cobblestone. Unavoidable, most likely. Two carriages collided. One of them... well, it tipped over into the river. The weight of it broke through the icy surface, and..." Pembroke shrugged his massive shoulders, but didn't go on. He didn't need to. Lara's parents were dead. "I'm truly sorry, my dear. I know this must be a terrible burden to bear, especially as I'm told this comes on the heels of your uncle's death and his family only a month past...absolutely dreadful," he muttered. "If there's anything..."

Lara shook her head, but couldn't find her voice to speak. *Go away!* Her mind yelled. Mr. Pembroke nodded solemnly, and then turned and bolted as fast as his heavy appendages could carry him, as if he'd heard her mind's angry retort. It was obvious to her that he didn't care for this particular part of his new job.

Sasha waited until the door to the sitting room banged shut, and then leapt from her chair. She quickly made her way over to where Lara sat, numb, unmoving, and not speaking. Joshua moved to her other side and knelt, taking Lara's stiff fingers in his large black hand.

"I'm so sorry, Miss Lara. So truly sorry."

"Is there anything that we can do, Lara?" Sasha picked up Lara's other hand, patting it gently, but Lara didn't respond to either of them. Her parents were dead. That litany refused to stop, pounding in her brain, getting louder and louder. Her parents were dead.

Lara pulled her hands free, laid her head down upon them, and closed her eyes. Images of her father and mother flitted into view. Her mother, Ava—a tall woman with raven-black hair and alabaster skin—just like she. In fact, she was the spitting image of her mother. Other than her eyes. The color of her eyes she inherited from her father. Her eyes were a dark emerald, while her mother's eyes were the color of the sky on a cloudless, summer day.

Her father, Travis, was a complete contrast of her mother and her—they were tall, he was short; their hair was black as night, his was a flaming red. The only thing she shared with her father, besides the color of his eyes, was his intellect, and a love of using that intellect. Her mother was smart, but her father was brilliant. Her mother was also the serious one, while her father loved to joke and play. Mischief danced in his emerald eyes and lined every facet of his face.

However, not all about Travis and Ava was contrasting, for they did hold one thing in common—a love for their unusual little girl. From the first, it was obvious that Lara was different from other children. She didn't care to play with dolls or to learn the fine art of crocheting and needlepoint. She much preferred to sit on her father's lap to help him balance the household accounts, sometimes catching a mathematical error that her father missed, much to his amusement and chagrin.

When Lara was nine, her parents started taking her to the family's boutique—a wedding gift to Ava. Owning a dress shop was Ava's dream, although had she married her cousin, she could have gone into the brick-making business. A very lucrative enterprise started by Ava's grandfather, Thomas Salter, in the mid-thirties[d].

When Ava decided to marry Travis, he'd given Ava her dream; one that turned out to be a business match made in heaven, and profitable, because the two worked in perfect harmony. While Ava handled business in the front of the store, Travis took care of the ordering and the financial end.

Her mother had suggested taking Lara to the shop to teach her a valuable skill, rather than simply allowing her to play hide-and-seek among the voluminous skirts. It was her hope that one day her only child would take over the running of the business; and while she was not completely opposed to Lara marrying into the Salter side of the family—a match that would see to her financial security even more so than a dress shop—Ava selfishly hoped that Lara would want to carry on with Ava's dream. However, Ava soon discovered that her daughter was ill-suited for the finesse of gown sales, preferring to settle on her father's lap in the store's office, going over the books with him. This propensity was when Ava determined that her only daughter needed to learn to be better rounded.

---

[d] Thomas Salter began brick making in the mid-1730s. His work was so important to the growth of Savannah and the surrounding area, that the island was named Salter Island. Due to a poor working environment, Salter died in 1751, leaving the brick making business to his heirs.

CHAPTER 2

Ten Years Earlier

"Mother, I have an idea on how you can expand your business and increase revenue." Nine-year-old Lara strolled out of the back office of the little boutique with all the confidence of a true businesswoman. "Oh, I do beg pardon." Lara stopped and closed the account ledger, placing it beneath her arm. "Do continue, Mother. I had no idea that you were engaged with a customer."

Ava smiled indulgently at her daughter and then turned to face the woman who was eyeing a dress that was obviously too small for her rather ample frame. With a practiced assurance, Ava steered the woman to a garment more suitable, and then persuaded her, with almost no effort, of the dazzling effects the gown had upon such a gorgeous body.

When the sale was complete, Ava turned back to her daughter, "Now, what was that you were saying, dear?"

"Well, I've noticed that you tend to sell gowns that are needed for everyday wear, but steer away from the evening attire and ball gowns that is a must in every woman's wardrobe."

"Well, aren't you a surprise," her mother declared with a laugh. "I wasn't even aware that you knew about gowns and other fineries, since you tend to keep your nose stuck in the account ledgers."

"Well I have seen different gowns hereabouts, and believe it or not, I do like to look at the circulars that come from Paris, on occasion, and this is where my point lies. It is with those gowns that you can make the most income, since we all know that women require those particular fineries in order to snare a husband." Lara finished her observation with a roll of her eyes, indicating just what she thought of the whole marriage thing. It was the only clue that gave away her age, for she was tall for a child of nine, thanks in part to her mother's six-foot genes. She was also extremely articulate, to a point that sometimes startled her parents. Ava often told Travis that it was Lara's reading material that provided fuel for, not only her imagination, but her intellect also.

"I appreciate the thought, Lara, but the reason we avoid the ball-gown sales is because of the expense in importing them, and I haven't skill enough to create the masterpieces like Sue Ann Harper does. That's why I take care of the simple sales and leave the complicated work to her."

"Ah, but herein lies the crux of my argument. We *can* afford it with a bit of flair." Lara retrieved the book from beneath her arm and opened it. "I've noticed that there are extra expenses here and there that can be cut back, if not altogether eliminated, such as right here, for instance: we don't really need to hire an extra hand every time we overhaul the display window, do we? And here..."

"Point taken, Lara."

"Good, because I found ample places in which to save money, which, as I stated, will enable us to acquire a few French gowns of latest fashion that we could sell at a premium, especially since those in the circulars are much more appealing than those Mrs. Harper designs. Sales from those gowns will bring in enough revenue to purchase more gowns, and so forth, until we've incorporated the French designs in with our day dresses. Thus making our boutique a must place to visit by women everywhere, and since many people are finding their lot in life improving greatly in the six or so years since the war ended, they will want to start dressing to reflect that improvement, wouldn't you say? You and me included, of course."

"And you wouldn't feel at all guilty over pushing another person out of business. Because if we do decide to bring in French fashions and do happen to outsell that poor woman, that's precisely what we'll do."

Lara blushed and lowered her head in chagrin, but just as quickly it snapped up, the twinkle back in her eye, "We'll simply hire her ourselves. After all, the gowns that we purchase will need to be altered in most cases and we'll need a seamstress to tend to it. It's brilliant, if I do say so myself."

"I approve."

Ava turned on her heel and saw her husband leaning against the counter. *When had he come in?* She wondered, moving over and placing a chaste kiss on his lips.

"Hey! The place is empty and that's the best you can do?"

Travis stepped onto a stool, grabbed his wife around the waist, and kissed her thoroughly. When he finally released his flustered wife, he looked over at Lara and winked. Lara giggled and hid her face momentarily behind the account book. When she lowered it again, she had composed herself, returning to the business at hand.

"You like my idea, Father?"

"I love your idea, and we'll implement it immediately."

"We will?" Ava asked.

"I don't see why not," Travis said. "It's obvious that Lara has given this a lot of thought, and since she will be taking over the business in future, she'll need to start making it her own eventually. Let me see the ledger, Lara."

Grinning, Lara turned over the account ledger. After a quick perusal of all of the notations Lara had made for her mother, and a few prodding questions, he closed it. "It's doable. Just as she says. So what say you, Mother?"

"Well, I suppose we could move in that direction."

They had, and the business flourished in the years following. Still, as Lara grew, her mother's concern over her future grew.

"You realize that if she continues in this vein, we'll not find her a husband," Ava worried one evening, after she and Travis had retired for the night. Lara, then thirteen, was not anywhere near interested in attending cotillions or having her parents introduce her to society. Not that any of the men in the neighborhood, or surrounding neighborhoods, had taken an interest. It wasn't due to a lack of beauty, for in point of fact, Lara was stunning, even in adolescence. It was the fact that, at thirteen, she was already five-foot-seven and highly intelligent. Both attributes of which were unappealing to the opposite sex.

"Would you prefer she be something she's not?" Travis asked, tracing a path down his wife's arm. He smiled when he felt a tremor run through her. *Even after all these years, the spark is still there,* he thought, eager for their conversation to conclude so he could take advantage of that spark.

"No, but shouldn't we at least encourage her to take on more feminine tasks so that she will have a small chance at marriage when she gets older?"

"Very well, but tread lightly. I don't want her to feel as if we are not proud of the person she is." Travis placed a kiss on his wife's arm. "Now, how about we discuss you and me."

The next day, Ava approached her daughter at the boutique with a deal that Lara couldn't refuse.

"If you wish to continue helping me with the store Lara, you're also going to have to make an effort to expand your horizons. Learn new things, so that you'll be a well-rounded young lady."

"What do you mean, Mother?"

"Well, for one, you need to learn how to behave like a proper lady of society." Lara rolled her eyes and started to protest, but her mother raised a hand to silence the outburst. "I want you to learn to prepare a menu, sew, do needlepoint, and run a household beyond the financial side, so that if the need ever arises, you'll be better prepared to care for your own home, married or not."

"You're trying to marry me off, aren't you?" Lara teased, knowing full well that doing so would take intervention from the Lord Almighty.

"Oh Lara, for goodness sake," Ava sighed, "didn't I just say 'married or not'?"

Lara laughed, "Yes, Mother."

"Very good. Now here's the agreement. You work for me, *not* just your father. That way, you will know *how* to sell the gowns to these ladies, and the business will continue to thrive once you take over. After all, what good is a dress store if you can't sell any dresses?"

"Fair enough," Lara said, and then turned to return to the office.

"Excuse me. Lara?" Her mother said, stopping Lara in her tracks. "That wasn't all, dearest."

Lara returned to her mother's side, "What else could there possibly be, Mother?"

"Well, didn't you hear what I said about running a household, dearest?"

"Yes, but I was kind of hoping to escape before you were able to bring it up. I guess my luck didn't hold."

Ava smiled, "Yes, well I guess it didn't. Here's the second part of the bargain..."

"You never said this was a multi-bargained proposition," Lara huffed.

Ava laughed. "Well, it is. And if you can't see fit to make the effort, I guess I can always sell the boutique."

"Mother, you wouldn't!"

"I'd rather not, no, so stop fussing and listen. Now, in the evening, when we return home from the boutique, you will strive to accomplish at least one task each night: preparation of the dinner menu, sewing, mastering entertaining skills, whatever I deem necessary. Do we have a deal?"

"What if I don't like the deal? Can we compromise?"

"Not this time darling. If you wish to inherit this store and continue working here, you will need to accept. Today."

"Oh, posh. Very well, Mother. Deal." In true Lara fashion, she stretched out her hand and waited for her mother to shake on it. It was a bargain she good-naturedly abhorred.

CHAPTER 3

6 Years Later

Lara's head ached, and she didn't want to move, but the insistent consolations of her butler and attendant were wearing on her now frazzled nerves.

She didn't realize she'd been crying until she lifted her head and noticed the puddle pooled on the oak between her folded arms. How long she sat there remembering, she didn't know, but it must have been quite some time for when she glanced out the window, Mr. Solow had made it to their street and was extinguishing the lanterns. Joshua had apparently lit a fire at some point, the flames of which were slowly dying to an amber ember.

It was nearly dawn, and her parents were dead.

She wiped her eyes and looked at the tired countenance of Joshua and Sasha, "Have you two been sitting here all night attempting to console me?" She whispered.

Weary of words the two merely nodded.

"Thank you. You are true friends." She rolled her neck, wincing as the kinks popped free.

"Are you going to be all right, Miss?" Joshua whispered, his voice hoarse. He rubbed his eyes, and then blushed beneath his dark skin when he was unable to stifle a yawn. "Sorry," he muttered.

"You needn't be, Joshua. We're all weary. But yes, I will be all right—eventually. I have to be, don't I?"

"Is there anything that we can do for you, Miss?"

"Would you like some coffee perhaps?" Sasha said, stifling her own yawn.

"We'd probably all better have some coffee since there is much to be done. Would you mind gathering the staff, Joshua?"

"Are you sure you want to deal with this right now, Miss Lara? I'm sure your parents will understand if you wish to wait a day or two."

"No, Joshua. I'll not disrespect my parents by wallowing in self-pity while their bodies decay beneath the icy waters of the Savannah River."

Joshua and Sasha winced at the harness of her words.

"I apologize," Lara sighed. "I shouldn't have snapped. I guess I'm more distraught than even I was aware."

"Isn't there anyway…I mean, isn't it possible to…" Sasha whispered, but was unable to continue in her discomfort.

"I'm sure if there was a way for them to bring my mother and father home in order to receive a proper burial then the constable would have done so. The means simply do not exist to remove two bodies from a submerged carriage, especially not in the dead of winter," Lara said, choking on the last word. She took a deep breath and closed her eyes, trying to maintain a grip on her grief.

"Oh, Miss Lara, I'm so truly sorry," Joshua whispered, patting her hand. "I wish I had the power to turn back the hands of that grandfather clock in the foyer so that this tragedy never occurred; so that you wouldn't have to suffer so."

Lara sniffed lightly and placed a hand on top of Joshua's. She opened her eyes and smiled encouragingly at her butler, a smile that was a stark contrast to the pain reflected in her eyes and the tears streaming slowly down her cheeks, "For my parents' sake," she said, her words emerging on a tremble, "I will get through this. At least I can thank the good Lord above that I have friends like you two that can help me."

"We'll always be by your side, Miss Lara," Joshua assured. "Just like we always have been. After all, who else will be able to see inside a person to discern whether there be a… ,"

"Dastardly fiend," Lara continued, "or a serial killer…"

"Or a mad scientist," Sasha joined in.

Lara smiled and then said softly, "Gather the staff, Joshua. Sasha, see to breakfast please, and then we'll begin making funeral arrangements."

CHAPTER 4

Sasha stopped in mid-step, her attention snared by the quiet-spoken conversation occurring in the secluded alcove off the study. As there were many whispered conversations taking place today, in deference to the mournful occasion, this particular one should not have warranted special attention; however, the few snippets in juxtaposition with the location, created an inexplicable dread in Sasha, which made her eavesdropping justifiable in her opinion. As she listened further, her concern grew, for this specific dialogue wasn't expressing sadness over Lara's loss, rather it was conferring over her future.

"How long before the bank takes possession?"

"She has six months to mourn and three months thereafter to marry or all assets will be repossessed and sold on the auction block."

"Perhaps she'll take an offer beforehand. Save time."

"Well we'll make an offer, of course, but it can't be too soon. She's still grieving, so making an offer this soon could result in hostility instead of acquiescence."

"Yes but if we wait too long there's a possibility that she could find a husband."

That statement was followed by a snort of disbelief, which raised Sasha's hackles.

"Highly improbable," The man replied finally. *"I mean firstly, she's had years to find one without success, and secondly, look at the girl. She's taller than most men, uses her brain far too often, and she's old. On top of that, she was running that business as well as her parents before she reached thirteen. If she was a man, it would be commendable."*

Sasha felt her temper elevate further, tempting her to step from her sheltered space and rebuke the two men for such an unfair assessment of her mistress. Of course, they'd probably have her thrown in jail for overstepping her bounds.

Even if a man could overlook her unsightliness, no one will ever be able to overlook her age. Good Lord, the girl is already nineteen and hardly an attractive prospect for a potential suitor.

Just goes to show that we won't have any difficulty with her marrying and keeping the house. In nine months, the bank will take possession of the property, and then we can proceed with our plans, unless we can persuade her of the benefits of selling ahead of that time. Her parents never should have turned down our offer. Nor should her relations, for that matter. If they hadn't…well, Lara won't have any options but to turn it over.

If she does turn it down, I can always pay another visit to our scar-faced business associate.

I don't think it will come to that. I'm certain that she will see reason.

Yeah, well, that's what we said about her family and they didn't.

Her family didn't have anything to fall back on, Lara has the shop. She can always board at her business, or live in relative comfort at the boarding house for the remainder of her years. That's the best a girl like that could hope for anyway. Certainly, she'll come to the same conclusion. No, in the case of Lara Esterhaus, we only need to wait. Time, and her lack of marriage prospects, are on our side.

Very well. We'll bind our time. Keep an eye open and an ear to ground. We certainly don't need any surprises. After all, a man could easily overlook her unappealing qualities when so much money is involved, especially if they discover her family connection.

Exactly, find a man that cares more for money and, voila—she's married. After all, there are just as many repulsive men as would be willing to settle down with her if it meant starting off that well-to-do.

Hopefully, that won't occur. We could ensure it doesn't if someone does show an interest. Still I don't guess there's any rush. I mean, it's not like anything's going anywhere. I'd say we're situated well at this point.

If I wasn't married already I'd possibly consider wedding her. Of course, I'd never have the courage to bed the woman. What about you? You're not married. Have a go at her and save us the waiting?

No, thank you. Fortunately, I'm wealthy in my own right but if becomes necessary, I'm sure that one of our friends could be persuaded to marry the twit, and then all concerns would be eliminated. If, as we say, it comes to that. In all probability, she'll willingly sell. If not, there's a higher probability that the bank will take possession.

Think our friends will be willing to wait nine months before proceeding? If, as you say, if comes to that.

Ooh, of all the nerve! Having heard enough, Sasha quietly moved from her hiding place. She didn't comprehend most of what the two men were speaking of, but she did comprehend enough to know that marriage was required for Lara and that Lara certainly needed to be made aware of it, if she wasn't already.

CHAPTER 5

"How are you holding up?" Sasha asked, kneeling beside her mistress.

"Oh, I've been better," Lara sighed. "Honestly though, if all of these people didn't mean well, I'd boot them out on their hind ends. I'm so tired of being gracious. Thank you by the way. I owe you a debt of gratitude for pulling me in here. Did you see that I was growing weary and decide to come to my rescue?" She made the comment half in jest; however, she wasn't prepared for the lack of enthusiasm in her attendant's reply.

"Actually, I pulled you in here…" Sasha paused, uncertain how her mistress would react to her eavesdropping, especially since she suddenly felt she could be overreacting to what she heard. She hoped.

"Is something wrong, Sasha?"

"Well, it sounded like it to me, but maybe I misheard. I was thinking that if I told you, you can set everything to rights again." Out of habit, Sasha lowered in her gaze in proper chastised fashion and waited for Lara to absolve her of her wrongdoing before speaking.

"I'll wait to see what you have to tell me before I admonish you for eavesdropping," Lara grinned mischievously.

"Thank you, Lara."

"Oh, for goodness sakes, Sasha," Lara snapped lightly, "when have I ever admonished you, seriously, that is?"

"I've never dared listen in on someone's conversation before though, and I know that's wrong to do, although it did sound as if these men were speaking ill about you."

"Perhaps you'd best explain what you heard."

"Well I overheard two men talking, like I said," Sasha explained, her anger elevating quickly again, overshadowing her feelings of remorse for spying, "and they said, a little too gleefully if you ask me, that you were going to lose the house and have to move into your shop. That, of course, means you'll have to sell all of your servants— including Joshua and me—to other households. Oh, Lara, tell me that's not going to happen."

"That's not going to happen," Lara replied automatically. "Still, why would I lose the house?" She asked rhetorically, knowing that her attendant couldn't possibly supply the answer. She sat up straighter, thinking. "It was paid for long ago. I know it was. Father was so proud that he showed me the deed. I have it in the safe…"

"It hasn't to do with ownership," Sasha interjected. "At least not that I'm aware of. What one of them said was it had to do with the fact that you're a woman. Apparently, a woman can't own a house."

"What?"

"That's what one of them said, and then the other one said that since you're too ugly to find a husband then the bank is going to walk in here pretty as you please in nine months and take it all away from you."

"Did you just call me ugly?"

"No, one of those two men did, and since you've never been interested in men and they seem to think that no man would be interested in you…well, they're convinced that you're going to be homeless. Honestly, they were like vultures circling. It's as if they can't wait for the bank to take it away so that they can buy it up. One of them even joked about proposing marriage to you himself but wasn't at all certain he could do his husbandly duty by you."

"Are you going to keep insulting me this evening, Sasha, because I'm truly not capable of handling…"

"Oh no, Lara, truly I'm not insulting you, I'm just saying what they said and well, I guess I'm not saying it very well," Sasha said softly. "If I wasn't so angry at them I might be handling this better, it's just…ah, blasted all to Hell."

"I see," Lara said, rubbing her temples, "well, I guess my appearance, appealing or not, is not really at issue here. What is at issue is the possibility of losing our home. I wonder if anyone was going to bother to inform me of this law. And watch your language, Sasha," She admonished absentmindedly.

"Sorry, and no, no one intended to tell you. Not the way these two men were talking. Dastardly fiends in disguise for certain."

"Without a doubt. So someone out there is interested in my home," Lara said thoughtfully. "Did you happen to see who they were or did they say *why* they wanted this property?”

“No. They were hiding in an alcove so I couldn’t see them, but they did say something about a project,” Sasha said, and then added quietly, “they also said they’d made an offer to your parents and to your uncle but it was refused, which they said was a mistake to do. Heartless cads.”

“Unfortunately heartless cads describe a majority of the men living hereabouts so that won’t particularly help with identifying them,” Lara snapped, trying to hide her hurt and anger over their callous comments regarding her person. “So where were you hiding, I wonder?”

“I wasn’t hiding,” Sasha defended. “I was emerging from the kitchen and heard voices as I was passing by the study.”

Lara laughed, “It’s okay, Sasha. I’m not angry with you. Obviously if you hadn’t left the kitchen when you did, I would find myself homeless in another…how long did you say we have before the bank shows up here?”

“Nine months.”

“But if I were to find a husband before that time there would be no question of maintaining ownership, correct?”

“That’s what they said, but they didn’t seem too concerned about that prospect.”

Lara sighed, “So you said, and they are probably right. Well I guess I’d better pay a visit to an attorney first thing in the morning to find out more about this law and see what my options are.”

CHAPTER 6

"Get married."

"That's it? That's my only alternative?" Lara asked. She didn't know what she expected when she walked into the law offices of Bingham, Barley, and Baxter at nine o'clock the next morning but having Mr. Bingham offer only one solution to her dilemma—a solution that seemed far out of reach—wasn't exactly encouraging. "Surely there's some ambiguity in the law…" she started again but he was already shaking his head.

"I'm sorry Miss Esterhaus, but that's the *only* solution in your case. Of course, without appearing callous, several interested parties have approached me regarding your property, parties who are willing to pay you a fair sum for its purchase."

"Well, in order to determine whether their price is a fair one, I will need you to pull out my father's paperwork: the will, deeds…"

"I'm sorry, but I can't do that."

"I beg your pardon?"

"The law prohibits you from engaging in any legal matter, including, but not limited to, the perusal of legal documents."

"You made that up."

"Certainly you aren't accusing me of being deceitful, Miss Esterhaus."

"As my father's sole heir…"

"You are not his heir. A woman cannot inherit, which brings me back to your only viable alternatives: either marry, or accept one of the offers on your property."

"You're contradicting yourself, sir."

"How so, Miss."

"If I have no voice at all in my own affairs, or the affairs of my deceased parents, I cannot entertain any offers related to the purchase of property; yet, here you sit telling me that the sale of said property is my decision to make."

"Ah, I see where your confusion lies, which isn't surprising since you're but a woman and ignorant of the law. I would act as your proxy in all matters legal. All you would need to do is sign a waiver, relegating all matters into my hands."

"And the alternative to this would be?"

"Get married, at which time it would be your husband's duty to peruse your father's records and make a decision as to your future."

"Do you find something amusing, sir?"

"Only your determination to act on your own behalf in matters far above your head."

"I think perhaps you should have chosen a profession in which humor was better suited. I consider your laughter at my circumstances as conduct unbecoming a man in your vocation."

"I merely find it mildly humorous that you should attempt to conduct your own legal affairs. I am hardly laughing at your circumstances."

"Strange but the smile on your face appears to belie your statement," Lara said, standing to leave, "If there were another attorney's office nearby, I would simply seek council elsewhere, but as you were my father's attorney and the only attorney around, I have no way of refuting your assessments. Still, be that as it may, I must endeavor to locate a husband so that he may see to my affairs, since, as you say, the law doesn't allow me to do so of my own accord."

"Miss Esterhaus, if I might suggest," Mr. Bingham said, trying to appear more sympathetic to her plight, but failing miserably, "take one of the offers. They are most handsome, and would ensure your security into your old age, along with the revenue from your business, of course."

"No thank you, Mr. Bingham," Lara said firmly. "I'll be keeping the house, but I will leave you with a bit of advice. Do try to control your emotions when dealing with your clientele. Your propensity to smirk during dire state of affairs is extremely rude at best. If you don't learn to be more sympathetic, then someone, somewhere, at some time, is going take offense in a way that's not going to be pleasant."

"If you were a man, I may perceive a threat behind those words, but as you are a woman, I will simply right it off as desperate hysteria and bid you a good day, with a word of advice of my own—take an offer. Surely you can see that finding a husband in the next nine months, when you've been unable to find one to date, is bordering on delusional; and, as I stated, the offers are very handsome indeed."

"What I'll do is bid you a good day, Mr. Bingham," Lara said, standing and moving toward the antechamber, "but in truth of the matter a good day is not at all what I'm wishing for you. In truth, I'm hoping that this building collapses about your ears for all the sympathy you've shown me and assistance you've given." Without waiting for a response to her uncharacteristic tirade, she yanked open the door and stormed from the office.

A moment after her departure, three men stepped from a side office, brows knitted and lips puckered in displeasure.

"Well, gentlemen," the lawyer said, "you heard her. Quite a pistol, that one. A disinterested pistol. Would you like me to try to re-present the offer? Perhaps add a few more dollars as added incentive?"

"There's not a huge rush. We'll just... ,"

"Keep an eye open and an ear to the ground," Alfred Garamond concluded.

"What happens if she takes her determination for information further, and seeks out alternate legal advice? She may not realize it yet, but there are more attorneys in neighboring towns who may just be willing to help her and petition to review her father's papers. If she discovers who she truly is…"

"We'll just do what we can to keep a lid on the matter; after all, none of it will matter in nine months. The property will be ours. All of it."

* * * * * * * * *

Lara stood in the foyer a moment bringing her breathing under control. When she was certain that she would not return to the office and kill the insensitive attorney, she placed her bonnet on her head, tied the laces beneath her chin, draped her woolen wrap about her shoulders, and then stomped down the stairs, and out onto the boardwalk.

Fighting against the tears that threatened to overwhelm her, she stood for an indecisive moment. She needed to go home, but facing the staff, all of whom were looking to her for uplifting news, wasn't a looked-forward-to moment. Time to think was what she needed.

Time to think, if she could.

She started down the boardwalk toward the shop. Her mind was in turmoil, but she forced herself to focus on where she was going, stepping gingerly to avoid slipping on the mid-morning icy patches. Maybe she could hide away in her office for a bit. She could always think at the office.

"Extra! Extra! Read all about it! President George Washington laid to rest!"

Lara stopped walking and turned to the newspaper boy, scanning the headline that stood out boldly in black-and-white.

"Buy a paper, Miss? Only nine coppers[e] today. Hot off the presses."

Before Lara could reach into her reticule, a horde of people shoved her aside unceremoniously in order to purchase a paper honoring the celebrated General, their first President, and a true American hero. She pulled out her coppers and elbowed her way through the crowd. She slapped the coins into the vendor's hand, snatched up a paper, and elbowed her way back the way she'd come. By the time she reached the open boardwalk the crowd had begun to disperse, the newspapers gone. She shook her head at the crazed display, and then continued toward the boutique, scanning the story about a man whom every American considered the father of their country, the founding father of freedom[f].

Still she wondered when that freedom would extend to every American; when freedom would change the laws to reflect equality for men and women alike. After all, a woman should have the right to remain in her home after the death of a male loved one or to sell the place and buy another home, should she so choose. To forbid a woman from possessing a home should be unlawful, not the other way around. Of course, the same sort of men who condemned her for being too smart and too tall were the same sort who wrote the laws, so was triple damned.

---

[e] Coppers were a source of monetary exchange in the late 1700s; however, the copper scare, which took place after the Revolutionary War, spurred the issuance of small change notes generated by private presses (http://www.coins.nd.edu).
[f] General George Washington died due to complications from the common cold (The Spector, Issue#235, Print date: Dec 16, 1799).

She sighed heavily and turned the knob to the boutique. It was locked. Her brow knitted and she moved to peer through the front window. It was dark inside. She looked up the avenue and then down. *Where was Mrs. Harper, and why was the boutique closed?* She wondered, and then realized that she'd probably read the paper and decided not to open today. She reached into her reticule and pulled out her key.

"Lara, honey? What are you doing out and about today?"

Lara turned around to meet the kindly gaze of the parishioner's wife. "Hello, Mrs. Dougherty. How are you this cold, blustery morning?"

"Oh what a precious child you are," the elder woman cooed gently. "You've only just lost your dear parents and here you are asking about my well-being. Well I'll not answer you until you answer me first."

Lara blushed and smiled down at the kindly lady, "Well despite my loss, there is much relating to my parent's affairs that must be dealt with, as well as my own; details that can't wait until I've had time to grieve." *Finding a husband for one,* she thought.

"It's so unfair, isn't it dear?" Mrs. Dougherty exclaimed. "Having to take care of unpleasant details that should wait until your heart has a chance to mend? Would you feel better if I took you down the street and bought you a sinfully delicious sweetmeat?"

"That's very kind of you Mrs. Dougherty, but I'll need to pass on your offer. Have you heard the news today, by the way?"

"What news would that be, dearie?"

"Former President Washington was laid to rest just nine days prior to his family's Christmas festivities. Such a tragic loss."

"Oh my!" The elder woman exclaimed. "He was such a simple man. I met him once, you know."

"No, I didn't know that."

"Oh indeed, yes. When he was still a General with the Continental Army. His men were passing through our hometown during the spring of seventeen-eighty, I believe it was, and stopped in at our home for a hot meal. Of course, that was before my husband accepted the ministerial position here in Savannah. He was a delightful man, simply delightful. General Washington, not my husband, although I suppose I could attribute that same characteristic to my husband; but not General Washington's vocalizations. He was very soft-spoken, he was." Lara watched the tears well in the old woman's eyes. "He will be sorely missed by all."

"Yes, I'm sure he will."

"Oh, how utterly despicable of me. Where has my tact gone," she exclaimed again in a dramatic fashion, wrinkled hand flying to her chest in a gesture of shocked dismay. "Here I am going on about a man you've never met, when your own parents passed only recently, and your uncle and his family only a short time before also. Such wonderfully kind folks they were as well—all of them. The funeral for your parents was so beautiful by the way. You did a fine job. Such a shame for you to have to hold a funeral so close to Christmas. Still, I'm certain you're grateful to have spent some of the holidays with them. I hope you know that I'll miss them as much as General Washington."

"It's okay Mrs. Dougherty," Lara assured, "I took no offense. Truly."

"You are too kind, child. What are your plans now, dearie?"

"I haven't decided yet," Lara said, the question bringing her dire situation crashing home again.

"Do you have other family from whom to draw support?"

"No." Lara shook her head, and realized that, until now, she'd not thought about family—or lack thereof—merely spent her time dwelling on the possibility of losing her home. She wasn't certain how to feel about the newfound realization, but did know that she couldn't dwell on it when other, more important things needed addressing first.

"Oh my. I'm so terribly heartbroken for you. Well, whatever course you choose, make sure you keep God on your side. He'll see you through. Remember that."

"Oh I will, Mrs. Dougherty."

The reverend's wife looked at the boutique and then sent a questioning gaze toward Lara, "You're not planning to open the store today are you, dearie? After all, you're still in mourning, as is the rest of the town."

"Not at all, Mrs. Dougherty."

"Very good then. Well I better be off. Don't want the sweetmeats to be gone before I get there. Takes me a bit longer these days," she said with a wink.

"Thanks for stopping by and I'll see you at Sunday service."

"Very good, dear."

Lara watched the elderly woman walk slowly across the street, her cane tapping out a rhythm on the cobblestones, and then she turned the key, unlocked the door, and went inside.

CHAPTER 7

Lara took a quick glance around and before she could prevent it, tears formed in her eyes. Her legs gave way as memory after memory assaulted her like physical blows. She slid down against the door; her gaze blurred by tears, and scanned the dresses on display. It was here she felt most at home, as had her parents.

Here, a common bond connected them. Here was where they spent most of their days and a majority of their evenings, going over the books, ordering new dresses, talking, and playing.

She blinked as a dim, ghostly image of her father appeared before her eyes.

"Father?"

She watched as the image tiptoed around the dress racks, peering between the large skirts.

Come out, come out, wherever you are, the ethereal image sang softly.

Lara smiled wistfully. He never could find her when they played hide-and-seek.

Where's my little girl hiding now, the ghostly apparition continued, pulling aside a dress quickly with a shout of *I found you!* But he hadn't found her.

"You never did find me, did you?" Lara whispered, as the image began to fade. "Even as tall as I was and as small as the store is, you never did find me. Did you cheat, I wonder? All to please a little girl?"

Lara, come here, dear.

"Mother?" Lara cried softly.

I'd like you to meet someone.

"Oh mother," Lara whispered, "you were always trying to find a Mr. Right, weren't you? Even when you knew that it was hopeless."

Lara, this is Mr. William Kimbal.

Lara couldn't see either herself or William, but she remembered that day well enough to know what had transpired. William Kimbal was new to their small community, and single. Obviously, her mother had seen an opportunity, and jumped on it; but when Lara came out from the office at her mother's bidding; William had taken one look—up—at her, and excused himself.

I'm sorry, Sweetheart, her mother had consoled her.

"It's okay, Mother. Truly," Lara said aloud in remembrance. "But I wish I could make you understand that I'm happy just as I am. And will remain so, whether I marry or not."

I know, dearest, her mother sighed, *and one of these days I'll stop trying, but you must promise me that you won't let the rejection of men cause you to feel less than you are: an amazing, brilliant, and exceedingly beautiful goddess.*

"If I ever feel anything less, all I need to do is look at my mother and know that I am everything that you say I am, for I am an exact likeness of you, and you found father."

You are such a sweet, giving child, and though you don't need a man to complete your life, one day you'll find a man who does—as I did with your father.

Lara watched as the image faded and then wiped her eyes with the back of her hand, "I may never find my perfect match, but I *am* going to have to find a husband or be forced to lose our home. What am I going to do?"

She drew in a deep, unsteady breath and slid up the door. She shook her head to clear the final vestiges of despair, and then bent to retrieve her newspaper. With steps of dejection, she made her way toward the back of the store to the office, settling in behind her large oak desk. She had no desire to do more than lie her head upon the desk and cry forever, but she would not dishonor her parents by behaving childishly in a moment of crisis.

With a long, drawn-out sigh, she opened the newspaper and started reading the story of General Washington's demise; however, before she completed the first paragraph, a thought entered her weary mind and she began to flip rapidly through the pages of the paper, ignoring the fashion section that she always scanned with interest, in lieu of another potential section of interest. Suddenly, she felt a small hope replace the weariness.

When she reached the section she was looking for, she read a bit, surprised at the number of advertisements upon the page. As she read each one, she began to doubt the wisdom in her line of thought and sat back, chewing lightly on her bottom lip, contemplating potential alternate plans. No other viable alternative was presenting itself. It seemed as if this was the only avenue open to her. She scanned the section again, and then leaned back in her chair, a thoughtful expression on her face, "Well if they can do it, why can't I?"

CHAPTER 8

"You can't do this! Have you gone completely insane?" Sasha asked as Lara settled down at the dinner table. Ordinarily, it was Joshua's turn to speak first about his day, but Lara had asked to break tradition, just this once.

It was a tradition she'd implemented many years before, with the approval of her parents; after she explained that she couldn't run a household properly, as her mother requested she try do, if she didn't have the ear of her servants and their trust to speak freely with her in a relaxing atmosphere.

Her parents had known it had more to do with budding friendships than duty, but conceded that she could dine with their butler and her attendant in the kitchen, except on formal occasions. To make it seem more homey and equitable, Lara had instituted a round-about method of discussion, so that she couldn't monopolize the conversation, nor would her servants feel disinclined to converse with her.

It took a bit of convincing that she was sincere in her interest, but eventually it became a looked-forward-to habit—by all three. Now, it was even more important that they continue with the tradition, as a way of sorting out this latest dilemma. A solution to which Lara thought she arrived, until Joshua and Sasha looked at her as if the strain of losing her parents had caused her to take a dive off a cliff—mentally.

"I'm perfectly sane you two," Lara said patiently, "so I wish you'd both quit staring at me as if you're thinking of having me committed."

"Well now, that may be for the best," Joshua said, scooping some sweet potatoes from a bowl and slapping the orange mound onto her plate. "I mean, what kind of a fool idea do you think that is, anyhow?"

"It isn't foolish, it's necessary. Why would you think it's foolhardy anyway?" Lara persisted. "After all, it works well for men, so why not for me?"

"And just how would you know if it works? Did you stop by every house between the shop and home to talk to the men residing there? See if any of them…"

"That's enough, Sasha," Joshua reprimanded. "You are not helping matters any."

"Well, even if she'd managed to determine it worked just fine for men," Sasha rejoined, undeterred, and then turned back to address Lara, "you're a woman, and what works for the goose does not always work for the gander," She paused long enough to take a bite from her black-eyed peas. "Why I've never heard of such a thing."

"Well, heard of or not, if it wasn't somewhat successful, there would not be so many advertisements," Lara interrupted quickly. "People don't tend to continue pursuing a certain method if it's proven a failure, unless they're insane. The success of my shop is another proof of success, since each year more women frequent my store than in years past. Women aren't flocking to Savannah for no reason; especially as Savannah is just now regaining its bearings after the colonists and French managed to drive out the British some seventeen years ago. Our town isn't yet a booming metropolis, so women need reason to locate here, and that would be the men advertising, offering tangible incentives."

"Do you really think the same thing that works for men will work for you?" Sasha pressed the issue.

"Have you forgotten that I have no other options open to me; that I'm not highly sought after, despite my wealth, a wealth that is not even my own at present. I merely subsist on the monies provided by my store, since that attorney won't release any information on my father's estate to anyone but a husband."

"Any man who can't see how beautiful you are, is blind," Joshua stated firmly. "I don't care what no man says, you aren't at all homely. And I'll say one more thing—any man who can't see what a wonderful wife you'd make, is just plain dumb. You just scare them is all, and if we could just find a man willing to look past…well…"

"I know," Lara sighed. "If I was four inches shorter, blonde, deaf, dumb, and mute, I might stand a chance of finding someone hereabouts, but since I'm not and our time is limited, then drastic measures are needed. Still, in deference to both of your reactions to my scheme, I will certainly hear any viable alternative plans either of you have. I certainly couldn't come up with another." Sasha and

Joshua looked at each other and shrugged.

"I admit that we don't exactly have an alternative, but certainly there's got to be one," Joshua argued, cutting a piece of his breaded chicken and shoving it into his mouth.

"Well I don't mean to put a damper on things," Sasha said, "but you made a point that may just make your smart idea not so smart."

Lara shook her head at Sasha's chosen words, but decided it best to hear her out. After all, it was their home too, which meant having to leave if she—or they—didn't devise a feasible strategy soon, "What did I say, Sasha, which makes my plan not doable?"

"You said that there isn't a man around here willing to overlook your height and smarts; that if you were shorter and dumber you'd be able to find a husband. So," she shrugged, "if that's true, then what makes you think a man from somewhere else will want you?"

"There probably isn't one, but I'm not interested in finding someone for me. I'm only interested in keeping the house, and out there, somewhere, is a man that might not be willing to marry *me* but will have no trouble marrying my money."

"What did you just say?" Joshua asked, the look of incredulity on his face comical.

"I said, I am going to find someone willing to marry me for my money," Lara repeated, lifting her head in defiance, daring further argument.

"This is a sad day indeed," Joshua sighed, shaking his head.

"I can't believe you're actually going to auction yourself off like this," Sasha muttered.

"Actually," Lara quipped, "I'm not auctioning myself. If anything, I'm the auctioneer, auctioning off my wealth. The winner doesn't need anything except a desire to wed a wealthy woman."

"I still say this is madness," Joshua said into his coffee cup. "If your parents were alive–"

"That's just it, Joshua," Lara interrupted, snappishly, "they aren't alive, and if I don't find someone willing to marry me before late next summer, then I'll lose everything that my parents spent their married life building."

"A heck of a poor way to usher in the new century, if you ask me," Sasha said.

"Actually, I have until a good nine months after the new century," Lara retorted.

"Sarcasm is *not* an attractive quality you know," Sasha huffed.

"Well I can just add that to my list of other unappealing traits then, can't I?"

"Oh Lara," Sasha exclaimed, only just realizing the insult, "I didn't mean anything by what I said."

Lara sighed heavily and then smiled reassuringly, "I know that, Sasha. I think we're all simply too upset to be thinking clearly right now."

"Since we're all a little hot under the collar right now, does that mean you're willing to forgo this crazy plan?" Joshua asked.

"Unfortunately no," Lara sighed. "Crazy or not, I can see no other way to go about acquiring a husband before the twenty-fourth of September, eighteen hundred. And since I am not delusional, I hold to the certainty that the bank will be knocking at my door only a minute past midnight on that particular day. That means that time is of the essence, so are you two going to help me or do I need to start finding employment for you both elsewhere?"

"What do you need us to do?" Joshua and Sasha asked simultaneously.

CHAPTER 9

Seven months later
Richmond, Virginia

"Brother, have a look at this advertisement," Andrew Bensley ripped out the ad in question and held it out for his brother, who merely sat looking at it in annoyance.

The fifth Earl of Ripon took a deep breath before responding, "Must you shred the paper in order for me to read something, Andrew? Surely it would have been just as simple for you to pass the paper to me in its entirety."

"Yes it would have," Andrew grinned, "but you know I like to get your ire up just to see you raise your eyebrow in that unusual manner. How *do* you do that, anyway?" Andrew laughed. "I see the twitching of your mouth so you may as well grin. You know you want to. Besides, this really is too comical *not* to read. Here, have a glance."

"Oh very well, you buffoon, hand it here." Philip Bensley snatched the paper, tearing it asunder. He huffed in annoyance, laid the two pieces on the table, and lined them up carefully. His eyebrow arched again as he read the advertisement.

Woman of means looking for business
partner to wed before September. Must be
willing to overlook obvious flaws. Applicants
respond in person to Thirty-eight Cornish
Mountain Road, Savannah, Georgia.

Philip scanned the advertisement three more times before looking up at his brother.

"There goes the eyebrow again," Andrew grinned.

"This isn't a true advertisement is it, Andrew?" Philip accused. "You had that friend of yours at the newspaper fix this up as a farce just to have me on, isn't that so?"

"Are you accusing me of being deceitful, dear brother, simply to get a rise out of you?" Andrew's tone held a mock innocence as his grin widened, making it difficult for Philip to ascertain his brother's truthfulness.

"Well since it's highly improbable that any lady would place a notice such as this, then I will err on the side of rationality and conclude that this is one of your childish pranks. You truly are a merry-Andrew. I think Mother must have had the sight when she named you, aptly as it turns out."

"Oh I'm wounded to the core," Andrew said dramatically, and then suddenly grew serious. "However, what if this advertisement is indeed the genuine article? It could very well be the solution to our rather embarrassing family dilemma. If you were willing to travel to Georgia…"

"Carrying this jest a bit further than you usually do, aren't you Andrew? You usually cease and desist once you've been found out."

"Ah but therein lies the truth, Brother," Andrew said, smiling mischievously, "I did *not* place this advertisement. It is indeed authentic, as unlikely as it seems."

"Impossible. I've never heard of such a thing."

"Well the evidence is right beneath your nose, so as I was saying…why don't we take a ride to Georgia and investigate this further. It may prove interesting, to say the least."

"Why ever would I do such a thing?"

"Well, the advertisement did say that the lady in question has money, did it not?"

"A woman of 'means' merely implies wealth, it does not necessarily mean money," Philip argued.

"But what else could it mean?" Andrew persisted.

"Any number of things. For instance, I knew a woman of means in Wales, whose sole claim to that title was an overabundance of horseflesh."

Andrew laughed, but refused to relent, despite his brother's pessimism. "But what if, in this particular case, it did infer money? If so, then perhaps we could pay off Father's debt, and if the funds are substantial, the King may see fit to grant us the return of the family holdings. Ah, I can see that I've caught your attention. I mean think about it, Philip," Andrew persisted, "this is precisely why we traveled to the Americas, is it not? To find a wealthy woman eager to part with her family money, as no woman in Britain seemed available?"

"Please, Andrew, do quiet yourself," Philip snapped. "You know how I abhor hearing about why we had to leave England."

"Yes I know. It's difficult being chased off family land, unable to do more than depart with tail tucked between legs. Even though it did take six armed dragoons to make it happen. Humiliating."

Philip stood suddenly, slammed his hands on the table, and leaned toward his brother, danger glinting in his sky-blue eyes, "I said enough, Andrew. You push me too far sometimes."

"I was talking about myself, Brother," Andrew grinned impishly, far from intimidated by his brother's outburst. He popped a grape in his mouth, chewing with exaggerated speed to prevent the laughter welling inside from escaping.

Most people, confronted with the fifth Earl of Ripon's rage, would wisely quiet and run, but not so his brother. After all, both men stood well over six feet and were deucedly lethal should the need arise, and though Andrew's temper was slower burning, it was never wise to rile either brother needlessly.

"Of course, there is the matter of her obvious flaws," Andrew continued after his brother settled back into his chair. "I do wonder what that could possibly mean. Do you think perhaps that she's horribly disfigured?"

"I'm simply wondering why a lady would need to advertise for a husband in the first place," Philip mused. "After all, where is her family? Surely it's a parents' duty to find their daughter a husband."

"Perhaps her parents are inept, and we both know what inept parents can do to their children."

"Must you constantly…"

"Just trying to make a point," Andrew interrupted. "So, what say you? Should we fire off a missive to let the lady know that you're interested in an introduction?"

"Why can't it be *you* who's interested?"

"You know very well why I can't be the one," Andrew grinned. "After all, you're the elder with the title, Brother; therefore it falls to you to protect our family's lineage."

"And I can see you are heartbroken over that detail."

"Yes well, there was a time when I probably would have been

bothered by the fact that you were born three years before me; had even contemplated your demise a time or two just to inherit the title; however, since Father and Mother passed along familial responsibilities to you, I'm more than happy to relinquish my bitterness and allow you to bear the brunt of the family obligations."

"Oh, without a doubt."

"Can't fault me for my honesty," Andrew laughed. It was a deep rumbling sound that proved contagious. Philip eyed his brother over the rim of his cup and felt his own lips twitch upward. He shook his head in bemusement, "You are truly a merry-Andrew, Andrew."

"Ah, but I'm an intelligent merry-Andrew."

"I could easily debate—and win—that particular point. Still, there is a small measure of merit in investigating this venture further."

"Excellent!" Andrew stood quickly, overturning his chair in the process, "I'll just go and let François know to prepare to deliver the letter and then have him and Pierre start to pack for the journey."

"I have a better idea. I'll simply hire Carl Standish…"

"Of the Pinkerton Agency? Why ever for?"

"Well I would think that was obvious," Philip said with a heavy sigh. "After all, it would be tremendously imprudent to travel all the way from Virginia to Georgia without first discerning whether this woman is a charlatan."

"Fair enough, but why not say we compromise?"

"And what sort of compromise could we possibly arrive at, my dear brother?"

"Well, we'll send Carl ahead of us, as you suggested, to have him suss out this lady's motivations, and her flaws, particularly. In the interim, we will begin our travels, at a more leisurely pace, of course, so that we may arrive all the more quickly should the lady be agreeable to a meeting and should Carl find nothing untoward in regards to her person."

"Thought this through, I see. And how are we to receive Carl's report if we are not where we're meant to be, pray tell?"

"We simply do a little research to determine at which point along our journey he may send word."

"And if this woman turns out to be *not* what she seems, or François returns to report that she's found a husband while we're in the midst of our travels?"

"No cross, no crown[g]," Andrew quipped and then sighed when his brother merely sat staring at him. "If the trip needs to be cancelled, we can simply return to Virginia. Consider it a short respite, a much-needed retreat from the trials of royal distress; however, should Carl find that she is truly in search of a husband, and not yet wed, then we'll be well on our way and can pick up our speed to arrive in all haste."

"Why not simply await word here, at the manor house?"

"Besides my being exhausted simply sitting around all day doing nothing, and the prospect of seeing a bit more of the Americas than Richmond, I thought that would be obvious," Andrew grinned when his brother's eyebrow arched in annoyance. "Fine, dull-wit, I'll spell it out for you. Firstly, if you hadn't noticed, we haven't had the success we thought we would in finding a suitably wealthy bride here in Virginia—or in any neighboring colonies—so this woman may very well be the answer to our monetary quandary. If so, it would be very unwise to allow someone else to nab her first, if someone hasn't nabbed her already during this rather extended discourse."

"You make it sound as if we're planning to kidnap the woman and abscond with her money," Philip snapped.

Andrew laughed, "No, I'm merely trying to ensure a successful undertaking, which may prove unsuccessful should we tarry and someone else reads this advertisement and…"

"Point taken, but might I refute a minor point?" Philip added, "There are plenty eligible and wealthy women available in these parts. Given adequate time…"

"We've been here for nigh unto a year, and haven't any success. So, if there are so many eligible women, as you say, then why haven't you wed any of them?"

"Because eligible and wealthy does not necessarily make a suitable match."

---

[g] "No cross, no crown" is an antiquated term referencing Jesus's suffering prior to crucifixion. Modern day equivalent could be "no pain, no gain"

"You mean that none has turned your head or caught your eye."

"Precisely."

"Not the wisest of reasons for rejection considering our quickly depleting funds. Still, if that is the sole reason for your lack of wedding prospects, then perhaps this will be a wasted effort after all, considering that this particular lady has admitted outright to certain obvious flaws."

"Ah, but that's the intriguing part," Philip said, sipping his drink. "What woman would readily admit to being less than perfect, yet within the same paragraph declare a need for a husband? If this advertisement is indeed genuine."

"One that hasn't all the apples for a bushel?"

"Perhaps, or one that's exceeding clever."

"I fail to see anything clever in being at cross purposes with one's self. After all, if she's seeking a husband, isn't it odd to declare the need while at the same time attempting to drive away those who might be interested? Kind of like trying to win a footrace with a broken foot. She's doomed to failure."

"Very odd indeed, but intriguing none-the-less, which is why we'll send a missive along first thing in the morning. You have François prepared to leave with the letter of introduction, and I'll have Pierre pay a visit to Carl to see if he's willing to travel to Georgia to investigate. Once we've dealt with those two items successfully, we'll begin making plans for our own journey.

CHAPTER 10

August 1800
Savannah, Georgia

"Well if you ask me," Sasha whined for the millionth time since they all concluded, reluctantly, that advertising for a "business partner" was the only course available, "placing that advertisement may have been foolish, but wording it the way she did, all but ensures its failure. It's like she wants every man who reads it to think she is unbalanced and unsightly."

"Now, now, Sasha," Joshua sighed for the fifth time during their conversation, "don't speak ill of the mistress. She's doing what she thinks is best, and I'm sure that if she's meant to marry, then God will see fit to send her someone *to* marry—unusual wording or not. She did state, rather truthfully, that it was unfair to advertise for a husband and not be forthright about her…well, what *she* considers her unappealing traits. I agree that it would have been a huge waste of many a man's time and ours, should dozens of men answer the advertisement only to turn away after meeting the mistress. By wording it the way she did, she eliminates those unwilling to bother with…how did she put it again?"

"Obvious flaws," Sasha snapped. "Goodness! I understand not wanting to waste valuable time, but she could see fit to give God a hand in the matter instead of appearing to harm her own efforts. After all, we've been waiting for eight months and not one person has responded to her advertisement. What does that tell you, Joshua? Had one of those imaginary dozen men you referred to showed up, there may have been one who took a liking to her. But a man can't take a liking to her if no man shows up."

"You know, Sasha, I've been listening to you rant and rave about this for the last eight months. Why don't you consider giving your wagging tongue a rest? I'm fair tired of having to justify Miss Lara's decisions to you. We still have a little over a month in which to locate a master for this household, and I'm certain as can be that God will send someone along, even if it is in the nick of time. Maybe then I'll find peace from your constant droning."

"Or in a little over a month you'll be apologizing to me because you'll see I was right the whole time; especially when Lara is forced to sell us to other households."

"The mistress isn't going to let that happen and well you know it."

"Well, all she's done to prevent it happening is resend that ridiculous advertisement each month to different newspapers and then go off to work every day as if time isn't ticking away from us."

"For the umpteenth time, Miss Lara is doing what she thinks is right, now do hush, girl," Joshua reprimanded, "I believe I hear the mistress now.

"Hello, is anyone about?"

"We're in here, Lara," Sasha called out a second before Lara came through the kitchen doorway.

"How did the dresses sell today?" Sasha asked, putting the last bit of icing on the carrot cake. She licked a bit of the creamy confection from her fingers and plopped onto a stool.

"Excellent. The last of the summer fashions arrived a few days ago, and are flying out of the store faster than we can unpack them. Not only that, but sales have been going so well, that I may have to hire on another seamstress to keep up with the alterations. Poor Mrs. Harper has her hands full. Still, that's not as important as this!" She exclaimed, waving a piece of paper in the air. "It was delivered today; hand-delivered by a French servant, no less."

"And what, pray tell, is that?" Joshua asked, placing three plates on the small kitchen table.

"As if you couldn't guess," Sasha exclaimed, leaping from the stool and snatching the paper from Lara's hand.

"Why do you want it, Sasha? You can't read it…and there's that man again," Lara said suddenly, her gaze shifting from Sasha to a movement across the street.

Joshua turned and glanced out the window, "What man? Wait, I see someone. It's difficult to say, but it looks as if he's watching the house."

Lara felt a chill run down her spine. "So it does. Perhaps I should go out and see who he is. It is possible he's the man I spotted following me earlier this week."

"You have men following you?" Sasha asked intrigued. "Perhaps that is a good thing. Still, I would not bother going out to confront him, as it looks as if he's been found out and is leaving. Do you think perhaps it is someone who read your advertisement and is simply trying to determine whether he wishes to announce himself after he's studied you?"

"I suppose that is a possibility."

"Perhaps you should let the constable know, Lara," Joshua suggested.

"Let him know what? That there is a man who stopped in front of my store and then again in front of my home? And how will I answer his query as to why I perceive this man a threat? He has done nothing to warrant scrutiny by the constable."

"Maybe it's the man who wrote this letter," Sasha interjected, waving the paper in front of Joshua's face. He took a swat at it, and Sasha laughed. "Read it, Lara? Maybe he showed up early and has been following you around a bit to see what sort of person you are before making his presence known officially."

"Well that would be a feat, considering that the letter only just arrived by courier at the store today, from Virginia, and I've never seen a man that can fly."

"Perhaps the suitor disguised himself as the courier, which would be far better than being a dastardly fiend in disguise…what?" Sasha snapped at the looks of skepticism on the faces of her friends. "Why couldn't the courier be the potential suitor?"

"I suppose that is possible, but I didn't get that impression. His demeanor was that of a servant; a servant that awaited my reply to return to his master."

"And what was your reply, if I may inquire?" Joshua asked, his attention suddenly snared, a feeling of hope welling inside that perhaps their search for a master may be coming to a close, at last.

"I agreed to a meeting, of course. After all, it would be foolhardy to place the advertisement only to reject the only potentially interested person to date, wouldn't you say? Of course, it will be nearly a month before the servant returns to Virginia and the gentleman in question arrives here in Georgia. Such a long trek."

"Well, if I weren't so weary with relief *and* starving, I would get up and dance a jig," Sasha said. "This puts us closer to getting you married within the deadline, doesn't it?"

"Perhaps," Lara said, suddenly not as enthused as when she'd first received the letter for an introduction. "However, I just came to the realization that this is no more than a request to meet. It does not mean that he will propose marriage."

"One response in eight months is certainly not a good thing, to be sure, but we will simply work to ensure that the man is so enthralled as to be willing to overlook your obvious flaws and propose marriage, or hope that he is desperate enough for money if he is unable to overlook…"

"Not one more insult, Sasha," Joshua snapped.

"I'm not insulting," Sasha said. "I'm merely stating the obvious. Right, Lara?"

"Without a doubt, Sasha; however, you inadvertently hit upon a point which may indeed influence his decision-making. He sent a servant."

"Which means he must be wealthy," Joshua concluded.

"So why would he be in need of your money?" Sasha continued.

"Indeed, and therefore why answer an advertisement from a woman in search of a man in need of money."

"Perhaps he had money once and has fallen on hard times," Joshua offered by way of explanation.

"That is a possibility, or he is a different type of fiend, one who is a poor manager of funds; a man who depleted his money on wine and women and now seeks to find someone like me who will replenish his coffers."

"Stop assuming will you, you two?" Sasha interjected. "If you continue on as you are, you will talk yourself out of meeting this fellow, who may be a decent sort."

"You're right, of course. It is wrong to make assumptions about someone with whom we are not acquainted. We will simply offer our hospitality and pray he is a decent sort, willing to marry someone like me, thus ending this rather extended nightmare."

"He may very well be the man of your dreams," Sasha said in a dreamy tone.

"There is no such man," Lara retorted automatically, "nor are there fairy tales with happily ever afters."

"I never understood why you could think like that, when your own parents are proof to the contrary," Sasha sighed.

"My parents were an exception. Mother simply got lucky, and we all know that my luck hasn't followed hers." Her attendant's propensity towards romantic notions such as knights in shining armor was amusing to Lara and they seemed forever in a silly debate over whether men of truly exceptional character existed. Had Lara not read *Pamela; or, Virtue Unrewarded*[h], and had she not been subjected to the ridicule of men for all of her pubertal life, she may be more inclined to believe in these fairy tale men of whom Sasha often dreamed. The closest knight she'd ever encountered was her father, and even his armor had a ding or two.

"Well, let us not allow doubt to influence your opinion before the gentleman even arrives, or you may start finding imaginary faults and destroy our only potential hope, as Sasha said," Joshua stated firmly, hoping to draw a close to the negative conversation before pessimism gained a foothold.

"For certain, so then does the letter state when our saving grace will arrive?" Sasha asked.

Lara sighed in exasperation over her attendant's chosen description, but wisely refrained from offering a sarcastic retort. "Unfortunately, he couldn't be definitive. It said that, if amenable to a meeting, he should arrive within a few weeks of my acceptance. So, in other words, we could have as many as six weeks to plan and fret."

"We'll make him feel right at home, Miss Lara, don't you worry none."

"Making him feel at home won't be the issue, Joshua. Getting

---

[h] *Pamela; or, Virtue Unrewarded* was written by Samuel Richardson in 1740, and is considered, by some, to be one of the first romance novels.

him to stay and marry Lara will be," Sasha said in her typically tactless manner.

Lara and Joshua looked at each other and let loose simultaneous long sighs. Lara shook her head and then looked down at the request for an audience again, suddenly finding herself hoping that the man turned out to be blind.

CHAPTER 11

"So what do you propose we do now?" Arthur Middleton asked, after barging into his friend's office moments earlier with what he perceived as dreadful news; however, his friend seemed unperturbed at his announcement, which agitated Arthur greatly.

"The letter she received doesn't necessarily mean that someone has decided to marry her." Alfred Garamond appeared calm and in control, but his mind was in turmoil. He'd counted on no one wanting Lara Esterhaus as a wife; had, in fact, allowed himself to feel smug with each passing month that the bank would foreclose as planned. Now, however, Arthur was in his office announcing that there may just be someone willing to marry the unappealing girl.

He now realized he'd grown complacent, as their fortune held month after month, both in Lara's lack of marital options and in her ignorance of the law.

"I tell you that that letter must be bad news," Middleton stressed again. "Had I not been walking past and seen that messenger hand her the letter, and wait for a reply, I may be more inclined to believe that it has naught to do with possible marriage. However, she was fairly alight with enthusiasm after opening the letter, and then closed up her shop and lit out of town like a dog after a cat. Is Henry still keeping an eye on her? I didn't see him anywhere about when she left the shop."

Just then, a breathless Henry barreled into the offices, "Well, it appears we may have a problem, gentlemen," he sputtered between gasps of breath. "Miss Esterhaus was fairly animated when she showed her house help a hand-delivered letter received at her shop…"

"I told you!" Arthur declared, standing with alacrity to pace the room. "Even Henry believes the letter a potential liability to our plans."

"You know about the letter?" Henry asked.

"We all know about the letter," Jeremy said, stepping from the men's wash room, drying his hands on a towel."

"I was across the street when the messenger arrived at her

shop. I didn't see you though."

"I was there."

"Would you two mind?" Alfred snapped. "So there was a letter! For all we know, she could be thrilled to hear that a long unseen cousin is coming for a visit."

Henry shook his head, "I was going to try to find a way to retrieve it just to make certain of its contents, but she spotted me standing across the street staring in her kitchen window, so I ran back to town and decided to seek out the messenger."

Alfred sat erect in his chair, and leaned forward in anticipation of further information, "Did you locate him?"

"Indeed. I got lucky. He was at the tavern. I bought the man a drink and, sure enough, he willingly disclosed that he worked for a man in Virginia who'd sent him to hand-deliver a request for a formal meeting, so definitely not from a cousin. Anyway, he was just having a quick drink before making the return trip with the woman's response." Henry finished his extended monologue and then flopped onto the nearest chair with a loud, dramatic "Whew!"

"Well, man! Did you not discover whether Miss Esterhaus sent a positive reply?" Garamond demanded.

"Oh, yes. She said yes."

"And knowing she was willing to meet this man, you didn't stop him leaving?"

Henry's brow knitted in confusion, "Stop him? I don't understand? Why would I stop him leaving?

"I think Alfred wanted you to prevent him delivering the lady's reply, you imbecile," Jeremy said, shaking his head.

"I am a far cry from imbecilic, Jeremy. Besides, Alfred, your dictate to me was to merely keep tabs on Miss Esterhaus, and I've done so. You said nothing about preventing someone leaving town."

"Think about it, will you? If it is indeed a response to that ridiculous advertisement, then the interested party will only make the trip if the messenger returns and informs him that the lady is willing to receive him. After all, what would be the point in coming if she…was he still at the tavern when you left?" Garamond asked suddenly, standing from behind his desk.

"I believe so, but was only minutes from leaving. What do you have in mind?"

"Perhaps we can pay him a goodly sum to state that Miss Esterhaus has already married. If she is no longer available, then the man who asked for an audience won't have a reason to come."

"*I* already paid a tidy sum to have her parents disposed of and her uncle and his family also. I can't keep paying out money like this." Arthur Middleton stopped pacing and returned to his seat, feeling suddenly deflated. He hated the thought of spending more of his inheritance on Alfred's scheme.

"We can and we will. We all know the value of acquiring the Esterhaus land; how rich we'll be when we do so, so we should just consider the money spent to ensure the acquisition a business expense."

"Yes, well, it's amazing how that business expense keeps coming out of my pockets and not yours."

"You are the money behind this venture, remember? I am the man with the plan, and Jeremy put down that decanter. It's too early in the day for whiskey. If you don't control your drink, you're going to ruin our plans. You talk too much when you drink."

"So says you," Jeremy huffed, but replaced the stopper in the decanter.

"Anyway, when I brought this plan to all of you, we agreed that your money would be used to ensure its success, Arthur. You know the rest of us don't have the funds needed."

"Yes, well, I didn't realize just how much of my money was going to be needed to make this plan of yours a reality. You initially told me that we'd have hold of that property quickly if we'd just buy off the owners, but you didn't take into account their unwillingness to sell; and then you needed more money to get rid of them. Then you were convinced that Lara would have no choice but to sell; but instead we decided to wait until the bank foreclosed because you were certain that she wouldn't be able to marry in time; but now…"

"Dear God, man! Shut up! I got your point. So, my plan has

had a few ruts along the way. I still say our man at the bank will foreclose and we'll buy it up for a fair sum…"

"Using more of my money," Middleton retorted angrily. "Plus you're banking on the fact that she won't discover…"

"She hasn't discovered anything yet, has she? As for your investments, I have told you that it will get returned to you threefold. You know that investigating I did at the onset? Remember what I told you three?"

"Yes. Lara's father sold that small stretch of land, back in eighteen seventy-six, near the Savannah River so that the government could build that earthen fort. Some protection from the British *that* turned out to be," Middleton snorted.

"Right and this planted that seed in my head at how valuable the property is. Well, here's something I didn't tell you all, because I wasn't certain it was going to become a reality, but you have to keep it under your hat—and you too Henry, Jeremy. Otherwise, those ruts we've run into will turn into an impassable canyon, and all the money you've invested will truly be lost."

All men nodded.

"I take it we're not worried about the messenger anymore?" Henry asked sardonically, as if the thought just popped into his head and had nowhere to go but out of his mouth.

Garamond closed his eyes and took a deep, calming breath, "I do believe that pigeon has done flown the coop, so we've lost that opportunity. Are you interested in my information, or would you prefer to chase him down regardless."

Henry's face reddened, "It seemed an important matter only moments ago, but as it isn't so important now, pray do continue."

"The Esterhaus' property is extensive. The land surrounding the old earthen fort, as well as most of the land south of here, is still in Ava's brother's name—Salter.; its future simply awaiting either marriage by Lara, or foreclosure by the bank. Anyway, before the Salter men met their demise, and Travis Esterhaus also, I heard a rumor circulating that Governor James Jackson is considering purchasing a bulk of that land running along the Savannah River, to do away with that old earthen, useless fort, in favor of better fortifications.[i]"

"Why on earth would he need to do that? The British were driven out years ago." Middleton asked.

"I can't say why, or whether or not it will actually happen. It's just a rumor. I do know that the Savannah River has a greater probability for attack by sea, and the Governor wants to deter anything like that happening."

"Why not just confiscate the land. He has every right since Lara is a female and there are no male heirs," Jeremy chimed in.

"I don't know. Maybe he isn't ready; possibly not prepared to plunge our state into debt over a potentially worthless endeavor—yet. Whatever the reason, we need to legally acquire…"

"Legally, ha!" Henry snorted, and then reddened again at the looks of disgruntlement aimed his way. "Sorry."

"I'll rephrase, shall I? We need to ensure that land is legally deeded to us, by whatever measures I deem necessary; so that when, and if, the governor decides to buy it up, we'll be the ones legally able to sell[j]. And if the governor doesn't buy it, there are always other people who might consider making their homes along the bank of the Savannah River. People are starting to discover the beauty of this place and are making their way south. Either way, we'll make a fortune. Plus, there's the matter of the Salter brick business. Lara has no idea that she's the sole heir to that establishment; its current wealth being deposited into an account in her father's name, who inherited it upon the demise of his all his brother's relations. We've eliminated all paths to wealth thus far, leaving only Lara, who only becomes a threat should she wed."

Henry, Arthur, and Jeremy sat in contemplation for a while, mulling over everything Alfred just said; and then out of the blue, Henry brought up a wholly unrelated topic.

"What do you propose to do about the Pinkerton agent?"

---

[i] Information regarding the history of Savannah can be found on most any website. Information here was obtained at www.civilwaralbum.com
[j] Interesting side note: In 1808 (only eight years after this conversation took place), President Jefferson commissioned the building of Fort Jackson, named after the Governor of Georgia, James Jackson.

"Pinkerton agent?" Alfred shook his head at the abrupt shift.

"While I was discussing things with the Frenchman—the messenger was French, in case you didn't figure that out—another man came into the tavern and started asking questions about Miss Esterhaus. Identified himself as one Carl Standish."

"How do you know he was a Pinkerton?"

"Sorry, he introduced himself as Carl Standish, Pinkerton Agent."

"You playing games with words right now isn't wise, Henry. There is too much at stake."

"Think the same man hired him, as sent the request for an audience?" Middleton asked.

"I suppose that's probable. If I decided to seek an audience with a woman who'd placed that sort of advertisement, I'd likely have someone investigate her prior."

"Great, those ruts are getting more numerous, eh Garamond?" Jeremy said sarcastically.

"How so?"

"He's a Pinkerton agent, which means he may ask more questions than needed just to ascertain Miss Esterhaus' credibility. If he's as tenacious as most Pinkerton agents, he may draw conclusions surrounding the deaths of her family members."

"Deaths pronounced accidental, so I don't see the concern."

"No, I don't suppose you would, but it concerns me. Their deaths may have been pronounced accidental, but there were quite a few in a relatively short time; which may arouse the Pinkerton's suspicions. Even our local constable started questioning the coincidental timing and we had to do away with him. This new constable is too thick to have sorted things out as yet…anyway, things feel as if they are beginning to come apart, and I don't like it."

"I can't see how you came to that conclusion. We've managed to stay one step ahead of every obstacle thrown at us…"

"Yeah, by process of elimination," Middleton muttered sarcastically.

"…so this will prove no different," Garamond concluded,

ignoring his associate's snide remark. "Henry, keep tabs on the Pinkerton agent, just to be safe. See if he becomes suspicious of our activities. There isn't any reason to suspect he'll do more than check out Miss Esterhaus, but better to protect our interests." Henry nodded and made his way to the door. "And this time, Henry," Garamond called, as Henry stepped into the corridor, "feel free to presume what I want you to do, if you think he's a threat to those interests."

"I'm not a murderer," Henry stated firmly.

"No, but Arthur here knows where to hire one, don't you Arthur? If you perceive a threat, ask Arthur and he'll direct you to our scar-faced associate."

Arthur Middleton nodded, a shiver of repulsion running along his spine as he recalled his first meeting with the scar-faced man.

Satisfied that he wouldn't have to do more than surveil, Henry left the office, at which point Alfred turned to Middleton, a determined look on his face, "I think maybe you need to call on Miss Esterhaus and declare your intent to wed her."

"I thought that wasn't necessary, especially after all of your assurances not two minutes ago about successfully avoiding obstacles." Middleton visibly cringed.

"Dear God, but you can be a nuisance. I feel extremely confident that our plans will reach a satisfactory conclusion; however, sometimes plans need a little help is all. To my way of thinking, now is the time for a little help."

"This plan of yours has required more than a little assistance, Alfred; and a lot of obstacles which keep having to be eliminated."

"Maybe, but don't forget that we only have a little over a month left before it all pans out. I don't want anything preventing the bank seizure of that property. What happens if we underestimate this potential suitor; if he decides to wed her despite all of her shortcomings?"

"I made it clear at her parents' funeral that I couldn't stomach marrying that woman, so why should I make a bid for her hand now?"

"Because, you can string along an engagement for a month;

and then suddenly call it off when it's too late for her to find a husband. The idea here is to have her cancel her meeting with this potential suitor, and also to prevent her from placing that advertisement any longer. Before now, I perceived that advertisement as a comedy, one in which no man would possibly take seriously, and it appeared as if that was going to be the case; however…

"Alfred's got a point, Arthur," Jeremy said, "We can't risk this man agreeing to marry her."

Middleton shuddered again, "Fine. I'll stop by the store in the morning and make my *interest* known. Eventually though, Alfred, you are going to have to do some of the dirty work. Thus far, it has been my money, my task to hire the killer, my duty to court the woman…all you've done is "plan"; and I don't see how any planning went into the discovery of the property's riches or her future inheritance."

"You've heard me say, 'If it weren't for me…' plenty of times, right? Well, hear it again now, because if it weren't for me, Lara Esterhaus and family could have remained on that property indefinitely, not even realizing the potential treasure right beneath their feet. If it weren't for my cunning, you wouldn't be wealthier than you already are in another month. So stop whining about your contribution and focus on keeping things on point. Bank seizure is right around the corner. Now go win that lady's heart. It shouldn't be too difficult a task. I want her so enthralled with you that the moment the other man arrives she will not even glance his way."

CHAPTER 12

"So, the letter was waiting for us? That's great. After two weeks of not knowing anything…well, what does Standish have to say?" Andrew asked.

Philip climbed from his saddle, threw the reins over a nearby branch, and moved to sit on a log next to the fire. "Don't know," he said, removing the coffee from over the flame. "I haven't read the note yet, nor have I asked François what Miss Esterhaus had to say."

"François? He's back too?" Andrew asked, searching for their butler. He could see no sign of the man, but then heard the faint sound of horse's hooves. He turned and looked over his shoulder, and then noticed the Frenchman riding toward camp from the opposite path. "Oh, such hilarity, Brother."

"What?" Philip grinned, sipping the hot brew.

"Haven't asked yet? You've only just noticed his arriving, so…oh God, why do I allow myself to be baited, and what about the letter? Were you planning on reading that sometime this evening?"

"As soon as I have some coffee. Besides, I wish to know the lady's response before I read Standish's report. Hello François. Nice trip?"

"Tiring trip," the Frenchman huffed, climbing down from his saddle. "I am only glad that I did not have to ride all of the way to Virginia to deliver the lady's reply as I do not know if these old bones could handle more time in a saddle." He reached for the coffee and then noticed the looks of questioning on the faces of both brothers, "Oh, *excusez-moi*," he grinned, pouring himself a cup. "My apologies. Of course, the lady is willing to meet you."

"And?"

"And what? Is that not what you wished to hear?"

Philip and Andrew sighed simultaneously.

"Are her flaws obvious?" Philip asked, his exasperation showing.

"Not to me," François murmured, "but then, I am French. A woman would have to be a man not to turn my head."

"I see. Would you care to expound upon that? For instance, is she fair to look upon?" Philip tried again.

"Again…"

"I know, you're French."

"*Oui.*"

"Well, it looks as if we're going to have to wait until our arrival to find out anything of value related to Miss Esterhaus," Andrew sighed. "François, thank you for making the journey ahead of us. Once you've rested, you'll have to climb back into the saddle if you wish to get back to Virginia in a timely manner."

"*Oui*, this I know," the Frenchman cringed, "but I must allow for my derrière to be well-rested before I go."

Philip and Andrew laughed and shook their heads. After a moment of silence, in which all three men sipped at their coffee, Andrew turned the conversation back to the letter Philip retrieved from the town Postmaster, "So then, now that we know we're continuing onward, what about Standish's report. Anything of value there?"

"A bit impatient, aren't you, Andrew? Can't a man finish his coffee?" Philip teased.

"Just give me the bloody paper, will you, Philip?" Andrew snapped.

"Tsk, tsk," Philip grinned. "Patience is a virtue, after all."

"Well, my patience is wearing thin, Philip."

"This trip was you're idea, Andrew, so why would you find yourself impatient?"

"Fine! You don't want to know what the agent said, so be it!" Andrew snapped. "Burn the damnable thing for all I care."

Philip laughed, "Goodness, you certainly became ill mannered rather quickly. So, what precisely has you so out of sorts? Need I remind you so soon that this trip was your idea, after all?"

"Yes it was, but sleeping on the hard ground when there is perfectly adequate lodging in the town you just came from is nonsensical at best."

"Ah, so then your mercurial temperament hasn't to do with the fact that I wouldn't turn over the letter, rather it stems from your inability to live in the rough."

"I wasn't born to live like this and neither should I have to.

Neither should you, for that matter. So while I may find some things amusing, your wit isn't currently one of those things."

"Well, to address your complaint about our sleeping arrangements…since we are not certain as to the outcome of this venture, it would be unwise to spend unnecessary funds on luxuries that we could well do without. If this woman is indeed a woman of means, as she says, and we do determine to form a union of sorts, then you'll be able to sleep in whatever hotel you deem suitable. As for your snappishness over my wanting to relax before reading Carl's letter…"

"You're doing this on purpose, Philip," Andrew snapped, "as some form of petty retribution for talking you into coming."

"Truly? Well thank you for telling me. And here I thought I had a mind of my own."

"Yes well, that mind is being unreasonable at present."

Philip grinned, and reached into his coat pocket, "Here, read the letter."

"I don't want to."

"Oh, do stop behaving boorishly, and read the bloody thing, so that I can relax. After all, I was the one who had to make the trip into town to collect it, and you are ten times more eager to know its content. Would you rather I hand it to François? His English is barely comprehensible…"

Andrew snatched the letter and ripped open the seal. Philip laughed. His brother loved to tease, but had a harder time with being teased; which is why Philip loved to give him a taste of his own medicine from time-to-time. His humor dissipated however when he saw brother's expression.

"Aren't you going to read it aloud?" Philip asked, watching his brother's reaction carefully.

"What? Oh, yes. Aloud."

"What is it, Andrew?"

"I'm not certain. Standish's letter appears to have been written rather hurriedly, as if he had much to say and no time to say it," Andrew replied while scanning the contents quickly. "And apparently there are wicked games afoot."

"So, she is a charlatan then?"

"No, his letter only mentions her."

"Perhaps you'd better read the letter."

"It's more a collection of incomplete sentences, but yes, perhaps I'd best read it. It reads: *Salutations. I hope this letter finds you well. Trip raising more questions than answers.*"

"Perhaps you'd best jump to the heart of the letter; the reason for our journey."

"Ah, yes. He goes on to write: *Lady in question genuine. Flaws apparent as stated.* He stopped, quirking a questioning brow at François, to which the Frenchman merely shrugged his shoulders. Andrew sighed and continued, *Flaws surmountable? For you to decide upon arrival.*"

"That's it?" Philip asked, quirking a brow.

"About the lady, yes, but then he goes on to write: *Deadly game being played by others. Will explain when you arrive. Still investigating.*"

"Deadly games? I don't understand." Philip's brow knitted in confusion. "And what kind of missive is that to be sending anyway? What of it, François? Did you ascertain anything that would lead you to believe that there are dangerous games afoot?"

"*Non*, but then again, I was there only long enough to await the lady's answer, and, of course, quench my thirst," He replied, grinning, but the grin quickly faded, replaced by a knit in his brow.

"You've something to add, François?" Philip asked, noticing his butler's sudden shift in demeanor.

"I cannot say whether this is of importance, but I was approached while partaking of my noonday meal."

"I thought you only stopped long enough to quench your thirst," Andrew quipped and François's face reddened.

"Well, a man needs sustenance in order to undertake such an arduous journey..."

"You said you were approached?" Philip interrupted.

"Oh, *oui*, there was a man who wished to converse with me about my business in town. He seemed a friendly sort of fellow, so I did not see a need for subterfuge."

"You told him why you were there?"

"*Oui*. Not everything, of course. Merely that I was only passing through, delivering a letter for my employer…that sort of thing. Did I get the feeling that there was danger in his inquiries? *Non*."

"No, I don't suppose you would, but I have a feeling that his nosiness ties into Carl's investigation."

"I concur. Still, what kind of deadly games could he be referring to?" Andrew asked, rhetorically, but his brother answered anyway.

"Perhaps the kind that gets a man, or woman, killed."

"That's a leaping assumption."

"Call it intuition instead, but there is something going on. The fact that François was questioned in conjunction with the tone of Carl's letter leads me to think that 'deadly' has already occurred."

CHAPTER 13

"Good afternoon, Miss Lara," Arthur Middleton said in his best genteel manner. He abhorred having to play this part, but abhorred greater the fact that he was having more difficulty snaring Lara's attention, much less her hand in marriage, than he'd anticipated. Apparently, he and his friends underestimated Lara Esterhaus' desperation to find a husband, for he'd been patroning her establishment under one pretext or other for the past week, with little more than a nod of acknowledgement from her. They'd all been certain—a little too certain—that someone in her position, as well as with her physical and mental shortcomings, would swoon after any man who even deigned show her a passing glance.

"Good afternoon, Mr. Middleton, isn't it?" He detested her businesslike manner as much as he did everything else about her, but was pleased that she'd at least recollected his name. He pasted on a smile, hoping that it portrayed his pleasure at her familiarity, but she'd already returned to her business at hand.

"I was beginning to wonder whether you'd noticed me at all, Miss Esterhaus," he stated in a morose tone, moving to stand closer to her side.

Lara paused at his tone and turned to face this man who had been coming into the store for the past week, irritating her with his lack of purchase. She'd considered calling the constable and complaining, for she could fathom no valid reason as to why he would continue coming into her shop for other than a place to duck the summer heat.

"I do beg pardon, sir?"

"Did it not register Miss Esterhaus that I have visited you daily in order to summon enough courage in which to ask you to dine with me?" He smiled, not at the fact that he'd finally snared her attention, but rather that his words were truer than she could ever imagine, for he had needed to summon every ounce of courage, daily, just to enter her place of business.

"Indeed it did not, sir," Lara answered candidly after a moment's scrutiny. Suddenly, she felt that her childhood game was about to become a reality, for a certainty flooded her heart and mind that this man was more than he appeared; a dastardly fiend in disguise. For a mere moment, before she responded to his statement, she wanted to believe him interested in her, but she knew it was a ruse, for his gaze contradicted the sincerity of his words. There was a disdain in his gaze that he attempted poorly to hide. He was after something, and should she fall for his pretty words, she'd prove no more than a means to his ends. Was he after her store? Her money perhaps? Had he seen her advertisement and decided to overlook her obvious flaws in lieu of a profitable arrangement?

Isn't that what she wanted?

As she looked at him, she wondered why she hesitated. Here was a potential answer to all of her problems, and even if he'd approached her merely because of her advertisement, shouldn't she be accepting his dinner invitation with alacrity, and doing all she could to convince him that marriage to her would be to his advantage?

Was she too cowardly to act upon her own whim?

Just then Mrs. Harper came bustling from the rear of the store, an armful of newly altered gowns thrown over both arms, "A little help, Lara," she called.

From the time it took for Lara to glance toward Mrs. Harper and back, Mr. Middleton vanished. Lara shook off his visit as a potential illusion, though she knew it was very real, before turning to assist her seamstress, "Fine job, Mrs. Harper. Let's get these wrapped for delivery before calling it an evening, shall we?"

The two ladies worked in silence, rather Lara did, for Mrs. Harper was never silent. Usually Lara listened to Mrs. Harper harp on about one thing or other with good-natured calm, but tonight that calm was outwardly only. Her mind was in chaos over her rather unusual visitor. It wasn't until Mrs. Harper mentioned hiring additional help that Lara returned her attention outside her mind.

"Do you have someone in mind? Mind you, she'll have to be as competent as you before I'll hire her on."

"Oh, she's competent all right. I've only been teaching her the trade since she was old enough to thread a needle."

"Referring to your daughter?"

"I certainly am. Would you mind letting her come to work here?

I've decided that you're right about the work load, and my fingers don't operate as smoothly and quickly as they once did."

"I have full confidence that your daughter will work out just fine; however, I'm sure you'll agree that I'll not be able to start her at your wages."

"I do, yes. I thought perhaps to pay her based on the number of dresses she completes effectively as a fair beginning. What say you?"

"I'd say that's fair indeed. She'll start on the morrow. I'll expect you to keep tabs on her work and provide an honest assessment on her abilities. Neither of us wishes our customers to find their dresses elsewhere, after all."

"I concur one hundred percent. Well then, that's the last of the dresses wrapped for delivery. I'll see you tomorrow, Miss Lara."

"Yes, tomorrow, Mrs. Harper, and thank you for the initiative in locating suitable assistance."

Mrs. Harper nodded, "Until tomorrow."

"Good night, Mrs. Harper."

Lara placed the packages in the delivery bin, collected her reticule, and then left the store. The moment she stepped onto the boardwalk and climbed aboard her buggy, her mind returned to her unusual visitor.

Should she take his pursuit seriously and accept his offer to dine should he deign to return and ask? If she did take him seriously, would that make it impossible to entertain any pursuit from the gentleman from Virginia?

"Well, that resolves that," she stated with finality, having reached a decision after only a minute of deliberation. "Still, it will be interesting to share today's rather interesting developments with Joshua and Sasha, and of course hear their opinion as to the decision at which I arrived."

She clucked her tongue at her horses and picked up speed, moving along the cobblestone street at a faster clip than normal, anxious to confer with her friends, but also to fill the gaping hole in her belly. She was famished.

CHAPTER 14

As was their nightly habit, the three occupants of the home settled at the servants table in the kitchen, recapping the day. Tonight it was Lara's turn to go last, which made listening to the others' tales of house chore horrors all the more difficult.

When it was finally her turn to speak, Lara eagerly recounted the visit by one of their townsmen and his less than apparent intentions.

"Sounds as if he may be after your home and store, Lara," Sasha observed.

"While I agree, I really haven't any evidence to substantiate that fact, thus it remains supposition. Am I doing us a disservice by dismissing his interest outright? Or do I heed the warning bells inside of my head and move on in the hopes that the gentleman from Virginia will prove a better option. Moreover, while I have never been in this position before, I feel it would be discourteous somehow to send consent for an audience to one man while dining with another."

"I thought you already reached your decision," Joshua stated.

"True, but I guess I need you two to offer a more justifiable reason other than the gentleman at the store seems disingenuous. Or that entertaining two males simultaneously is uncouth. My decision was based solely on the latter. After all, to tell the gentleman from Virginia that I will entertain his pursuit only to dismiss his pursuit upon his arrival, merely because another man seems interested in a courtship—thus potentially reaching an end to our plight sooner— seems crass. Wouldn't you agree?"

"I think that this—what was his name again? The man from the store?" Sasha asked.

"Mr. Middleton; however, I don't recall his given name."

"His arrival at the store seems too timely, or am I the only one thinking along these lines?"

"Do you recall the conversation you overheard in the alcove, Sasha? At the masters' funeral?" Joshua asked. When Sasha nodded, he continued, addressing Lara, "Well, those men seemed convinced that you wouldn't be able to find a husband and the house would be taken by the bank and auctioned off, correct?"

"So you think that this was one of those men? That he, and the other man possibly, no longer view my inability to wed as a certainty and now are seeking to prevent my taking notice of potentially genuine suitors?"

"Sounds as if you already figured it all out in your head before we even started this conversation," Sasha laughed, taking a bite out of her dinner roll.

"Not all," Lara said thoughtfully. "Talking to you two helped me gain necessary perspective. So what say you about refusing this man's advances? If I do, and the man from Virginia decides against marriage, we would, inevitably, lose everything."

"From what you tell me, I do believe that this Middleton is a dastardly fiend in disguise for certain, and it would bode far worse for all of us were you to take his pursuit seriously," Joshua said, his tone dire.

"Then we'll await the arrival of our mystery man from Virginia and hope he sees fit to make an offer."

"We will see to it that he sees you for who you truly are, Miss Lara," Joshua said affectionately. "If he can't, then he's blind."

"I was kind of hoping he would be," Lara laughed nervously. Joshua sent her a look of rebuke, but decided not to comment.

"I know that we are risking a good deal by turning away the only man who may prove our salvation, but I can't bear seeing you marry someone whose true person is the devil, just to save our hides," he said instead.

"That reminds me of one more matter that I was thinking upon on the ride home today."

"An awful lot of thinking for such a short buggy ride," Sasha quipped.

"More than you know."

"What else possessed your thoughts, Miss Lara?"

"You and Sasha."

"Hmm, and what thoughts might those have been?"

"Probably who best to sell us to," Sasha whined.

"Now don't you go assuming about Miss Lara's thoughts, Sasha," Joshua admonished.

Lara smiled, "Actually, I thought that if things turned against us, that I might find a place for you two at the store. Living and working quarters would be snug, but if you two are willing to make a go of it…" She stopped speaking at the look of shock on both faces. "Neither of you would prefer that option?"

"It sounds absolutely lovely," Sasha whispered.

"You'd really keep us on?" Joshua asked in awe.

"I wouldn't be able to keep the entire staff on, but you two are more my friends than any friends I've ever had, and if we can stay together, I was hoping it would be preferable to finding new households."

"Indeed it would, Miss Lara. You have our deepest gratitude."

"Now Joshua, don't you dare cry, or you'll make me cry," Sasha admonished, swiping at the tears welling in her eyes.

"Don't anyone start crying…"

A knock at the door brought their conversation to an abrupt halt. "Joshua?"

"On my way, Miss Lara."

A few minutes later, Joshua returned to the kitchen, a look on his face similar as to the night of the constable's visit, "What is it, Joshua?"

"There's a Mr. Arthur Middleton come to call."

Lara visibly stiffened. "So that's his given name. Oh well, this is a rather unnerving surprise. I suppose now would be as good a time as any to inform the gentleman of my decision. Hopefully put an end to his determined courtship. Joshua, escort him to my sitting room and then prepare tea. Sasha, ready yourself to act as chaperone and send Elizabeth to act as attendant this evening."

With no further word needed, Sasha and Joshua jumped into action while Lara made her way to her bedroom to change into proper attire for receiving a male visitor and to compose her nerves. She knew she was going to meet up with Mr. Middleton again soon, but had not counted on his resolve bringing him to her home.

Elizabeth was waiting in her room when she arrived.

"We'll do the burgundy gown," Lara said without preamble, and then settled on the settee to await Elizabeth's ministrations. The maid ran a comb through her hair, pinned it atop her head and placed a rose colored bonnet as a finishing touch. Once completed, she asked Lara to stand. She unbuttoned the back of her gown and had Lara step into a less elaborate French brocaded silk taffeta open robe in a shade of burgundy which complemented her hair and eye color perfectly.

"All done, Miss Lara," Elizabeth murmured.

"Very good. Thank you, Elizabeth. You may return to your duties."

Elizabeth curtsied and left. Lara stood before her mirror, taking shallow, comforting breaths. When she was certain her outward appearance did not give away her inner tumult, she left her room and made her way towards the sitting room. Sasha was waiting outside the door.

"If you wanted to turn this gentleman's head more so than you've already done, you'd succeed in this gown, Lara. I always favored it as well-suited to you."

"Thank you, Sasha. I am not at all certain I know how to entertain a gentleman caller, as I've never had one. Mother taught me the skills…"

"Well then, now is the time to put those skills into practice," Sasha interrupted, knowing her mistress was simply postponing entrance into the sitting room.

"Very good. Would you do me a favor, Sasha?"

"Anything."

"Would you sit where you can surreptitiously observe Mr. Middleton's demeanor, especially his eyes."

"See if I can see the same dastardly fiend as you, or do you want to somehow find him worthy of your hand?"

"I want you to form an opinion of the man using your own brain, and try not to jump to an opinion based upon our earlier conversation. For today, I must turn Mr. Middleton away, but if you feel there is the slightest chance that I may have been wrong in…"

"You don't want to quash any hope entirely if our gentleman from Virginia turns out to be even more of a fiend?"

"Precisely." Lara drew in a nervous breath and let it out on a whoosh then turned the doorknob. "Shall we?"

CHAPTER 15

"Mr. Middleton, what an unexpected surprise," Lara said graciously, extending her hand. Arthur took it and placed a very light kiss on the back, then released it with rapidity. "Might I introduce Miss Sasha Blackwell?"

"You're introducing me to your servant?" Arthur Middleton's eyes widened absurdly, and Lara knew she'd committed her first faux pas. She glanced at Sasha's face. Her expression revealed that even she, a servant, was aware of Lara's mistake. She did her best to cover her ineptness as quickly as possible.

"Sasha is a friend, acting as chaperone this evening." It was a lie, but as lies went, Lara justified tacitly, a harmless one.

"Ah," Mr. Middleton glanced over Sasha's less than fashionable attire, dismissed her as poverty stricken, and lightly kissed the back of her hand, "A pleasure, Miss Blackwell."

Sasha grinned at her temporarily elevated status, and then settled onto a nearby Rococo Chaise, "Do go on, as if I'm not even here," Sasha said in imitation of the upper classes. Lara smiled and rolled her eyes, but settled on a chair opposite Arthur, hoping that Sasha would be able to peruse their guest without appearing too obvious.

"Of course," Arthur smiled graciously, and then turned his attentions to Lara. He struggled to keep it in place when he saw that, even seated, he had to raise his chin a notch, just to look her in the eyes properly. "Well, Miss Lara, I had hoped to continue our conversation of earlier today."

Just then a knock sounded, and Lara jumped. She sighed quietly, silently telling herself to unwind her taut nerves, "Enter."

Joshua opened the door and entered, bearing a tray with tea and a few sweetmeats. He set the tray down on the small table and turned to address the guest, "How would you like your tea, sir?"

"Two sugars."

"A sweetmeat?"

"No."

"Miss Lara?"

"A sweetmeat sounds lovely, Joshua. Thank you."

Arthur watched the exchange and again cringed at the

casualness, the intimacy, at which this woman conversed with those of lower class distinction; even deigning to look them in the eye. He was of a sudden grateful that his pursuit was merely a deception, for he found it unimaginable to bring this woman into his home only to have her befriend his servants; to slowly find those servants more than running his home but in control of it also. He had a difficult time keeping the shiver, which raced along his spine at the thought, in check.

Joshua completed his task, bowed at the guest, and took his leave. The moment he departed, Arthur again began his attempts at making his intention known. He decided it was better to be straightforward in his intentions than hem and haw about the subject; a luxury neither he nor Lara Esterhaus had the time for, nor inclination. Of course, he also wanted to finalize his insertion into her life as soon as possible, so he could put this charade behind him quickly. He disliked her immensely, and abhorred being in her company, although she'd been nothing but cordial since his arrival. He realized his perceptions of her stemmed not from her personally but rather from his own feelings of ineptness. He was wealthy, but his wealth was inherited; and while part of Lara's wealth was also inherited, or would be once she married, she had also proven successful at establishing her own wealth. Moreover, he felt inadequate as a man when standing or even seated next to her, for her height was obscene for a woman.

"Mr. Middleton?" Lara hedged when he merely sat staring off in contemplation.

Arthur visibly jumped, startled, "Oh dear, my apologies." He cleared his throat and started his rehearsed speech, "As I stated at the store earlier, it is my intent to…well, to start with a nice dinner, and then perhaps…what I mean to say," Arthur stumbled, his rehearsed speech falling into a jumbled mess, "is that it is my intention to court you. Not that you don't have a say in the matter…"

"Mr. Middleton, please relax."

"My apologies again." Arthur took a deep breath, determined to get through his speech smoothly, but before he could start again, Lara interrupted him. What he'd failed to perceive was that his presence annoyed her almost as much as she annoyed him. Sitting and listening to him speak, made her quiver with repulsion. She quickly decided that despite her need for a husband she wouldn't allow desperation to saddle her with this type of man. She'd rather move into her shop than live in abject misery.

"Mr. Middleton, I think perhaps it is best to stop this before it even begins. While I am sincerely honored at your attention, and while I am certain that your motivations in coming here are pure, I must decline your offer of courtship and bid you a pleasant evening." Lara stood to leave; however, instead of rising to escort her to the door, and himself from the house, Arthur sat in stunned disbelief. Breaking with etiquette, which she didn't feel obliged to follow anyway, Lara curtsied lightly and left the room.

After a moment, Sasha stood to follow, only to be stopped short by a query from their guest.

"Is your friend insane?" Arthur whispered.

For a moment, Sasha forgot that she wasn't a servant who could address his question; rather Lara had temporarily elevated her to someone of his rank, which meant she was quite able to converse with him—should she choose. Although she knew she could speak, no words emerged, and she stood immobile, until he speared her with a haughty look that incensed her. She raised her chin a notch, remembering that this man could very well have been the one in the alcove laughing at Lara at her parents' funeral.

"Lara always keeps her wits about her," she said in a puffed-up tone.

"Apparently not," Arthur rejoined, "because if she were at all rational she would appreciate that I am the only man willing to marry her. Is she not in danger of losing her inheritance, including this home?"

"Indeed she is; however, Lara did not feel it was respectful to…" Sasha stopped speaking, trying to find the proper words for a reply so that she revealed only that which Lara may have revealed.

"Respectful to what?" Arthur demanded.

Sasha jumped, took a deep breath and hoped she didn't sound like a servant when next she spoke, "Lara has already accepted someone else's courtship and didn't feel it polite to accept yours also."

Arthur's eyes narrowed, "Someone else's."

"I fear I've said too much," Sasha said, wishing to depart in all haste. She wasn't capable of maintaining a pretense with this man, and she feared that anything she said could come back to hurt Lara. "I think perhaps Lara intended to tell you, but wanted to spare your feelings. Now, if you will excuse me, I really need to…" Sasha nearly said, 'tend to my duties', but caught herself, choosing instead to curtsey and flee.

Arthur sat there enshrouded in fury. It would have been humiliating having someone worth his time reject his pursuit, but to be rejected by someone like Lara Esterhaus was beyond the pale[k]. He stood and had to balance himself when the blood rushed from his head. He closed his eyes to steady both his body and his thoughts. When he opened them, Joshua was standing in the doorway, watching him intently. For Arthur, that was simply too much.

He stormed over to the older black servant, stopping only when his face was mere inches away from Joshua's startled gaze, "When Lara loses everything and you are put on the auction block, I will make certain that I win the bidding; then I will make certain the time you have remaining on this earth is nothing short of hellish." With that, Arthur shoved Joshua aside and stormed from the house.

Joshua wiped the spittle from his face and then went in search of Lara. He found her drinking a cup of tea at the kitchen table.

"Mind if I join you?" He asked softly.

"Only if I can too," Sasha said, following behind. "I saw what that heathen did to you, Joshua, and heard what he said. You didn't deserve that."

"What happened?"

"That man threatened to buy Joshua at auction when you lose everything and abuse him every day until he dies; then he nearly pushed him down…"

---

[k] Unacceptable; outside agreed standards of decency
(http://www.phrases.org.uk/meanings/beyond-the-pale.html)

"Now Sasha, don't go exaggerating the matter. He was merely distraught and I provided an outlet."

"You really are too generous, Joshua. Any other man would have punched him in the face," Sasha snapped.

"Any man not a servant," Joshua concluded.

"Are you alright, Joshua?" Lara whispered.

"I am unharmed, Miss Lara."

"I should have a word…"

"I would advise against doing so, Miss Lara," Joshua interrupted. "The man is fickle in the head, and I do believe he is not above causing bodily harm to a person."

"He reminded me of a petulant child who pitched a hissy fit when he didn't get what he wanted, even though it was obvious he didn't really want it," Sasha murmured.

"So we can all agree with my earlier assessment that his intentions could not possibly be honorable and therefore it was the right decision to turn away from his pursuit. I'd say that the dastardly fiend hiding inside this one was similar to a Samuel Mason[1]…"

"Who?" Sasha asked.

"Oh, father told me about him. A former militia captain with a fondness for taking lives."

"He's got a temper to be sure," Joshua said, "but we can hardly compare him to a killer."

"I don't know about that, Joshua," Sasha said, "you didn't see the look he speared me with. If looks could kill…"

"Joshua's right," Lara interrupted, "I was just over exaggerating the man's character. After all, it's one thing to have a tantrum, as you two appeared to have witnessed, it's quite another to transfer that into physical harm upon a person. We will just mark this down as a timely learning experience and move on to our other potential suitor arriving in a little more than a fortnight."[m]

"I certainly hope that he doesn't end up being a fiend in disguise like Mr. Middleton."

---

1 http://truecrimeus.com/database/samuel-mason/
[m] A fortnight is a British term which means 14 days or two weeks.

"While I said that Samuel Mason could be the fiend hiding inside, I truly believe that Mr. Middleton wore no disguise. His fiendishness was quite transparent. Anyway, I do believe we are all hoping that this man from Virginia proves a more affable fellow," Lara sighed. "Well, we'd better continue our preparations on the morrow. In the meantime, I will bid you both a good night. Sasha, are you coming?"

Joshua touched Sasha's arm, delaying her departure silently.

"In a moment, Lara. Comb out your hair and I'll be along to help you with your clothing."

Lara nodded, stifling a yawn.

"Goodnight, Lara," Joshua said. When she'd left the room, Joshua turned to Sasha, "I think we'd best keep our eyes opened wide, Sasha, so as to keep all of us safe, especially Miss Lara, because I don't think we've heard the last from Mr. Middleton."

CHAPTER 16

Arthur wasted no time deciding upon a plan of retribution, his friends' wishes be damned. He would not be rejected by the likes of the Esterhaus woman and not make her pay for it. Had he been of sound mind, he may have taken time to consult with Alfred about his intentions, but he wasn't and therefore he didn't.

He glanced at his pocket watch. Still early enough in the day for a buggy ride. He left Lara's home, climbed aboard his phaeton, slapped the whip toward the horses and sped down the cobblestoned streets towards the wharf. It was time, again, to find his scar-faced associate.

CHAPTER 17

"It wasn't very clear on whether we're to meet him somewhere or…"

"Well, I suppose he'll come straight here when he arrives. He didn't specify, and since he also didn't say *how* he'll be arriving, I wouldn't know where to meet him anyway."

"So, in another day or two," Sasha said, grinning, "we'll get to meet your knight in shining armor. Cutting it close though, if you ask me. We've only a little more than a week remaining before the bank takes what's rightfully yours."

"Oh, Sasha," Lara sighed, "don't be so dramatic." She took a bite of her pudding, which reminded her of her thoughts. She was definitely pudding headed right now; her nerves a jumbled mess.

"Well he would be your rescuer, in a manner of speaking," Joshua said. "Wouldn't you say? A rescuer to us all, if truth be told."

"Well, you're counting on him to propose immediately upon arrival. For all we know, he'll take one look at me…"

"And fall madly in love," Sasha concluded.

"I can't say that's ever happened to me before. Most just turn and hightail it the other way."

"Well before was then. This is now."

"And what has changed about me *now* that would make a man's head turn, I ask you?"

"Well you're twenty now and there are plenty of men who prefer an older, more mature woman."

"Sasha, the next time the mistress asks a question, make believe it's hypothetical."

"What did I say?"

"Let's just say that if you'd written the advertisement, she wouldn't have even gotten this little nibble."

"Well I most certainly wouldn't have said she has 'obvious flaws', for goodness sake."

"No, you would have listed every one of them in alphabetical order," Joshua snapped.

"Okay you two," Lara sighed, "enough bickering please. I know Sasha means well, Joshua, so there's no need to come to my rescue. And Sasha, Joshua's right. It's not necessary to constantly point out my flaws or agree with me when I mention them. It doesn't bode well for my confidence."

"Oh, Lara," Sasha whined, "I don't mean any disrespect. You know I love you like a sister."

"I know, Sasha," Lara smiled, "which is why I try to overlook your wayward tongue. Now since we are going to have a visitor rather soon, we need to make arrangements, wouldn't you both agree?"

"Most assuredly," Joshua said.

"I'll be happy to get up early to get the cleaning staff started," Sasha offered.

"Pshaw," Joshua scoffed, "You can't ever get out of bed before the sun's well on its way to the top of the sky."

"That's not true…"

"You know, I don't think you two have ever bickered this much. Could be the stress is getting to more than me?"

Joshua and Sasha lowered their gazes and remained silent.

"I think that's perhaps the case, and I do understand it well enough, but you two need to curb your enthusiasm a little. Either way, I didn't mean that we needed to do more cleaning, Sasha. After all, we've all been scrubbing non-stop for the last two weeks. I don't think there isn't anything left that doesn't gleam. I was thinking more along the lines of our menu. Joshua? At what time are the extra hires due to arrive in the morning? It's important our kitchen runs efficiently."

"Five in the a.m., Miss Lara, and I've planned a trip into town with some of them come sunrise tomorrow to buy additional supplies, while the others start preparations for the noonday meal. Is there anything else we can do to make this go more smoothly besides providing memorable meals? We want to make you look doubly good."

"Then it might be a good idea to solicit prayers from everyone. Specifically that this particular individual is blind or has no objection to tall, slender business women with intellect.”

“Sounds like a sound request to me,” Sasha said, jokingly.

“Oh do hush yourself, girl,” Joshua snapped.

Lara sighed, “There is one important thing that you two can do to ensure our guest isn’t put off. That is to maintain a respectful decorum; none of this nonsensical bickering in front of him. I know you two mean nothing by your nonsense, but a stranger may be put off by it. Agreed?”

“Of course, Miss Lara,” Joshua said, his tone subdued. When Sasha remained quiet, he leaned over and nudged her, “Well, speak up, girl!”

When Sasha merely glared at Joshua, Lara grew concerned, “Sasha. What’s wrong?”

“You’ve never treated us like servants, Lara, but you telling us to behave made me realize that this man that’s coming may very well treat us like the hired help; and that made me think about your own behavior. What if this man is good enough to marry, but expects you to start acting a certain way. This could very well be our last dinner together. We could lose your friendship.”

Lara sat back, a thoughtful expression on her face. She sighed several times, mulling over what Sasha said, her gaze drifting back and forth between the two worried gazes of her friends. Eventually, after composing her words carefully, she addressed their concerns.

“I don’t know what to expect any more than you do. For all we know the gentleman coming won’t remain any longer than others who’ve met me. On the other hand, he may not have an objection to my person and decide marriage is an option. How that will affect your position in this household will have to be seen; however, I hope you both know that you are more than servants and always have been. I will introduce you two as my friends and ask politely that this gentleman respect my decision to continue to allow you to dine with us as such.”

“Miss Lara, I love you as if you were my own daughter,” Joshua said softly, “and I hope you don’t mind if I speak my mind about this matter.”

“Of course not, Joshua. What’s transpiring affects you two as much as it does me."

"Well then, I don't think it would be wise to be placing demands upon this man; especially if he does seem interested in making himself at home here. We may be your friends, and always will be, but until we suss out this man's character, I say we act appropriate to our station. After all, we need to make certain you look real good."

"I understand and I guess I do agree to a certain extent. Ok, so let's come to some sort of conciliation, shall we? I won't introduce you as my friends, but I won't treat you as common servants either. Hopefully my attitude towards you will represent your standing in this household, and our guest will pick up on that readily. Until we determine the sort of fellow he is, I will simply have to try to find a decent compromise and hope that our rapport isn't as off-putting as it was for Mr. Middleton. I guess we must ask ourselves—do we want a master for this home who is unkind, someone who cannot fathom crossing the imaginary master-servant line? I would prefer a man like my father; a man unafraid to look a servant in the eye and speak to him or her with respect. Still, with that being said, I won't abide any silly bickering, you two. At least for the time being," she concluded with a smile.

"We understand, Miss Lara," Joshua smiled, "and we did just say we wanted you to look doubly good, didn't we? So we aren't likely to do something to jeopardize this meeting. Isn't that correct, Sasha?"

Sasha nodded, her expression still registering all of the doubts flooding her mind. Still, to her credit, she remained silent—this time.

"I never doubted your dedication to this endeavor, because I know how much this means to all of us; and while I sympathize with your concerns, we really do need someone here whom the law recognizes as master of the household. Without him…well, we'll discuss those events should it become warranted. In the meantime, I'll be off to bed. We all should consider getting a good night's sleep. With our nerves a jumbled mess, while awaiting this man's arrival, I have a feeling we're going to need all the rest we can get. And Sasha, try not to look so grim."

"I'll do my best," Sasha grumbled.

Lara shook her head and grinned, "You're such a silly girl." She stood and stretched and then made her way to the door, "Now do come along. The sooner you attend me, the sooner you can get to sleep also. Goodnight, Joshua. Sleep sweet."

"You too, Miss Lara."

Joshua made his way around the house, locking doors, checking windows, and extinguishing lanterns. He snuffed out the light in the entryway, casting the foyer into darkness. As he made his way through the kitchens to his living quarters, he glanced out of the window and stopped short. Although Mr. Solow had long ago extinguished the lamp flames lining the street, the full moon radiated the street across from the house with ample light so that he was able to make out the silhouette of a man. The bright red tip of a cheroot[n] showed bright against the darkness, confirming that it was indeed a person and not simply his imagination run amok.

"There seems to be an awful lot of interest in Miss Lara of late," he whispered to himself, wondering if this was the same man whom Lara had seen on prior occasions. Inwardly, he debated whether he should collect one of the muskets from the gun cabinet with which to scare away this person, but decided against it. Not that it mattered now, as the silhouette started walking away. "I have feeling that, one of these days real soon; I am going to have shoot somebody dead."

---

[n] A cigar cut square at both ends.

CHAPTER 18

The thud was just loud enough to jar Lara from sleep, but not enough to keep her tired lids up. She started to drift back into her dream when another thud sounded. It was if a drunkard was stumbling about on her front porch. She shook off the vestiges of sleep and sat up against her headboard, straining to hear if another thud sounded.

It didn't, instead the faint tinkle of glass shattering reached her ears. Her nerves pricked and she felt her heart increase its rhythm to where only pounding could be heard inside her head.

She knew it was foolish to go investigate the noise, but if she didn't ascertain what was happening, she'd never be able to return to sleep. She tiptoed across her bedroom floor, careful to avoid the boards that creaked and groaned with every footfall. She cringed when she landed on one of those boards, hoping that the noise didn't echo loudly in the rooms below. After a moment of deep breaths to steady her nerves, she began her movement again.

The hinge to her bedroom door squeaked as she opened it, and she flinched. If there was someone in her home, they would be as capable of hearing her movements as she had been theirs. When she was almost certain that no one detected her presence, she slowly made her way across the landing, leaning over the railing as far as she dared to see if she could see anything. It was too dark below, even though she could see through the far window the start of a new day peeking over the horizon. Apparently it was later in the morning than her brain realized.

She slowly made her way down the stairs, stopping occasionally as the sound of voices drifted toward her. No longer did she doubt there was someone in her house, but who? What did they want?

As her feet continued forward, she again questioned the wisdom of investigating this on her own. "Perhaps I should wake Joshua?" She whispered to herself and then realized that his quarters were on the other side of the kitchen from where the voices were issuing. She sighed. As she reached the foyer, her gaze fell upon her father's gun cabinet. She didn't know how to shoot a musket to save her life, but the intruders may be unaware of that. With stealth she didn't know she possessed, she made her way over to the cabinet and retrieved a musket, and then turned and headed for the kitchen. She hadn't bothered loading it, because she really didn't have any intention of firing it; however, she hoped that the mere sight of the musket aimed at their bellies would be enough of a motivator to have the intruders flee her home and think twice about returning.

She moved slowly down the hall toward the kitchen, taking deep breaths with each step. The last thing she needed was for her nerves to be wound so tight that the musket shook in her hand. The idea was to appear confident, not comical.

When she reached the door, it opened suddenly. Lara screamed and dropped the musket. Her hand flew to her chest and she began laughing when Joshua stopped short in alarm at seeing her there.

"Goodness, Miss Lara, what are you doing up and about, and why do you have the master's musket?" He asked, reaching down to retrieve the weapon.

"Oh Joshua, was that you making all that ruckus?" She gasped between laughs.

"I'm sorry if the new kitchen staff woke you. I told them to keep it shushed up, but they was like a pack of cows coming in the back door. They haven't been here half hour and I already had to send the one packing because she broke one of the mistress' favorite crystal glasses."

When Lara continued laughing, so hard that tears started streaming down her cheeks, Joshua grew concerned that one of the bolts in her head had finally popped free from all of the strain she'd been under.

"You okay, Miss Lara? I told you that the extra kitchen help would be arriving at five this morning, and I sure am sorry that they disturbed your beauty sleep... goodness girl, are you going to keep cackling like that. You're scaring me but good."

"I'm sorry, Joshua," Lara gasped, trying to gain a modicum of control. She took breaths between laughs and swiped at the tears in her eyes, but it took several minutes more before she regained control of her near-hysteria.

"I think maybe you need to have some tea. All of the anxiety you been under is starting to show, and we can't have you breaking apart like that when our guest arrives." Joshua took Lara by the elbow and ushered her into the kitchen, and then settled her at the table. He snapped at one of the new hires to get some tea and biscuits prepared faster than fast, and then settled in a chair next to Lara.

"How are you doing now, Miss Lara?"

"Much improved, Joshua, thank you," she responded, stifling a yawn. "Goodness, but that was a scare. Far too early in the morning to have my nerves jostled about like that." She glanced over to where the new kitchen staff bustled with the bread dough, "So, this is what early morning looks like," she quipped. She was never in the kitchen when the cooking was taking place, only after when Joshua, Sasha, and she settled down to eat. Lara stifled another yawn, "My stars, but this has been an exhausting morning already."

"Skulking about the house after imaginary intruders atop the tension you're already carrying over the arrival of your new suitor, can certainly fatigue a body."

Lara laughed, "Yes, and add to those my earlier than usual wake up time and I'll be surprised if I can manage to stay awake during our noon-day meal."

"I will just make certain that the coffee steeps a bit longer than usual. That should keep the pep in your step."

Lara laughed again, "Your attentiveness to my vigor is certainly appreciated, Joshua. Well," Lara said, standing quickly, "since the staff is preparing an early meal, I guess I'd best head on back upstairs and prepare for the day. Will you send Sasha to attend me? She is probably going to grumble over having to rise this early, but remind her that she'll survive it and not to complain."

Joshua laughed, "That she will. I'll send her along Miss Lara, and I'll just return the musket to its proper place, shall I?"

"Most assuredly. Thank you."

"Um, Miss Lara, it wasn't loaded, was it?"

"Of course not. I haven't the slightest notion how to load a musket."

Joshua let loose a sigh of relief. After all, a loaded weapon dropped could discharge causing injury or death to bystanders. He shook his head, collected the musket, and followed Lara from the kitchen.

"We should have a small repast completed by the time you come back down. Are you planning to open the shop today? I meant to ask last night."

"Yes, I'll go in early, since I'm up. I can work on the books and prepare some orders before opening. It's better to keep myself preoccupied while we await the arrival of our guest. If I stay here, I'll be underfoot and fretful."

"That's completely understandable. I'll see to waking Sasha now."

"Thank you again, Joshua. I'll see you for breakfast shortly then."

He watched as she ascended the staircase, and then returned the musket to its place in the cabinet, all the while issuing thanks that she hadn't known how to load it; that had him thinking that, perhaps, he needed to show her how; and also show her how to shoot one. With so many people hovering around their home and her place of business of late, it might not be too long before someone really did enter their premises unannounced. If that ever happened, and Lara decided to investigate, it was best she was prepared to protect herself.

CHAPTER 19

Philip and Andrew arrived in Savannah that same morning. Both had ridden harder than necessary in order to arrive earlier than anticipated. "After all," Philip stated the prior evening, "I would like a chance to bathe and rest in a decent bed, rather than arrive last minute and call upon the lady dusty and sleep deprived. I also want us to suss out any information we can on Lara Esterhaus before I make my appearance at her home."

Andrew had been too tired to argue, and only hoped, after the already long and arduous journey, that he'd be able to stay seated in the saddle for the final leg. The jarring gallop assisted with this hope and he sighed heavily when they finally slowed to a gait, moving down the main street of Savannah just after the breakfast hour.

A short time later, they drew their mounts to a halt in front of the only hotel in town.

"You check us in, Philip. I want to visit the local saloon. See if I can discover anything of interest."

"More like imbibe a few shots of whiskey?"

Andrew laughed, "After the journey we just made, a few drops of whiskey may be just what my aching bum needs."

"Your bum has nothing to do with it," Philip laughed.

"True, but no, it's too early in the morning for whiskey. I just want to see if anyone is there; see if there isn't information to be gleaned."

"I'll check us in and order up a couple of baths for later. Then I'll call 'round to Carl's room, to see if he's discovered anything more of interest. Maybe you can ask a few prying questions while you're giving your bum a refreshing cup of coffee."

Andrew laughed and headed down the boardwalk. Philip watched him go and then headed into the hotel.

"Can I help you, sir?" The proprietor asked.

"Yes," Philip said, approaching the gleaming oak reception desk, "I need two rooms if you have them available."

"We do indeed, sir," the gentleman said congenially. "And for how many days would you be in need of these two rooms, may I inquire?"

"Unknown, but let's start with two weeks," Philip answered, and watched in amusement as the proprietor eyed him cautiously. Although he knew himself to be a well-bred gentleman of honor, his fine clothing meant nothing to this man.

"I'll need payment up front for such a lengthy stay, sir."

"Do I strike you as a charlatan?" Philip asked, far from offended.

"Certainly not, sir!" The proprietor exclaimed, his eyes widening.

"Just satisfying myself that I didn't look disreputable," Philip said, smiling.

"On the contrary, sir," the proprietor reassured quickly, "you are one of the finest dressed gentleman we've had stay in our establishment in quite some time."

"Much appreciated. Now, can you assure me that I will be reimbursed should mine and my brother's stay be shortened?"

"Without a doubt sir," the proprietor said, sliding a registration form across the surface. "If you will just take a moment to sign the register, I will get your keys."

"Thank you," Philip said, handing over three golden eagles.

"Sir!" The proprietor exclaimed. "This is far more than the necessary amount, I assure you," he said, sliding one of the golden eagles back across the counter.

"That's quite all right," Philip said, sliding it back. He picked up the quill and began filling in his pertinent information. "Just put it in your safe. I'm sure that our needs will justify the amount paid…how much will our stay amount to, precisely?"

The proprietor picked up his quill, dipped it in the ink well, and scratched out some figures. "Meals included in your stay, sir?"

"Certainly."

He scratched some more. "Warm baths weekly?"

"Daily."

"Very good," he said, dipping his quill and scratching some more numbers on the paper. "All totaled, you should manage the two weeks nicely on fifteen dollars for both you and the other guest." He smiled, again sliding the last coin across the counter. "Two should suffice, as I said."

Philip grinned, "Very good, and I appreciate your integrity. Therefore, if the fortnight passes without incident, and all is in order, I will leave you the remaining coin as a way of offering my thanks."

"You are too kind, sir."

"Let's just hope you're as proficient at running the place as you are with your calculations."

"Indeed I am…" the proprietor turned the registration book around to address his guest by name, his eyes widening as he read the name and title. "My Lord, I had no idea we would be entertaining royalty."

"It's hardly worth mentioning."

"But you're an Earl!"

"Relax, my good man," Philip said. "I put my pants on one leg at the time, just the same as you."

"As you say, my Lord."

"Now, I'm looking for one of your other guests," Philip said, pocketing the keys to their rooms. "A Mr. Carl Standish with the Pinkerton Agency."

The proprietor turned his guest book around and started flipping through the pages, "When did he arrive?"

"Approximately a month ago."

"Ah, here it is," the proprietor said, pointing his long, bony finger at a name scrawled on the page. "Checked into room one-hundred-six. Checked out yesterday."

"Checked out? Are you sure?" Philip asked.

"Well the notation here says that he paid his bill…no wait, his bill was paid for him."

"I don't understand."

"It means that someone other than Mr. Standish closed out his room."

"Can someone do that?"

"Well, not normally," the proprietor said, seeming suddenly nervous, "but this gentleman had a note from Mr. Standish requesting that he be checked out. Something about urgent business out of town. Oh wait, here's another notation," the proprietor said, and then stopped and turned to face the desk behind him. He scanned the numbers lining each cubbyhole, and then pulled an envelope from an unnumbered one. "Here, this is for you, my Lord. It would appear that the day before he checked out, Mr. Standish left you a note."

"Thank you."

"No trouble, my Lord. Would you care to have your baggage taken to your rooms now?"

"Yes, please."

"Breakfast sent up?"

"Just for one," Philip said, turning the envelope over and over in his hand. "When my brother, Andrew Bensley, arrives, send something up for him at that time."

"As you wish, my Lord."

Philip moved toward the stairs, a shiver of apprehension tracing along his spine. Did Standish really get called away on urgent business or did something untoward happen to him? "Dangerous games afoot," he muttered, turning the key in the lock and swinging his door wide.

"Sir?"

"Nothing," he said. "Just put the luggage on the bed. Thank you." He pulled a farthing from his pocket and handed it to the porter.

"Thank you, sir."

Philip waited until the door closed before he broke the wax seal. He quickly scanned the contents, and then turned and stormed from the hotel.

CHAPTER 20

Andrew entered the saloon a few minutes after parting company with Philip, and wasted no time attempting to pry out information from the bartender with both a handsome purchase and an even larger monetary incentive.

The bartender brought a pot of coffee over, and slid the extra coin in his pocket, "Well now, there's not too many men who'd take a shine to Miss Esterhaus, which is why she's still unwed at her age."

"What's wrong with her?" Andrew asked, his curiosity over this woman piqued for the hundredth time since beginning this journey.

"What ain't wrong with her, is the proper question," the bartender quipped and then excused himself to attend to his other customers.

When it didn't appear as if the bartender was going to return to answer any more questions, Andrew settled at a corner table and poured himself a drink, wishing it *were* whiskey, anything that would quash his feelings of frustration. He'd only just started on his second cup of coffee when a man approached from the bar.

"Excuse me, sir?"

Andrew turned at the voice behind him. "May I help you?" He said politely, trying to see the man beneath the low-brimmed hat.

"Well, sir," the man continued in a near whisper, leaning closer, "It is I who may possibly be of help to you."

"Truly? And what assistance do you perceive that I'm in need of, pray tell?" Andrew asked, uncertain whether to be amused by the gentleman's attempt at subterfuge or wary.

"I overheard your inquiry into a certain lady. If you are in town because of the reason I believe you to be..."

"And your belief would be?"

"To meet said certain young lady, perhaps?"

"Ah," Andrew exclaimed, deciding to be amused. "And you have something to tell me about this young woman, perhaps at a price?"

"Ah, no," the man said, moving a step closer, but using caution to remain in the shadows. "I am here to offer a goodly sum to forget said woman, and continue on your way."

Andrew's brow knitted. That was certainly *not* what he'd expected. If the woman was indeed flawed, as her advertisement proclaimed, what would make a man eager to part with his own funds to prevent another from even meeting her. Unless those flaws were a ruse, as his brother suggested, and the man was merely attempting to eliminate whatever competition he may by means most agreeable. Then again, the bartender's cryptic reply to his inquiry made that seem just as improbable. *Damnation!* Andrew railed in his head. *Who is this woman?*

"And should I decide to decline such a handsome offer?" Andrew asked. He couldn't wait to tell Philip of this latest development, once he parted company with the strange individual. The man's answer however, gave him pause, and changed his amusement to one of wariness.

"It would be in your best interest to do so, sir," the gentleman said. "I will return in an hour to receive your reply," he said sharply, and then turned and quickly exited the saloon.

"Well, that was interesting," Andrew muttered, downing his rapidly cooling brew. He was about to leave when he spotted his brother enter the saloon. He waved him over and then asked a passing server to bring an extra cup and another pot. It didn't take him long to fill Philip in on what he'd discovered.

"Think he'll actually return in an hour to see if I accept his offer?"

"Hmm, sounds a reasonable assumption that he may," Philip said thoughtfully, "especially since he appears unaware of my presence and sees you as the suitor. It also appears as if these men, whomever they are, have been anticipating our arrival; or at least the arrival of one of us."

"You have inadvertently hit upon something which would make an intriguing proposal, Brother."

"And that is?"

"That this man, or these men, may perceive me as the suitor, in which case, I can act as a distraction that could provide you the opportunity to pay your respects to Miss Esterhaus without interception or interference."

"Indeed; however, I don't plan to call upon Miss Esterhaus until tomorrow. Certainly these men will discover that you do not travel alone long before that time comes."

"True, but if I appear as the suitor, it stands to reason I will be the one bearing continued scrutiny, which means you can make your way over to Miss Esterhaus' home without detection. Further, your visiting alone, will afford me time to investigate the source of these dangerous games while you get acquainted with your intended," Andrew concluded with a grin.

Philip smiled, "Thought this through, have you?"

"Only just," Andrew said, still grinning. "If alarm bells were not ringing loudly in my ears, I'd be having a grand old time over this whole affair."

"As would I, I'm sure," Philip said less convincingly, and Andrew laughed.

"You're too stuffy, by far, big brother," Andrew said, pouring them another drink.

"And you are, by far, too much a Merry-Andrew," Philip retorted, picking up the coffee, and holding it for a toast, "Not exactly the best drink for this, but here's to you and me. May we survive this meeting with Miss Esterhaus. Speaking of survival," Philip said, suddenly serious, as if he'd only recollected the reason he'd sought out his brother. "Read this."

He watched his brother's brow knit as he read. In his mind, he saw the words scrawled on the page in Standish's barely legible hand.

29 August 1800

My dear friend,

Have encountered disturbing information directly relating to the lady in question. It appears there is speculation circulating that her parents died most foul. Although their deaths appeared accidental, many still feel as if it were not so. I befriended a man during my stay, one Jeremy Weston by name. Mr. Weston, during a night of carousing and quite unintentionally, I haven't a doubt, disclosed that the deaths were indeed intentional and that their daughter, the woman with whom you presently seek an audience, is next on their agenda should she not part with her property before too many more weeks have past, or if she finds a husband before the bank forces her to part with it. Unfortunately, at our next encounter, Mr. Weston was tightlipped as if warned not to speak further on the subject or he was made aware of my profession and felt it best to hold his tongue. He disappeared two days after our second encounter.

As for the advertisement, it is my attestation that the lady wisely chose the only course of action available to her in locating a husband forthwith, in order to prevent losing the property of her parents. It has been imparted to me, by several individuals who've heard rumors of your arrival (from me, I must confess), that you are the first to answer her advertisement since it first appeared in circulars many months ago. However, I have also heard it mentioned—and only under the influence of whisky, mind you—that keeping the property seems to be something someone does not wish her to do, so the parties involved may go to great lengths to prevent any union between you and the lady, should you choose to pursue her hand in marriage.

I'm writing this, instead of informing you in person upon your arrival because I fear I have inquired too extensively into this matter, and my own life has now been placed in jeopardy. Further investigation is warranted, but will not be done by me. If you do not receive a bill for my services within a fortnight of your arrival in Georgia, assume the worst my friend, for it will no doubt have occurred.

I will close with this dire warning. Dangerous games are afoot, and if you are wise, you will forget your meeting with the lady, although beauteous, and return home in all haste.

Forever your humble servant,

C. Standish

"You think the worst has happened?" Andrew asked softly, passing the letter back to his brother.

"I do," Philip said grimly.

"So what is it about this property that has men going about committing murder, I wonder, and what is it about this woman that men are unwilling to wed her? Standish stated she was a woman of beauty, so you'd think that men would be beating down her door for the right to court her, especially if she is a woman of means also."

"I don't know. I simply don't have any answers, just more confusion tumbling about in my brain. Still, men of ill repute will not dissuade me from my path, so I'll continue on with my plans to meet Miss Esterhaus. Perhaps she can shed some light on what all of the clamor is about surrounding her and her property."

"If she is indeed aware. You know, I think it's a good thing we have stubbornness as a family trait, Brother, or we may have decided against meeting this woman after all we've learned. These men have no idea who they've pitted themselves against."

"If they persist in their own course of action, they'll find out readily."

"My curiosity is aroused by this cloak and sword° affair, so much so that I now wish I were the heir and you were me."

"You're forgetting that I may wind up dead, Brother."

"In which case, I *would* be you," Andrew quipped, the twinkle in his eye evident.

Philip laughed, "I wish you were me too sometimes, but not at this moment. As of this moment, I am going to break with protocol and drop in on a lady with no further notice that I've arrived in town. It's high time I met this strange woman."

"I wish I could join you, but I have more cloak and sword business to attend to." Andrew wriggled his eyebrows in comic fashion, and Philip laughed again.

"We should consider taking these men seriously, Andrew," Philip chastised lightly. "After all, we know of at least four people who have died by their hand."

"I do. Humor just helps me cope with the seriousness of this business, but where do you come up with four deaths."

"It is my assertion that both the man Carl was speaking to, and Carl also, have met their demise. Carl also stated that Miss Esterhaus' parents may also have met with untimely deaths. Those are the people I know of. There could very well be more casualties in this affair…"

"…which I will attempt to ascertain while you are conducting your meeting with Miss Esterhaus."

"With caution, Brother. You are not above being murdered."

° The term *cloak and sword* precedes the term *cloak and dagger* in literature by about forty years, appearing in French literature in the early 19th century. I took some liberty and used it in the final year of the 18th century. However, in defense of my choice, Giacomo di Grassi used the term *rapier and cloake* in his late 16th century work, "His True Arte of Defence" to describe deceptive combat methods.

"I don't need to remind you what I am capable of if crossed, Philip."

"Nor I, but remember, you may not see the sword that attempts to strike you down."

"Words of wisdom imparted from our otherwise unwise father." Andrew flipped open his pocket watch. "The time is drawing near for the stranger to return for my answer to his offer. Perhaps it is best if you return to the rooms and remain out of sight."

Philip nodded, "I must confess at being mildly uneasy about this whole affair, so I will bid you to use caution again, Brother. I do not want you to become a casualty also. Oh, and when you get back to the hotel, stop by the front desk and give the proprietor your name. He's been advised to have a meal and a hot bath prepared upon your arrival."

"You know it's possible that Standish had it wrong," Andrew said suddenly, stalling Philip's departure momentarily.

"What? The beauteous part?"

"No, the lack of interest in the advertisement. Remember when we arrived? That man approached me and offered me a goodly sum to forgo my meeting with Miss Esterhaus. If that is the way things are, perhaps others have answered her advertisement, but decided to accept the payoff offered."

"I too had my thoughts on the subject, for if it wasn't for the letter that Standish left, I'd be inclined to believe a rejected suitor played a hand in keeping the woman from marrying."

"It has been known to happen," Andrew said, "but as you said, Standish indicted that it was the woman's property these men were after—not the woman."

"So why not just sell it to them," Philip said. "Why hold onto something…"

"Because it belongs to her," Andrew interrupted, a sudden ferocity in his tone. "It's like our land in England. We wouldn't have parted with it, given the choice. And you are willing to marry a stranger just so we can regain possession just as she seems to be willing to do. Why bother? Why not just accept its loss and move on?"

"Because it belongs to us," Philip said, nodding in understanding.

"Precisely," Andrew said, "And to be honest, Brother, what these faceless men are doing makes my blood boil, despite my attempt at maintaining my humor."

"Might be interesting to see what they do if I decide to wed the lady," Philip said, grinning.

"It may redirect their attack in your direction," Andrew said. "Of course, talking about marrying her and actually doing so are two completely different things; you realize that, don't you?"

"Yes, but I may be better equipped to handle whatever problems head her way than she." Philip stood with a sigh, "It really is time for me to go before this faceless adversary realizes that there are two of us."

"For certain. I will be along shortly to give you an update. In the meantime, go bathe and remove the travel from your body."

Philip stood and made his way toward the saloon doors, not realizing that he passed the faceless adversary on the way out.

CHAPTER 21

Andrew watched with bated breath his brother's departure. The man with the low-brimmed hat entered, no curiosity registering in his body language at all. Andrew relaxed, until another man entered, following closely behind the first man. They conversed for a moment confirming Andrew's suppositions that there were more people involved than just the one man.

Instead of coming to his table, the man with the low-brimmed hat found a spot at the far corner of the bar. It was the other man, unconcerned about being identified, who approached Andrew.

When Andrew saw his face, he understood his lack of concern, for the only way he could be identified was through the extensive scarring of his face. Andrew tried not to stare, but it was hard not to.

"Most people are so repulsed they tend to look away," the man muttered, taking a seat opposite Andrew. That snapped Andrew out of his daze. He didn't like that he'd been thrown off his guard by mere appearance.

"And most men have the courtesy to ask before being seated."

"You know why I'm here."

"Why don't you explain why?"

"It has been brought to your attention that a certain young woman needs to be ignored. Someone earlier offered you an incentive for doing so. I'm here to receive your reply."

"And what was the incentive again? I've had too many cups of coffee, the amount of which is hindering my recollection."

"The men I work for are willing to pay you fifty dollars if you take your leave this day."

"And what is it precisely about this woman that would make avoiding her worth that much money, I wonder?"

It was a rhetorical question, but the stranger answered just the same. "Enough that you don't need to ask questions. Just mount up and ride away."

"If I just mount up and ride away, how do I know that I'll see even a shilling, much less fifty dollars?"

"Because I say you will," the man replied.

Andrew grinned, "Well, your word is your bond, I'm sure," he said sarcastically, "but unless you have a pouch full of coin hidden beneath that ridiculously oversized coat of yours, I'd say you can forget it. Besides, I am fairly certain I'll be staying the night, at the very least."

The man reached into his coat, and Andrew's hand went instinctively to the butt of his pistol. He relaxed when the man retrieved his billfold.

"Perhaps I can whet your appetite with this." He pulled out and counted twenty crisp bills. Not British pounds, but the newly minted American paper money.

"That's not equal to fifty dollars. I can count, you know?" Andrew observed.

"You aren't intending to leave this minute, so the price just dropped. I suggest you take this, tour the town for a bit, and then ride out of town tomorrow at first light." He slung the bills across the table, but Andrew just sat there, staring at him.

"You're mighty rude for someone who wants me to comply with something," Andrew observed casually. "And since I'm not of a mind to be agreeable with someone whose isn't agreeable, I'll take my leave of you."

Andrew stood but was prevented from departing when the man's hand shot out and gripped his shirt, "Where do you think you are going?"

"I have an appointment to keep," Andrew said in a tone that suggested the man would be exceeding wise if he released his shirt in all haste. The man caught the tone and did just that.

"You might want to reconsider the offer," the man said softly.

"I have and I've decided that a woman worth that much money is worth meeting and, most likely, marrying," Andrew said, shoving his hat on his head. "And I'd suggest that you steer clear of me and mine, or I'll feed you that money, should next we meet."

"You may reconsider the offer when you take a look at the girl," the man said, and Andrew saw his thin lips form a malicious smile.

"Not a concern," Andrew said, wanting to punch the man's indiscernible face. "Money wears blinders."

"Use caution, or you may regret these rash decisions," the man called as Andrew started away.

Andrew stopped and returned to the table. He leaned down until his face was inches from the scars. "Was that a threat?" He whispered.

"Consider it good advice," the man rejoined, not the least intimidated by Andrew's size or anger.

"Well here's some equally good advice," Andrew said, menacingly, "tell your cronies to forget all about Miss Esterhaus, because if another person disappears, and her name is associated with them, I'll find out who you all are and come after you with a vengeance unlike anything you'd ever be able to match."

Without awaiting another reply, Andrew turned and stormed from the building. A few minutes later, the man with the hat left the bar and made his way over to the table.

"Apparently money isn't the motivator it should have been, and from his reaction to you, I'd say he doesn't intimidate either."

"Which leaves only one option," the scar-faced man muttered, gathering the bills and returning them to his billfold.

"As much as disposing of this man would bring us both considerable pleasure, I'd rather you take care of Lara Esterhaus first. Eliminate her and we eliminate the need to worry over potential suitors."

"I thought Garamond wanted to steer away from that course of action. Might raise too many questions?"

"Garamond doesn't call all the shots, and I say Lara Esterhaus' death is well overdue. It's time we put an end to this nonsense."

"You're the man who pays me, so I'll do what you want."

"Good, then go take care of it now."

"Accidents generally take planning. We can't afford for there to be any inquiries."

"Fine, then start the planning now. I want it done before that man decides to walk her down the aisle and take over her family's fortune."

The scar-faced man nodded, slid his hat onto his head and left the saloon.

Arthur Middleton sat back in his chair and smiled. It was long past time he did some of the planning, instead of allowing Garamond to call all of the shots. Besides, the way he figured it, Lara Esterhaus deserved what she had coming to her. "That's the last time she'll reject me."

CHAPTER 22

The afternoon sunlight filtered into Philip's room, striking him in the face as an offended suitor seeking a duel; and Philip reacted as violently as he would in that instance, bolting erect and wide-eyed from a sound nap.

It took him a moment to orient himself, as he blinked rapidly to adjust to the intensity of light hitting his pupils. He rubbed his eyes several times and attempted to right his thoughts. Then it registered where he was, and that his brother had not sought him out as he stated.

With mounting concern, Philip tossed the covers back and jumped from the bed, dressing quickly. In mere moments, he was across the hallway, pounding on his brother's door.

"Andrew, are you in there?"

His pounding abated only after he heard a muttered curse from within. The sigh of relief he let loose would have been audible all the way to the dining hall, had anyone been in there to hear it at that time. A moment later, the door jerked open.

"Why are you banging at my door?" He growled, his eyes mere slits against the light streaming in from the hallway. Philip laughed, relieved to see his brother was suffering from no more than having his own nap disturbed. He must have been too exhausted to remember his promise to fill Philip in on his meeting. As tired as he looked right now, Philip would be surprised if Andrew even remembered why he was in the saloon to begin with. More than anything, his laughter stemmed from relief at finding his brother unharmed.

"Come brother," he boomed, "join me for an early meal, as it would appear that we both slept much of the morning away, and there is much you must tell me about your encounter earlier this morning."

Andrew grumbled, leaning heavily against the door jamb, "Can't you return a little later, Philip? What time is it, anyway? I feel as if I haven't napped at all."

"It's eleven in the a.m. and we haven't a lot of time before I must leave to meet with Miss Esterhaus."

"Not a lot of time! Good God man, you've decided upon tomorrow as a good interview time, surely you can afford me another hour of sleep! Wait! Are you saying that you've decided to meet with her today?"

"Yes. I feel an urgency that will likely run its course, once I converse with you at length about what transpired with our mystery man this morning; however, I fear that the urgency will not abate entirely until I ride out to meet our mystery lady. Today, rather than wait for someone to prevent it occurring."

"Of course," Andrew stepped aside to allow his brother entrance.

"You get dressed. I will order meals to be brought to your room instead of us going to the dining room. Better to keep our acquaintance anonymous for the time being, as you suggested."

Andrew grumbled something more unintelligible, but Philip simply ignored him and headed down to the front desk to see if the kitchen was open. The proprietor, unlike Andrew, was wide awake and working at a small desk behind the front desk. He looked up when he saw Philip approach.

"My Lord enjoyed a nice repose?" he greeted amicably.

"Indeed, and it is my hope that your kitchen staff is available to prepare two meals," Philip inquired lightly.

"Lunch, sir?"

"Yes. Sent to room my room, if you please. Coffee also."

"Cream and sugar?"

"Black."

"As you wish, my Lord."

"Thank you, good sir." Philip returned to his brother's room and was pleased that Andrew was dressed and seated by the window. From his demeanor, it was hard to tell he'd awaken in a foul disposition less than five minutes prior.

"Coffee on the way?" He inquired the moment Philip strolled in.

"On its way. Very soon."

"Ugh. Soon may not be soon enough," Andrew muttered.

"You appear quite alert, Andrew."

"Appearance can be deceptive, dear brother, as I can assure you that I am teetering on the abyss and can only be pulled away from sure mental downfall by a cup of steaming coffee."

Philip laughed, and stood as a knock resounded at the door, "If you did not get sufficient rest," he said, as he opened to admit the porter, "it's your own fault, and thus you must suffer the consequences. However, as you can, it took no longer than the time I left and returned for it to arrive. Now do come and partake of your saving grace." Philip handed the porter a shilling and shut the door. When he turned back, he had to laugh yet again, for his brother had made it to the table in a speed unfathomable by Philip, and was downing his first cup of coffee.

He shook his head and settled in the seat opposite, dishing up a serving of mashed potatoes and fried ham. He ate in silence waiting on his brother to speak first.

"You passed the mystery man on your way out of the saloon this morning," Andrew said after finishing his first plate of food.

"You recognized him even though he kept his face obscured on your first meeting?"

"Different man." He downed his second cup of coffee, and then sat back in his chair with an audible sigh.

"Better?"

"Much."

"Then do continue."

Andrew grinned, "Of course. Anyway, this new man didn't bother masking his face, hideous though it was."

"Hideous?"

"Scarred in its entirety," Andrew clarified before continuing. "I gauged him as the hired gun. Threatening sort."

"And did he? Threaten?"

"After a fashion."

"Explain."

"That was my intent, brother," Andrew quipped, but his demeanor changed to one of irritation as he started telling Philip about the abbreviated encounter.

"He sat without invite, which was telling, and immediately offered fifty dollars if I were to mount up and ride out within the hour. The buffoon. I informed him that it wasn't my intention to ride out at that time, so he withdrew from his billfold twenty crisp bills of the newest American currency."

"That's sounds quite a lot of money."

"And I was tempted to take it, although it didn't add up to the promised fifty."

Philip quirked his brow, which told Andrew what he thought of that possibility and then continued with his train of thought, "Men with that much money generally have an equal level of power."

"And men who are willing to part with their money as a means to an end can prove quite dangerous."

"As Carl discovered, no doubt," Philip concluded, shaking his head in frustrated anger.

"When I told him that I wasn't interested in his boss' money, he resorted to those threats we were expecting. Intimated that it would be unwise to be in town come sunrise. In fact, before you came in from ordering lunch, I was sitting here looking out of the window. He's not out there, but there are several unsavory types that seem interested in the goings-on here at the hotel."

"So, now that we know that these men are serious and are willing to resort to bribery and possibly murder, to gain possession of Miss Esterhaus' property, what do you propose we do?"

"I am going to pay a visit to the constable. File a report regarding threats issued by a scar-faced man, and also make inquiries into suspicious deaths, particularly of those individuals related to Lara Esterhaus."

"Think you'll make it to the constable's office before getting a musket ball in the back?" Philip asked, only half in jest.

Andrew grinned wryly, "That's the funny thing about it. While I was watching those unsavory characters milling about, I also happened to notice that the constable's offices are located right across the street from our hotel. I could run the distance before any of them manages to draw his weapon, if that's the intent. What about you?"

"I'll leave you to play the part of an investigator, while I intend to break with etiquette and pay an unannounced visit to Miss Esterhaus."

"So you mentioned. Let's just hope that she isn't put off by your lack of decorum."

"I'm more of a mind to hope that my lack of decorum doesn't cause her to reject me outright."

Andrew laughed, "So you're going to make an offer of marriage, sight unseen, just to stick a lance in their plans?"

"Well, I'll obviously see her when I propose."

"You know what I mean."

"Yes I do. And yes, I'm seriously considering proposing immediately. Might be interesting to see just how determined those are who want to prevent a marriage from taking place."

"Could be placing yourself in quite a lot of danger, brother," Andrew said, growing somber. "Especially for a woman and her property that may be unworthy of such a valiant defense. Are you certain you really want to do this?"

"You think I ought to let them toss her off her family land? After that speech about keeping what's hers? If I allow those men to intimidate her out of house and home, I'd be no better than the men who did the same to us."

"You're right, I suppose," Andrew sighed.

"I know."

"I only hope that her obvious flaw isn't mental, or we may be biting off more than we can chew."

"We?" Philip said wryly. "It's not as if you'll be wed to her too."

"After a fashion, I will. After all, I will be her brother-in-law, which means I'll have to put up with her just the same."

Philip laughed, "Well if she's too unusual, I'll just wed her for her money, and then move back to England. That way, she can keep her property and I won't have to worry about her instability."

"So you say, but you haven't the ability to be unchivalrous, Brother, so let's hope she makes a decent impression when you arrive."

"Are you certain you wish to stay behind and snoop around more? It could be more dangerous for you; especially as those men appear to be mistaking you for me."

"Despite your brave talk about breaking protocol and arriving unannounced, I do believe you are stalling, Brother," Andrew stated with a wide grin, "but to answer your question, yes, I want to see what happens now that I've rejected their offer."

"Be careful, Brother."

"It's highly probable that those men now know there are two of us milling about town and will attempt to eliminate us both, so I will say the same to you. Now, stop delaying and go meet your intended."

CHAPTER 23

"Tell the staff that I appreciate their efforts in providing such a lavish lunch. I almost bust loose from my corset, I ate so much," Lara laughed, collecting her riding gloves from the table in the foyer. "I'll return at approximately six o'clock to dress for our evening meal. I trust that you'll have our new staff in tiptop shape by then? No more broken dishes?"

"Of course, Miss Lara."

"I know you will, Joshua. It's my nervousness causing me to blather on so. Oh," Lara continued, pulling open the front door, "and do have Sasha prepare my turquoise evening dress. I think that should suit for dinner. Goodness, but where did this fog come from. It was clear earlier in the day."

"Comes off the river, Miss," Joshua said, following her down the steps to her waiting buggy. "If you would feel safer, I could take the reins for you. You aren't used to riding in this type of weather."

"I'll give the horses' the rein this afternoon. They know the route to the store as well as I do."

"On a sunny day they might," Joshua quipped, "but not when the fog rolls in thicker than whipped butter."

"Well then, I'll just trust my own judgment. I'm certain that I've traversed the route to and from the store enough times to do it blindfolded."

"Which you'll be doing in this fog. You could ride right into the middle of the Savannah River before you even noticed you was there."

"Ok, Joshua, I get your meaning. I will go slowly and carefully." She clucked as she slapped the reins, "I'll see you in a few hours," she called over her shoulder, and then disappeared quickly into the thick bank of fog.

"Ok, God," Joshua muttered as he headed back into the house, "You know all about them ill feelings that cling to my gut every now and again, so I'm asking that you watch over Miss Lara this afternoon. Keep her safe from harm."

Lara started down the street at a decent clip, but it soon became apparent that going faster than a walk could prove dangerous, so she pulled back on the reins until the horses were moving along at a crawl, especially as she drew closer to town and heard other hoof beats nearby, with occasional shouts of "Ho, driver approaching!" or "Ho, rider nearby!"

She quickly realized that this was others' way of warning nearby passersby of potential collisions; an assumption borne out when a horse galloped so close by that the wind rocked her buggy. The speed of the other rider also startled her horses and they reared slightly.

After calming her mares, she decided to give a shout out so that some unsuspecting rider didn't run into the rear of her buggy and get seriously injured. She felt foolish, but necessity overruled her feelings, so she called out, "Be careful, there's a buggy over here."

All other calls fell silent and Lara giggled, "Well, as my former nanny would say, *'Qui a mis leurs culottes dans un noeud*[P]. Her horse whinnied as if in understanding and Lara laughed, "As if you comprehend French."

It was then that she heard a return whinny and another set of horse hoofs pounding at a faster clip-clop than the other horse which had come at her. She couldn't see them, which meant they couldn't see her, "Ho, buggy here," she called, shouting louder than before.

Her horses instinctively began sidestepping, as if it would prevent the imminent impact, "Whoa Nellie, whoa Molly, easy girls. We don't want to wind up in the river, do we?" Her nerves pricked as the horse drew nearer, and she was about to shout out another warning, when she heard a loud whinny just to her rear. She turned and saw a massive stallion rearing back on its hind legs; kicking enormous hoofs in the air.

She squealed and slapped her whip in the air near her horses' rumps. The mares leapt forward, yanking the buggy into motion. She fell back against her seat and dropped the reins. She looked back as the mighty stallion dropped its front legs with a loud thud. Had she not noticed the beast rearing, it would have landed too close to her head for comfort. She shivered.

Her mares, startled by the nearness of the male horse, and now leaderless, shot down the street, fear their guiding force. She held

---

[P] English translation: 'That put their knickers in a knot' onto the buggy seat tightly, thankful for only one thing at present—that the fog was lifting, so she could see other nearby riders. "Move!" She shouted. She wanted to call out for help, but knew there was little anyone could do to assist with runaways. The only hope she had now was that her horses calmed themselves of their own accord and slowed, preferably before smashing into someone or something.

She looked over her shoulder and was frighteningly surprised to see the stallion racing along after her. It was as if its rider wanted to keep her mares in a state of startled anxiety. The same effect it was having on her.

When horse and rider suddenly veered off onto Main Street, Lara breathed a sigh of relief, until she turned back around in her seat. Her eyes widened in dread for her mares were racing upon a phaeton too quickly, which was moving slowly along the river's edge, and there was no way to prevent colliding. Lara threw her hands up in front of her face instinctively, as the mares dodged the phaeton. Their sudden directional shift destabilized her buggy and it skid sideways, slamming into the rear of the phaeton, unseating Lara.

She thought, absurdly and irrationally, that she didn't realize she could fly and then felt a tear prick at the corner of her eye as the water quickly rose up to meet her rapidly descending body. She slammed into the surface with an impact that knocked the breath from her lungs and quickly began sinking, the heaviness of her clothing acting as an anchor.

* * * * * * * * *

Philip was approaching the end of Main Street when two occurrences snagged his attention: there was a runaway buggy racing along the river's edge, and a lone horse and rider had turned suddenly onto Main, nearly running headlong into Philip.

Philip pulled back onto his horse's reins, but had little to fear as the rider quickly righted his own horse, galloping by with little care for his actions.

Philip's nerves jumped as he noticed something particular about the rider, something related to what his brother had said about his mystery visitor's face from the saloon, 'Scarred in its entirety', his brother had commented. It didn't take a genius to realize Miss Lara's adversaries' gun man has just ridden past as if chased by the hounds of Hell. Within another second, he connected the rider to the runaway buggy and his heart began to race with dread.

"Let's go, boy," Philip called, slapping his reins and squeezing his calf muscles tightly against the horse's haunches. The horse leapt forward, picking up speed quickly; but just as quickly, Philip was reining his stallion in, as they approached the overturned buggy.

There was chaos at the scene of the crash, but what snared Philip's attention were the men diving into the water. Moments later, two of the men were trying, with little success, to haul a non-responsive female from the depths. Two more men jumped in and attempted to assist, but all kept sinking beneath the surface, the weight of the woman's clothing pulling them continually under. The water at that depth wasn't overly deep, but the men doing the rescuing were too short to touch bottom.

Philip wasted no more time taking in the scene. He jumped from his horse's back and ran to the water's edge, diving in—boots and all. It was a more difficult swim with his clothing acting as a drag, but he soon reached the struggling foursome, who'd all started to sink below the surface yet again.

"Here, let me!" He called out, wrapping his arms beneath Lara's. He quickly began to sink himself, and pulled his feet beneath his body, hoping he hadn't misjudged the depth. Within a few seconds, his feet landed on the rocky floor, the water slapping at his face just below his mouth. He hoisted the woman higher to keep her own face above water and then began trudging along toward the edge.

The other four men began paddling toward the water's edge, and had to be assisted in climbing up the bank. Each sank to his knees, drawing in deep breaths. The doctor, who'd been summoned, examined each man quickly while he waited on his actual patient to arrive.

Philip reached the bank several minutes later. Two other men raced up and relieved him of his burden, and then he collapsed next to the original four men who'd attempted the rescue.

"Thanks mister. We'd have all drown for certain if you hadn't come along," one man huffed between breaths. The other men nodded in concurrence. Philip could do no more than nod.

"Are you going to be okay, mister?" The physician called, as he led his horse-drawn cart down the street. "I really need to get Miss Esterhaus back to my offices, so can't stop to examine you right now. If you think you need my help, have someone bring you along to see me."

"I'm fine, just take care of my fiancé," Philip waved a hand to show he was just tired, ignoring the gaping expressions of those nearby who'd heard his pronouncement.

When his legs felt more stable than wobbly, he carefully righted himself and slowly made his way back to his waiting, faithful, stallion. He smiled inwardly at the murmurings as he passed, but that smile quickly faded when some of the comments registered.

"How did Lara Esterhaus land a beau like that?"

"How did she land a beau at all?"

"There must be something wrong with him to hitch himself to that girl."

"Has to be. No man in his right mind would take her."

What is wrong with these people, Philip thought tacitly *I could see nothing wrong with the woman, so why do these people mock her so?*

He'd made his announcement loud and clear because he'd wanted word to spread along the rumor mill quickly, that Lara Esterhaus was engaged. It was his hope that it would either spark her adversaries into revealing themselves or cause them to cease attempts at claiming her property. He hadn't counted on the derision his declaration would elicit.

"Excuse me," he took his horse's reins and approached a man standing nearby, "could you tell me where I can locate the doctor's offices."

The man looked up at him and his jaw dropped, "Is it true you're planning to marry the Esterhaus girl?" He asked, his tone awestruck.

"I am." Philip drew in a breath and nearly asked the man to explain his, and others, reactions to the news; to explain to him what it was about Lara Esterhaus that caused such an effect; but he refrained. The last thing he was interested in was obtaining information from a biased source. He would wait to make his own determination about the girl.

The man merely shook his head in wonder, and then sighed,

"Well, just head straight up the street here until you find yourself headed out of town. You'll come upon a small path on your left with a hand-painted sign. That path leads up to the doctor's place.

"Thank you. Have a good day, sir."

"You also, sir."

Philip climbed into his saddle and started down the street, ignoring the looks of incredulity aimed his way. He sighed for he felt it a ludicrous thing that he should find these peoples' reactions so strange, and that those reactions should concern him in the least.

The he realized why he felt ill at ease.

These were the same sort of looks and the same type of murmurings he'd heard when armed dragoons had come onto his family lands and escorted him, Andrew, his mother, and his father away with bayonets aimed at their backs. It was a feeling of humiliation then—for himself. Now, he felt humiliation for a woman whom he didn't even know, but somehow knew didn't deserve the disrespect of these people.

He saw the hand-painted sign in his periphery and stopped his mount. 'Doctor', it read.

"Well, there's no mistaking that this is where I need to be," he murmured. He pulled his reins to the left and his horse started along the pathway beneath overhanging trees, covered in Spanish moss; a prominent part of the landscape he'd discovered upon his arrival in Savannah.

It was a short trek to the house, and he pulled his horse to a stop in front of a lovely white-washed home with a porch that wrapped around the entire front. A woman, who must have heard his approach—or was expecting his arrival—came from inside followed by a young black boy.

"The doctor said you'd be along," she murmured quietly. "Emmanuel will see to your horse."

"Thank you, Emmanuel," Philip said, handing the reins to the startled youth.

That was something else which always intrigued Philip, the attitudes people reserved for their house staff. Yes, he understood the dynamics of class and rank, but he still held that people were people and deserved respect and courtesy. A feeling not shared by those he'd met here in the Americas.

Here, those of elevated class treated those less fortunate and those in the position of servant as less than human. Some, he'd noticed frequently, treated their dogs better. It angered him, but it was the lay of the land and none of his concern. He had to admit that things were not very different at home, in England.

"I'm afraid that I'm more than too wet to enter your premises, madam," Philip said as if suddenly aware that he was sopping.

"I noticed," the woman smiled kindly, "which is why I sent my maid ahead with some towels with which to dry yourself, as much as is possible."

"My sincerest appreciation, madam, but I fear that it may not be enough to prevent dripping onto your floors."

"We've had more than water dripping on these floors at times. At least water is easier to tend to, and if you'll simply remove your boots and leave them here on the porch…"

"Oh, for certain," Philip said, sitting onto the porch swing and tugging mightily on the wet footwear. There was a loud sucking noise as each boot finally broke free from the watery suction holding them to his feet. He looked at the lady of the house in mild embarrassment at the noise, but she simply smiled, and handed him several towels with which to dry himself.

"How is Miss Esterhaus?" Philip asked, as he squeezed the water from his clothing and then ran towel after towel from head to toe, attempting to rid his clothing and body of as much water as possible.

"The doctor is tending to Miss Esterhaus now and…"

"But how is she faring?" He interrupted.

"I'm afraid I don't know. The doctor had her taken straight to his office where he's been hole up ever since. He said for me to make you a cup of tea while you wait. And as I also need to tend to Miss Esterhaus' wet clothing, I really must escort you indoors now."

"I do apologize," Philip said, following her indoors.

"Not at all. I am quite sympathetic, I assure you."

She just finished her statement when a door at the rear of the house opened and a man, whom Philip recognized as the doctor, came toward him, hand outstretched in welcome.

"I'll get tea," the woman murmured, curtsied, and disappeared down another hallway.

"Doctor Jacob Malloy, at your service, sir."

Philip shook the doctor's hand.

"Lara is going to be just fine. A good thing about women's undergarments which you may be unaware is that the corset is so constrictive, that little water is able to get inside a body. Fortunate for Lara as she could have drowned. My biggest concern was the lack of oxygen, which could have been just as deadly. Fortunately, she coughed up that little bit of water intake the minute I removed her corset, and soon oxygen found its way back in. A few more minutes underwater could have seen a different outcome. Anyway, she's weak as a newborn babe, but in fine spirits knowing she avoided crossing over death's threshold."

"Is it possible for me to go in to see her?"

"British, are you?"

"Yes," Philip answered tersely, wondering if the doctor was simply curious or stalling.

"So, Lara's your intended? You must have answered that advertisement she placed."

"Doctor, while I appreciate that your curiosity is piqued, I really would like to ascertain for myself that my fiancé is in good health."

"Of course. My apologies. I'll take you back."

"I'd rather see her alone, if I may. It's that door at the end of the corridor, correct?"

"That's right, although she may be sleeping."

Philip extended his hand, "Thanks for bringing her back to me. I appreciate your skill in this matter."

The doctor shook Philip's hand and then stepped aside. He watched Philip walk down the corridor and then murmured under his breath, "Good looking man, and very tall. Hmm. I couldn't have ordered up a more perfect mate for Miss Lara myself."

"I think we can credit God with this find," the woman who'd greeted Philip said softly, moving to stand beside the doctor.

"He does seem to know what He's doing more times than not," the doctor replied, placing his arm around her waist. "He found you for me, didn't He?"

"Indeed He did," she smiled, a light blush tinting her pale cheeks. She cleared her throat softly, "Do you think he'll want his tea now?"

"I think perhaps I'd better partake of the tea and let him alone for a while."

The doctor's wife handed her husband the tray, "I do need to ensure Lara's clothing has been hung up in front of the fire properly to dry," she said. The doctor placed a light kiss on her cheek and then retreated to his office.

CHAPTER 24

Philip stood beside the bed, staring down in awe at the beautiful alabaster face in repose. Occasionally her brow would knit and her head would move indicating that her dreams were disturbed by unpleasant memories.

He could easily guess as to which memories they were, recent and potentially deadly. He wouldn't be able to sleep peacefully either, if he'd been in her buggy at the time of the crash; if what happened to her, happened to him.

Her face relaxed again and her breathing returned to soft inhales, exhales. This helped him relax also, and he resumed his perusal of her features, trying, but failing, to locate any flaw in her flawless face. She was far and away the most beautiful woman he'd seen in all his years of noticing the opposite gender.

Perhaps it hasn't to do with her physical appearance, he pondered, settling onto a chair near the bed, *but rather an internal one. Perhaps Andrew was right, that her mind may be imbalanced.*

A disturbance in the corridor brought him to his feet. He was about to investigate when the door opened and the doctor peered inside. He glanced over at Lara, and then stepped into the room without uttering a sound. He moved aside and two people, obviously distraught, filed inside.

The woman made a beeline for Lara's bedside, tears streaming down her face. She hadn't even noticed Philip standing there, but the elderly black man did, and his gaze, though reddened from tears, held a challenge that both amused and startled Philip.

"Remember what I said," the doctor whispered sternly, "you aren't to waken Lara with your histrionics or I'll see you're removed."

The black man nodded assent, but did not remove his gaze from Philip's. When the doctor closed the door, Philip stepped forward, with his hand extended. Whoever this man was, he obviously held a place of high esteem in Lara's life, or he wouldn't be standing here now, challenging him with his gaze.

"Philip Bensley, Fifth Earl of Ripon," he announced formally, albeit in a quiet tone. He waited for Joshua to acknowledge him and accept his outstretched hand. He grinned when he saw the black man's eyes widen and, for a moment, he thought he was going to ignore his overture. After an obvious struggle to regain his composure, the man straightened his shoulders and clasped Philip's had firmly.

"Well, your Grace, I may just be Miss Lara's butler, but I think that, under these circumstances, I got the right to know who you think you are, announcing to all and sundry that you be Miss Lara's fiancé."

"Do you think it would be possible for us to continue this conversation elsewhere? I would hate to waken her. She's been through quite a bit in so short a time."

Joshua's gaze quickly took in Philip's own wet clothing and he shook his head in bemusement, "You was the one that jumped in and saved our Mistress?"

"One of many men that came to Miss Esterhaus' aid," Philip acknowledged.

"Well, that may not excuse your impertinence, but it certainly does make me less hostile towards you at present. Sasha," Joshua hissed, "come here girl."

For the second time in less than five minutes, Philip was startled. This time at the way in which he addressed the white woman in the room; a woman whom Philip mistakenly assumed was Lara's relation.

Sasha sniffled and stood, moving over to stand by Joshua. Her eyes widened when she realized they weren't alone. Joshua took her by the elbow, leading her toward the corridor, nodding at Philip that he should follow along.

Philip inexplicably felt the need to comply.

When they all were standing in the hallway, Joshua turned to introduce Philip to Sasha.

"Sasha, I'd like you to meet the man I'm assuming sent the letter of introduction to Miss Lara?" He looked toward Philip for confirmation and then continued. "This here is Lord Philip Bensley, the Fifth Earl of Ripon. Did I get that right?"

Philip smiled and nodded again, "Your Grace, this is Miss Sasha Blackwell. She is Miss Lara's attendant."

Philip's eyes widened a fraction, but then he recovered and bowed low at the waist, "A pleasure, Miss Blackwell." A gesture overly formal given the circumstances, but it afforded Philip the opportunity to compose his features. He'd never had a black servant introduce him so formally to another servant.

Sasha nodded, but couldn't speak. She was still having trouble digesting the part of the introduction about this man being royalty; and to top it all off, he was exceedingly tall and handsome. Each stood staring at the other trying to decide where to go from the introductions.

Finally, Philip spoke up, "I'm not Your Grace," he said simply. "That title is reserved for Dukes, although I'm flattered to find myself elevated in the hierarchy." He smiled, hoping that it appeared a friendly gesture and not a snooty one.

"What do we call you then?" Sasha replied shyly.

"My Lord is acceptable or just Philip."

"That would hardly be appropriate," Joshua said, finalizing that part of their conversation. "Sasha," he said, "stay by Miss Lara's side. I am going to walk back with his Lordship to his hotel room so that he can change his attire. Wouldn't want him to catch his death. If Miss Lara wakens, come find us immediately."

Sasha nodded. She gave a quick curtsey to Philip and then returned to the room.

When they were alone again, Joshua turned and again gave Philip the once over, "I'd offer to take you back to the house to dry your clothes out, but there isn't anything in the master's wardrobe that will come close to fitting a man of your size."

Philip laughed. "My hotel room is probably closer anyhow; however, might I suggest we ride rather than walk? If Lara wakens, we need to get back here as quickly as possible."

Joshua nodded.

Both men left the doctor's house and mounted their steeds. Joshua followed behind Philip at a short distance, an arrangement Philip was about to rectify, but then he remembered Joshua's comment about propriety and continued on his way.

The glances aimed his way bespoke of how quickly word had spread about his engagement to Lara.

"Looks as if you might be a man people notice," Joshua called from behind him.

Philip laughed, both at the comment and Joshua's selectivity over matters appropriate. He wouldn't call him by his given name, but he didn't have any qualms about addressing him informally in a public setting. "Strange man," he muttered.

He dismounted in front of the hotel and was immediately met by his brother, Andrew.

"Philip. Glad to see you're in fine form. I heard there was a commotion down by the river that had you pulling a woman from the drink; also heard that you got yourself engaged to that same unconscious female."

Andrew tipped his hat toward Joshua who'd dismounted and was standing nearby.

"Indeed. Well, today's events have confirmed Carl's suspicions that there are dangerous games afoot. Seems our scar-faced man attempted to put an end to Lara Esterhaus' pursuit of a husband by putting an end to her," Philip said dryly. "It was just fortuitous timing that I happened to be riding by. I shudder to think what may have occurred had I not decided to break with protocol. Oh, forgive my rudeness, Joshua. This is my brother, Andrew. Andrew, this is Lara's butler. He was determining whether or not to put a musket ball in me earlier for audaciously announcing to all and sundry that Lara was my fiancé. Isn't that right, Joshua?"

"Well, now that I know you aren't a dastardly fiend in disguise, I'll forgo. It's a right nice pleasure to make your acquaintance, Master Andrew."

Andrew shook the outstretched hand, a perplexed look on his face.

Philip just laughed, "Well, I think we need to take this conversation indoors. I need to get out of these wet clothes, and there is a lot that we need to discuss."

"Mind if I sit in on those discussions, my Lord? I know it isn't my place to be discussing Lara's affairs, but after all I just heard…"

"I was quite expecting you to, Joshua," Philip said, slapping the elderly man on the back. "Go and wait with Andrew in his room. It won't take but a moment for me to get changed."

"Yes, my Lord."

"And Joshua, if you've got the gumption to stand up to me the way you did, you can summon up enough gumption to call me Philip."

Joshua merely smiled and followed the two men into the hotel.

CHAPTER 25

Philip had no sooner walked into the room, when Joshua began to query over the comments made outside, "What did you mean about someone trying to stop Miss Lara finding a husband? Are you saying that her buggy crash weren't no accident?"

"I can tell you with near certainty that the buggy crash was intentional. It's assumption, to be sure, but…Andrew, do you remember telling me that the man who threatened you had a severely scarred face?"

"Indeed."

"Well, I passed a man matching your description riding away from the runaway buggy at top speed. It was as if he knew that the crash was going to occur and didn't want to stay around the area."

"But why would someone want to hurt Miss Lara?"

"I can answer that," Andrew said. "I paid a visit to the constable. A bright fellow and definitely full of theories; theories that, I'd say, wouldn't hold water, unless combined with the happenings of late."

"How so?" Philip asked.

"Apparently, there have been a lot of deaths ruled accidental over this last year and a half, including that of the former constable. More interesting is that a majority of those accidental deaths have occurred within the Esterhaus family."

"Joshua? What can you tell us about that?"

"I did find it a might suspicious that Miss Lara's family suddenly started dropping like flies, but each and every time the coroner, he says that there wasn't anything foul about the deaths. Still, for Miss Lara's uncle, aunt, and cousins all to die in a house fire followed not two months later by the death of Lara's parents…"

"How did they die?"

"Not too dissimilar to the way in which Miss Lara nearly died. An accident in December toppled their buggy over into the icy waters of the river. There wasn't no way for anyone to retrieve their bodies, like you did with Miss Lara, not with it being winter and so cold, and iced over. So with their deaths, that makes Miss Lara the last surviving member of the family."

"And that brings me back to the answer to your question. Why would someone want to harm Lara Esterhaus? And the answer is—to gain possession of her properties. Apparently, she is heiress to quite substantial properties. Her great-grandfather was Thomas Salter. He owned all of the lands south of Savannah proper, which has been passed down through the years to his heirs, along with the family business. The family was in the brick-making industry which garnered the heirs of Thomas Salter quite a tidy fortune. Lara's uncle ran the business and it was his sons who stood to inherit it all, since Lara's a woman; however, with their deaths…"

"Lara is the sole remaining heir, but without a husband…"

"The bank takes possession and Miss Lara loses it all," Joshua finished, his eyes widening with comprehension. "No wonder those men were eager to get Lara to sell or to marry that no-account man who came to call a few weeks back. We knew something smelled funny about him, but now I know he must've been one of the men in cahoots with the others trying to steal everything. Well, as God is my witness, I won't be letting anyone take what Miss Lara holds dear to her heart."

"What's wrong her?" Philip asked suddenly. "Why couldn't she find a man willing to marry her? Why did she need to resort to advertising for a husband?"

Joshua stood gawking at Philip for a moment and then he slowly regained control of his emotions, took a deep breath and let it out with a whoosh, and then sank into a nearby chair, "I like you," he said finally, "which is why this conversation is going to be so much easier than if I decided you had a dastardly fiend lurking beneath that skin of yours."

"I beg pardon?"

"Nothing to worry over," Joshua said. "Just suffice it to say, I'm glad you're the one who answered Miss Lara's advertisement."

"Which means you're going to explain precisely what she meant by obvious flaws? Because I'm telling you now, I got a good look at the woman and I couldn't see any flaws whatsoever."

"I reckon I can tell you some things, since it's obvious that you don't mean her no harm," Joshua said.

"I'm listening."

"As am I," Andrew said, pulling his chair closer to the other two men. "Curiosity over this woman has been eating at me since we first read her advertisement."

"Fair enough. You see…well…let me start by saying that Miss Lara was very close to her parents. None closer. You ever heard that expression 'two peas in a pod'?"

Philip nodded and Joshua continued, "Well, it may be a might bit crowded, but there would have been three in their pod. Right from the start, me and her parents could tell that Lara was special. Even early on, she could run that business and keep the store's books better than her daddy."

"Store?"

"You had her investigated, but don't know about her family's business…well, her business now."

"My investigator didn't feel the need to mention that particular aspect, especially as there seemed to be more important things he felt I should know. Pray, continue. What sort of business does she own?"

"Her family—I mean Lara. Lord, but it's still hard to acknowledge her parents' deaths. Anyway, Lara owns a dress shop," Joshua said. "A very successful dress shop."

"I see. Do go on," Philip said, now knowing where the woman of means entered into the picture.

"You don't see where I'm going with this?"

"Not yet."

"Her obvious flaws," Joshua said. "You can't see them, can you?"

Philip looked questioningly at Joshua, brow knitted in confusion, "Hence our conversation."

"Okay, I'll explain in a way that you might be able to get where I'm going," Joshua said. "You know what she said when she placed that advertisement of hers?"

"No, but I expect you're about to tell me," Philip said.

Joshua nodded, his countenance suddenly saddened, "She said that if she was only a few inches shorter, dumb, blond, and mute, then maybe she might just be lucky enough to find herself a husband in time to save our home."

"Dear Lord above," Philip said, understanding dawning. "She's tall and smart."

"It's a little hard to overlook her height, but you haven't had a taste of her brain power yet, that be for darn sure. She is one of the most intelligent women you're ever apt to meet."

"I easily overlooked her height because she's been in the prone position since I've seen her. I have yet to see her upright," Philip stated automatically, his thoughts trying to come to an understanding over people's prejudices.

"Well, she's a might bit shorter than you are, my Lord, but she's a sight bit taller than most men."

"And that's why…"

"Men don't want her; don't want nothing to do with her. It's bad enough her being as tall as she is, but when a man gets wind of how smart she is too—it's a courting death sentence, it is. It was a sad thing to watch when she reached the age of maturity. Her mother was tall too, you see, but Missus Ava held out hope for her little girl because she'd been fortunate to find a man. Master Travis was a sight bit shorter than Missus Ava, but that didn't seem to make no never mind." Joshua sighed. "But it didn't seem as if the same fate awaited Miss Lara. You see, everyone that her mother introduced from far and wide, bolted the minute they took one look at Miss Lara. Most didn't even stick around to find out about her smarts. Most likely didn't like the fact they all had to look up. Men don't fancy feeling small. The very few who decided to overlook her heights, and I do mean precious few, left the minute she began speaking about the business. That acumen of hers was even more intimidating than her height. There were many a times I wanted to chase after a few of those suitors and put an end to their cruel parting words with Master Travis's pistol, but that wouldn't have been fitting. If Miss Lara had the capacity for putting on airs and pretense, she would have been more likely to find a husband by acting brainless, but there ain't a deceitful bone in that girl's body, let me tell ya. Don't get me wrong, Missus Ava wasn't deceitful either, she was just more able to adapt to societies demands. Plus, Miss Lara got Master Travis's smarts, but that wasn't no fault of hers, so why men have to make her feel so small is beyond me."

"Dear Lord above," Philip repeated with a sigh.

"Yeah, you just said that," Joshua sighed. "Anyway, when your letter arrived saying that you wanted an audience, it was an answer to our prayers, and now that I've gotten to know you, well…I guess God knew what He was doing is all I've got to say."

"Good heavens, what an affair this is turning out to be," Andrew said finally. "Quite the adventure, eh Philip?"

"Quite the adventure," Philip murmured.

A knock sounded at the door startling them; bringing their conversation to a close. Each jumped to his feet, and retrieved his weapon. When all had checked their load and quietly prepared to fire, Philip nodded at Andrew who nodded back. Both men moved into strategic locations, should the need arise to mount a defense; a possibility after what they'd discovered.

"Could you answer the door, Joshua?" Philip whispered.

Joshua nodded. He shifted his weapon from hand to hand, wiping his sweating palms on his pants leg and then pulled the door open with a whoosh. It was Sasha.

"Joshua, Lara's awake."

CHAPTER 26

"How are you feeling, Miss Lara?" Joshua asked, kneeling next to the bed. He took her hand in his and held it gently, renewed tears forming in his eyes; tears of relief. Sasha knelt on the other side of the bed, which left Philip and Andrew standing awkwardly at the foot.

"I'll recover, Joshua," Lara said softly. She felt tired, drained, and battered, but grateful to be breathing. "Who are y'all[q]?" She whispered, her gaze moving from Andrew to Philip and back.

Joshua looked up at the two men, twirling hats in their hands, but before either could respond to Lara's question, Joshua piped up, "I should have introduced these men the moment we entered, but we are just so relieved to have you with us that our brains are still a bit scattered."

"It's alright, Joshua." Lara turned her head to look at her butler and long-time friend. It was so unusual to see him flustered that she automatically assumed that there was something wrong; that these two men had somehow brought all of these latest woes crashing down upon their heads. When Joshua next spoke, she knew her suppositions had no basis.

"I want to introduce you to the man who saved your life, and his brother." Joshua stood. Swiping at his tears, he went to stand next to Philip. He squared his shoulders and proudly announced, "This is his Lordship, Philip Bensley, Fifth Earl of Ripon."

Lara's eyes widened, but Philip didn't notice. He was too busy finding amusement in Joshua's demeanor. He smiled at the ease in which Joshua introduced him this time around. Gone was the awkwardness with his title, and in its place was all of the formality of a butler.

"And this is Master Andrew, Philip's brother; and might I add, that it was his Lordship who sent the request for an introduction. Moreover, both of these men have been instrumental in discovering much about what happened to you today and also to what happened to your parents."

Philip leaned over next to Joshua's ear and whispered, "You

---

[q] The origin of the contraction y'all traces back to the late 18th Century.

remind me of a peacock at present."

Joshua smiled widely.

Lara watched the exchange in growing wonder, "How long have I been unconscious?" She asked, having immediately made yet another invalid assumption that such a rapport between servant and master must have transpired over weeks or months.

"Only an hour or so, and I must confess that I'm pleased to see that you weren't badly injured," Philip answered, moving to the place vacated by Joshua.

"You saved my life," Lara stated, growing drowsy again.

"I only but assisted," Philip said bowing slightly.

"What was that Joshua said about my parents?" Lara's speech slurred and she barely finished the sentence before sleep reclaimed her. The last thought to drift through her mind was she was hallucinating, for nothing she witnessed made sense.

For the third time, her assumptions were incorrect.

The doctor entered a moment after Lara drifted off to sleep, "My wife told me that you'd all returned. I didn't have the chance to tell you that I'd only just given Lara a sedative. You all may as well return home for the evening, as I expect she'll sleep through the night. She should be okay to return home tomorrow, but I want to give her a final check in the morning before releasing her. After all, she suffered quite a traumatic event."

"Thank you for everything, doctor," Andrew said, shaking the doctor's hand.

"It was my pleasure. I was there to deliver that young lady, and I would have been sore displeased if I were to attend her funeral before my own. Any ideas what happened? I know it was foggy, but Lara's a fair hand with the horses."

"We have a notion, but nothing that can be substantiated. Right now it appears as if the mares got spooked and she dropped the reins. Since it was busy on the thoroughfare, a collision was inevitable," Philip answered. "At what time may we come around to pick up your patient, doctor?"

"After breakfast should be fine—my breakfast, not yours. So, that will be around seven in the a.m."

"Very good. You should expect to hear a knock at your door at seven a.m. sharp then. Thank you again, doctor, for providing such excellent care to my fiancé."

"Oh, which reminds me, I didn't have the opportunity before to congratulate you on your pending nuptials." Philip nodded and the doctor stepped into the corridor, "I'll bid you a good day. You can find your way out, I presume?"

Philip nodded again. The door closed and he returned his gaze to the woman sleeping; again in awe of not only her beauty, but now also her manner of speech.

"How could anyone not be enthralled?" He whispered.

"Far too easily," Sasha stated.

"Sasha," Joshua scolded, although he knew that Sasha didn't mean any harm. In all likelihood, she'd meant to express her disgust of men and their poor opinion of Lara, but, as usual, it wasn't expressed well. Joshua realized that, but he worried that Philip and Andrew wouldn't understand.

"What did I say now?"

And thus the promise to Lara to hold off on their silly bickering ended. Philip and Andrew both cleared their throats simultaneously, which elicited laughter from everyone. Only when Lara moaned in her sleep at the ruckus did they all file quietly from the room.

"It sure feels nice to find laughter again. All of this worrying of late creates a pounding in my brain something fierce," Joshua said, his spirits light, but it didn't take long before those spirits were restrained again.

"Unfortunately, this whole affair hasn't drawn to a close. I'm afraid there'll be more worrying to be had before all's said and done," Philip said, his tone subdued. "Would you mind if we were to move our things into your home? I know it's presumptuous, and may cause a few tongues to wag…"

"Sasha and I will help you pack your belongings. After all that happened over the last few hours, having an extra pair of strong men around the home certainly won't go amiss. Of course, Miss Lara has the final say on whether you gentlemen stay, but I've never known her to be unreasonable when there's sound logic involved."

"Understood," Philip said and then addressed his other concern, "We also need to consider Lara's safety. If the person who tried to have her killed discovers she's still alive, he may make another attempt; and while the doctor is an excellent physician, I'm not certain we can count on his being a crack shot."

"Round the clock watch?" Andrew asked.

"Round the clock," Philip confirmed. "At least until seven in the a.m. How are you with a gun, Joshua?"

"A crack shot, sir."

Philip smiled, "Glad to hear it. You'll take first watch."

The four of them stepped from the doctor's home just as the loud report of a musket reverberated through the late afternoon air.

"Now what?" Andrew snapped.

"Miss Lara!" Joshua exclaimed, but Philip prevented him from returning inside the house.

Philip's first thought too was that someone had snuck in the back of the doctor's home to finish what was started, but after reason returned, he realized "the shot came from further down the lane," he said, voicing his thought aloud. "Joshua, where's your gun?"

"On the nag," Joshua said, heading down the steps to retrieve his weapon.

"Sasha, you head on home. I don't think you're in any danger," Philip instructed. When Joshua returned, Philip addressed the men again, "I don't think there isn't anyone who didn't hear that musket fire, and the constable is probably already on his way; but I still want to see what's happening. It's probably nothing to do with us, and yet my gut tells me this could be a distraction to get to Lara. Joshua, your watch starts now, keep a sharp eye out and walk the perimeter. Andrew will relieve you at dusk. Andrew, let's go see what we can see."

Joshua watched Andrew and Philip mount their horses and head down the path in the direction from where the musket sounded. He checked his load, removed the safety, and started his first circuit around the house, more than ready and equally willing to shoot first and ask questions later.

CHAPTER 27

"Apparently, I didn't make it clear enough that I didn't want Lara Esterhaus harmed?" Alfred Garamond asked the moment Arthur opened the door to his home and permitted admittance.

"It's lovely to see you too, Alfred."

"This isn't a social call, Arthur," Garamond growled. "You deliberately went behind my back and tried to terminate Lara, against my express instructions."

"She rejected my courtship; has accepted the courtship of another," Middleton stated petulantly. "There was no other recourse to prevent her marrying before the deadline. How did you know anyway?"

"You didn't think I'd find it too much of a coincidence that another Esterhaus just happened to have a near-fatal buggy ride? Why didn't you come to me with the information about the other suitor?" Garamond moved to Arthur's liquor cabinet and poured a tumbler of Scotch. After that disturbing news, he needed a drink. He knew that there was a letter, but hadn't heard the gentleman in question had arrived in town already.

"What would you have done? Planned something? You even told Henry that if it was warranted to take action, to "assume" what you wanted done. Well, that's what I did."

"Oh, I'm sure your motivations had nothing to do with your ego; so what happens when it traces back to us?"

"How would that happen? It isn't as if our hired killer will turn himself in."

Garamond sighed loudly, "What's done is done, but you should know that the coincidental buggy accident isn't what tipped me off that you were up to something," he took another swig, refilled the glass, and settled on the chair near the window.

"How then?" Arthur asked, when it didn't appear as if Garamond was going to offer up any more information.

"I was stepping from the hotel…"

"What were you doing there?"

"Not that it's any of your concern or at all relevant, but I paid a visit to Rita. Anyway, as I exited, I heard two strangers and a black man, who looked suspiciously like Lara's butler, conversing. From the snippets I heard as I passed by, they know about the scar-faced man and even connected him to efforts to prevent Lara marrying. Since that connection was made, it stands to reason that he will be the prime suspect in the buggy crash, if it is determined not to be accidental."

"There isn't a reason to suspect anything but an accident. I think the scar-faced man chose a good time to make it happen. Accidents during heavy fog take place frequently."

"You met with a man in the saloon this morning, and accompanied the scar-faced man there again soon after, correct?"

Middleton's eyes widened, "Having Henry keep tabs on *me* now?"

Garamond shrugged, "After your hysterical outburst when we discovered someone answered Lara's advertisement, I felt it wise to…well, let's just say that I didn't want you to transfer your histrionics into stupid actions. Keeping the brim of your hat low on your brow isn't the most intelligent of disguises, but it showed you were capable of some level of rational thought. That's why I was surprised when you went off into the realm of irrationality, going against my dictate not to harm Lara Esterhaus."

"I did what I thought was right."

"And yet you were wrong. You allowed your damaged sense of self-worth to dictate your actions and put our entire plan at risk. Now, I have to find a way to sew up the gaping hole in our plan that your actions caused before we lose the Esterhaus fortune." Garamond walked over to the fireplace during this rebuke. After a moment he glanced at his pocket watch and then reached up to retrieve an antique Flintlock rifle which hung above the mantel. "You keep this loaded, don't you; always thought that was foolish."

A knock sounded at the door, startling Middleton.

"You going to answer that?" Garamond asked when Middleton remained seated.

"You planning to put that rifle back?"

Garamond shrugged, "Why don't you see whose come to call? Unless you think it might be the constable. Any reason to think he might have linked you to the buggy crash?"

Middleton's nerves were jumping. Garamond was examining his Flintlock too closely, was speaking to him too calmly. "I don't see why he would."

The knock repeated and Garamond arched a brow in question. Middleton took in a deep breath and stood, slowly making his way toward the door. He heard Garamond's footfalls behind him and his heart began pounding. *Surely he wouldn't shoot me in the back with a witness just outside the door*, he thought, somehow knowing that his partnership with Garamond was about to come to a tragic end, just as Jeremy's had. All because Jeremy had gotten drunk and revealed too much to that Pinkerton agent.

He picked up his pace, suddenly eager to admit the visitor. A shot in the house could easily be explained away as an accident. He could hear Garamond now—'I was just examining the weapon that Arthur holds so dear and must have squeezed the trigger without realizing it. I didn't know he kept it loaded'.

His standing in the community would keep him from going to jail; however, if there was another person in the house, it may just deter Garamond and extend his life.

He reached for the doorknob, opened the door, and flinched as the Flintlock discharged.

CHAPTER 28

"Constable," Andrew greeted as he and Philip met up with the man near the area of the musket fire.

"Hello again, young man. Andrew, isn't it?"

Andrew nodded acknowledgment, "This is my brother, Philip."

"Pleasure."

Andrew then nodded toward the riders following the constable, "I take it we weren't the only ones to hear the shot?"

"I think everyone may have heard that shot," the constable said, his tone grim. "I am only hoping that someone decided to hunt deer near town rather than the other option."

"I gather hunting game this close to town goes against certain ordinances?" Philip asked.

"Indeed." The constable pulled on his reins until the horse finally stopped walking. He then turned to face the men following, "Well I do believe this to be the general vicinity; however, there are numerous residences from which the shot may have derived. I think our best course of action is to fan out, see if we stumble upon anything of note."

"That won't be necessary, constable," Alfred Garamond said, riding out from the nearby tree line. "I'll take you to the body."

"Mr. Garamond," the constable greeted. "Found something in the woods?"

"Experienced something, more like," he said, pulling a few leaves and twigs from his hair. "The trek through the woods was a more expedient exit for which to come to get you." Alfred pulled on his reins, "If you'll follow me. The shot came from Arthur Middleton's place."

The riders filed in behind Garamond as he made his way up the lane. After a short ride, he turned onto a wide path which led to a clearing where a beautifully crafted, sizable cabin was situated. Even from the edge of the yard, it was easy to see the body of a man sprawled out on the front porch. Another man was seated on the steps, hands cradling his face, in apparent distress. He looked up as he heard the riders draw near and blanched, remembering…

"You shot him."

"He was becoming a liability."

"How did you know…?

"I gave him the hour to be here."

"We may have had further use of his services," Arthur Middleton whispered, unable to take his eyes from the gaping hole in the scar-faced man's face; unable to wrap his mind around how close he came to death. 'Why him, and not me?' he wanted to ask, but was afraid the answer would be, 'You're next.'

"I want you to know that his death is your doing. I may have pulled the trigger, but if you hadn't gone off in an offended rage and hired him against my will, he may have been of further use…well, what's done is done. He had to die because I couldn't risk his making another attempt on the girl, since his first attempt failed," Garamond said, also unable to draw his gaze from the body sprawled on the porch. He'd never killed anyone before.

"How are we going to explain all of this?" Middleton asked, his mind a jumbled mass of confusion. Was Garamond going to get rid of him by making him take the fall for murder?

Garamond stepped onto the porch and signaled that Middleton should do likewise. With careful steps, he crossed over the threshold and went to stand next to the porch swing, but continued watching Garamond warily.

Garamond moved to the door again, stepped inside and shut it. Middleton's brow knitted as he heard the lever tumbler lock[r], installed only last year, click into place. A moment later, Garamond appeared at the window, slid it open, and crawled back onto the porch. Without uttering a word, he moved back to the door, lifted his foot, and slammed it into the area just above the knob, splintering the wood. The door flew open.

Middleton understood what Garamond was doing, manipulating the scene, but the only thing that ran through his head was that it was going to cost money to repair the damage, and he was already spending too much on Garamond's plans.

Garamond took a step back and surveyed his work and then moved to stand beside Arthur, "There isn't any way that that shot went unheard, so we can assume that company is on the way. Since his face is obliterated, there will be no way that anyone will know it's the scar-faced man. That means there will be no way to connect him to either of us. So I'll go over what we're going to say, and

---

[r] The lever tumbler lock, which uses a set of levers to prevent the bolt from moving in the lock, was perfected by Robert Barron in 1778 (Wikipedia).

then we'll discuss what's to be done about this potential suitor."

"What about Lara?"

"She's not the threat to our plans. The suitor is. Keep him from walking down the aisle, and Lara's property is ours."

Middleton returned from his musings as the men on horseback drew along the front of the house and began dismounting. His eyes widened and he stifled a gasp when he recognized one of the men as the potential suitor; the man he'd attempted to buy off in the saloon only this morning. He shot Garamond a look, which made Garamond's eyes narrow in question. Middleton slowly tilted his head toward Andrew and Garamond turned to look at the man who'd dismounted next to the constable. He sent a return nod to Arthur and Arthur sighed audibly. The noise drew the constable's attention and he walked over.

"Mr. Middleton, isn't it?" The constable asked.

Arthur nodded, summoning the courage to speak, running the explanation given him by Garamond through his head again.

"Very good," the constable said, acknowledging the nod as confirmation of his identity, "so then, could you explain what happened here this evening?"

But Middleton didn't answer. He made the mistake of allowing his gaze to wander in the direction where Andrew stood. His gaze collided with Andrew's and his mind went to racing. *Does he know I was the man beneath the hat that tried to dissuade his proposing to Lara? If I speak, will he recognize my voice and alert the constable?*

He remained silent.

Garamond's brow knitted at Arthur's silence, but rather than try to force his cohort into speaking, who may raise suspicions, he decided to offer the explanation himself.

"If I may relay the version of events, constable? I was visiting with Arthur when this horrible tragedy transpired."

The constable nodded. Only when he moved off did Arthur manage to tear his gaze away from Andrew. He returned his head to his hands and remained that way, fearful that his very look could portray his guilt.

"You gentleman can return to your homes now," the constable

said, addressing the men, all of whom were gawking at the corpse with looks ranging from disgust to inquisitiveness. "It doesn't appear I'll be forming a posse after all, since the shooter is sitting right here."

Middleton's eyes squeezed tight and his shoulders slumped. He kept his face buried in his hands. The men murmured among themselves as they mounted and rode away.

"You'll let us know if you need assistance?" Andrew asked. He'd seen the look the man named Middleton gave him and his curiosity was piqued. While he would have preferred to stay and hear what had happened, he couldn't think of a justifiable reason to do so, not when there were more important things to look after.

"Thanks for asking, but I have quite a few questions to ask before I write up a report; decide whether an arrest is warranted. Actually, there is one thing," He said, stopping midway up the steps.

"Most certainly."

"Could you ride over to my office and tell Josiah and Moses to bring along a wagon to remove this body? There isn't just cause why it should remain here."

Andrew nodded and he and Philip mounted and rode back towards town.

"Now, you were going to offer an explanation?" The constable asked, turning back to Garamond.

"Oh, yes, well, as I stated, I was visiting with Arthur this afternoon when without warning, we heard a banging on the front door, dreadfully loud it was. Arthur instinctively reached for his father's Flintlock, as this is the only weapon he possesses. I always thought it foolish for him to keep the thing loaded as he does, but after today I feel it was the wisest thing he could have done. His actions no doubt saved our lives. Anyway, here is what happened.

'It's probably that black bear returned for a bite of my venison. Broke in last week and stole a slab that I had cooking over the fire. Right beneath my nose, it did. Stood on hind legs, roared deafeningly, walked over pretty as you please, nabbed my food, and sauntered off.'

"A bear." The constable stopped jotting notes on his small pad and speared Garamond with a look of incredulity.

"Well, that's what Middleton said to me. As I wasn't present when the bear made its first appearance, I can hardly attest as to the validity of his words. We do have black bear in the area though. Weren't you aware of that, constable?"

The constable shook his head, "No, I wasn't made aware of that when I was given this post. My apologies for the interruption; pray continue."

"Well, as I was saying, Arthur grabbed his Flintlock and we slowly made our way to the front door when another loud banging sound shattered the air. If it was the bear, we hoped to make it to the stairs and out of harm's way, should it manage to break the door down. We made it to the foyer when the door flew open with a bang. Arthur fired instinctively. It is possible that the door flying open in his face caused him to react. Either way, we didn't know that he'd killed a man until the smoke cleared. Arthur is devastated, as you can well imagine."

"Yes, only just," the constable glanced down at the body nearby, "he managed to shoot so accurate as to eradicate his face, so we can't say who it was banging at the door, unless, of course, either of you managed to get a look at who it was before who it was became unidentifiable?"

"We were discussing that very thing before I came to get you. Who it could have been trying to bust through Arthur's door? Arthur is a wealthy man, as you are probably aware, constable."

"I am."

"Well, the person could very well have had burglary in mind."

"To burgle in daylight hours takes a brave man; and an even braver one to bang upon a door to a home he intends to burgle.'

"Or a man deep in his cups.[s]"

"But one has to wonder as to whether a man deep in his cups could steady himself well enough, or wield enough strength, to down a door." The constable suddenly sniffed at the air, which made Garamond's brow knit. The constable caught his look of confusion and smiled grimly, "Just wondering at the lack of aroma. If he wasn't cooking his supper, what would have drawn Mr. Middleton to the

---

[s] Deep in his cups means very drunk.

conclusion that the bear had returned for another feast?"

Garamond merely shrugged, unwilling to delve further into the pit of lies he'd dug. He hadn't counted on the constable being the curious sort; had, in fact, pegged him as a little on the dull-witted side. A mistake, he now realized. A mistake that needed to be rectified, he wondered, as with the previous constable? He inhaled sharply through his nostrils, trying to tamp down on the anger that flared. With less than a fortnight to go, things were spiraling out of control and it was all Middleton's fault. If he'd let his bruised ego heal instead of seeking retribution then none of this would be transpiring; they would still have the scar-faced man to rely upon to rid them of Lara's potential suitor.

Now all they had was trouble.

"The door had a lock?" The constable asked again, moving to inspect the damage.

"Um, yes," Garamond answered, following along behind.

"I didn't realize this latest invention had made it to the Americas," the constable murmured.

"Well, like I said, Arthur is a wealthy man. When a friend returned a few years ago from visiting Britain, he came with news that his cousin, a man named Barron, had designed this new locking system to keep intruders out of homes. Had one shipped over…"

"But why was it locked?" The constable interrupted.

Garamond's face took on an even more perplexed expression and the constable sighed, "I suppose I'm wondering why you or Mr. Middleton felt the need to lock the door, while he was entertaining. Had he mentioned the expectation of trouble?"

"He liked showing it off whenever I came 'round. I still think he's the only man in Savannah to have purchased such a lavish mechanism. Must have latched it and forgot to undo it before we came into the study to have a drink." Garamond was grateful he had the ability to think quickly and that he'd decided to answer the constable's questions. Had it been Middleton, the sod would have turned himself in and confessed everything, all because the constable turned out to be the curious sort.

"And he liked to brag about that fact?"

"Repeatedly," Garamond said with a roll of his eyes.

The constable laughed softly and then grew serious again, "And yet a man chose this home to burgle; the only home in Savannah known to possess the latest in home security. Nice Flintlock," he observed, his foot nudging the weapon still on the floor in the foyer. "Just dropped it after he fired?"

"Yes. I guess he was in shock about discharging his rifle in such haste."

"Indeed, and he appears to be as adept at dropping things neatly while in haste, as he does at firing expertly while under duress."

"I don't take your meaning, constable," Garamond said, his nerves beginning to jump. This man was finding too many things to nitpick over; too many small details that many a man would readily overlook.

"Yes, well, I've dropped my weapon a time or two, and it never seemed to fall in precisely the direction in which I was pointing." He nudged the Flintlock again with his toe, drawing Garamond's attention to the fact that the muzzle was aimed directly at the front portal. He then picked up the Flintlock, took aim, pretended to discharge the weapon, and then let it fall. The rifle bounced heavily and then landed with the muzzle pointed toward the study door. "I could probably drop that a thousand times and never will that muzzle land the way it lays now. It's as if Middleton simply lay it down."

"I can assure you he dropped it in haste," Garamond said. "Maybe one of us accidentally kicked it..."

"Of course," the constable interrupted.

Garamond fought to maintain a calm demeanor, but his mind was formulating his next course of action—how to rid himself of Arthur Middleton. Had the constable simply overlooked the flaws in his rather hastily executed plan, then Middleton may have remained an asset to his plan, at least his money would have. However, if the constable were to take Middleton to his offices for further inquiry, Middleton could relay all he knew thereby destroying all that they'd worked to gain. He'd have his own wealth to rely on once he possessed the Esterhaus land. Middleton had to die next.

"Is there anything further for now, constable? I feel I should bring Arthur in for a strong cup of tea with a dollop of laudanum to help him sleep. He's suffered quite a shock today."

"Laudanum?"

"Oh come now, constable, don't tell me that you Brits never used laudanum before," Garamond laughed, guiding the constable by the elbow towards the front door.

"Couldn't live without it," the constable said. "It keeps these old joints lubricated; however, I really should speak with Mr. Middleton prior to his tea."

"He may not be in the right frame of mind until after his tea, constable."

"Of course. Understood. Well, once Mr. Middleton has recovered from his shock and awakened from his nap, I would appreciate it if you could bring him down for me to have a further word with him. It would help matters if he could corroborate what you've told me."

"I daresay he's quite unable to corroborate his own existence at present," Garamond said, nodding to where Arthur still sat, unmoved from the time the constable and he entered the house. "Perhaps tomorrow would be a better time to speak with him, when he's more himself."

"Indeed. Well then, I'll see you two gentlemen on the morrow."

"I will come by in the morning and collect him; personally escort him to your office."

"Very good, then I'll bid you a good day. When my men arrive to remove the body, would you like one to remain behind and scrub the mess away?"

"I'm certain that Arthur would appreciate that."

The constable nodded and then moved down the stairs and mounted his horse. With a tip of his hat, he left.

Garamond watched the constable ride away and then muttered to himself, "Let's see just how much laudanum a man can take before it kills him."

CHAPTER 29

"What's on your mind, Andrew?" Philip asked as they rode back towards town.

"What? Oh, on my mind, right. I can't be certain, but when the owner of the house looked at me, I got the feeling my being there caused him as much distress as the dead body had; which led me to believe that he may have been one of those trying to keep me…us…away from Lara. Unless I simply reminded him of dreaded relative."

Philip grinned, but it held no humor, "I got a funny feeling too because that man's face may have been mangled, but the man's build and the clothes seemed all too familiar."

"The rider that sped by you earlier this afternoon right after Lara's carriage accident?"

Philip nodded. "Good guess, and yes. I only mention it because of your gut feeling and my unease over the whole affair. After all, we're both wearing similar clothing right now to that dead man, and there are plenty of men with his physique, so he could very well be completely unrelated to everything that's taking place with Lara."

"Or he, and those other two men, could be the ones trying to deter Lara from marrying."

"Yep, that's what my gut is telling me."

"So what are we supposed to do now?"

"There isn't too much we can do, since our theories are based solely on supposition. For all I know, we could simply be making more of everything than there is, because of all that's happened. Those men may have absolutely nothing to do with anything."

"True, but my gut is screaming at me too, and I don't think both of our guts could be wrong."

Philip opened his pocket watch, "It's suppertime. Let's go inform the constable's hires about the body and then go eat. Afterward, you can relieve Joshua. As soon as you relieve him, have him meet me at our hotel to pack up our belongings. Once we've settled in at Lara's place, we'll start preparing."

"It's difficult to prepare for something when all you have is speculation."

"True, but while there are a lot of unknowns, we do have some idea of what these men are after and should try to plan accordingly. Even if those men at the house have nothing to do with this, there are men out there who are still trying to prevent our involvement with the Esterhaus woman, and that is what we need to be ready for."

Andrew sighed heavily and shook his head, "And I'll say it again, it's hard to plan for something when you don't know what or when it's going to happen."

"There has to be some sort of deadline to all of this, some agenda being followed. Lara's advertisement mentioned needing a husband before September, which just so happens to be this month. Perhaps Lara or Joshua can fill us in on everything and we'll know what we're up against."

"You're looking forward to conversing with her, aren't you?" Andrew asked as they dismounted in front of the constable's office.

Philip smiled, "Admittedly my curiosity, while aroused earlier, has more than tripled now. She is beauteous; and to discover she is intelligent also…well, let's just say that that particular trait isn't as off-putting to me as it may be to others."

"That's because you're not a half-wit to begin with, as are most men, but what about her height? Is that a bother?"

"I have yet to encounter a woman that matches either of us in height, Brother."

"We were blessed with genes of a giant, weren't we?" Andrew quipped as they stepped into the constable's office.

"Help you?" A stout black man asked, standing from his seat in the corner of the room. Another black man came from the rear, wiping his hands on a rag.

"We're looking for Josiah and Moses," Philip said.

"That be us," the man with the rag said.

"The constable sent us. He has a dead body up the road at…what was the man's name again, Andrew?"

"Middleton, I believe it was."

"Right. Needs it cleared away, and asked us to come get you two to see it done."

The two men nodded. Job done, Philip tipped his hat and he and Andrew continued on their way to the hotel.

"You know, I was thinking about what Joshua said, about God knowing what He was doing. Perhaps Joshua's correct. Perhaps you were meant to find that advertisement, God knowing that no other man would have Lara," Philip said thoughtfully.

"I'm not certain I hold to divine providence, Brother."

"Me either, but don't let mother hear you say that, Andrew. She'll think she didn't raise proper Protestant sons." The men tied their horses to the post out front and made their way through the lobby of the hotel and into the quaint dining area. They settled at a table and quickly ordered a light repast. Once the server left the table, Andrew commented on Philip's spiritual view of what was happening.

"I guess if we looked at everything irrationally, there might be a stance made for divine intervention."

"Goodness! I half expected you to continue to argue against my observation not agree with it. I guess I'm so used to you babbling on nonsensically about how we make our own destiny…"

"Well, I can't help it if I think we're in charge of our lives; still, there have been a lot of coincidences of late which can't be completely overlooked; the two greatest of which: we are in dire need of an advantageous marriage and the only woman to meet the criteria happens to be in need of a husband in all haste."

Philip laughed, "And you can't see how God might have had a hand in it?"

"Perhaps, but if we are going to credit God with a part in this, we may as well give the devil his due too. That rascal certainly is having a heyday, causing all forms of mischief and mayhem, wouldn't you say?"

"I'd say that certain men don't need the devil to assist in causing trouble. Most seem quite capable of conflict all of their own accord."

"Very true indeed, but since you don't think the devil assists in causing trouble how can you insist that God assists in assisting."

Philip laughed, "My my, but that was a mouthful. Ah, and speaking of mouthfuls…"

The food arrived and both men grew quiet as they ate their soup, both contemplative. As quickly as the meal arrived it vanished, and soon they were leaving the dining area.

Philip stopped at the foot of the stairs, "I'll start packing up our belongings, and you send Joshua on over. I'll relieve you shortly after one in the morning."

Andrew nodded and headed toward the door.

"And Andrew," Philip called, just as Andrew pushed the door open, "You're right. If I truly think God is assisting, then I have to believe the devil is hindering."

Andrew grinned.

"Be careful out there," Philip warned. "The devil may be a mischief maker, but he doesn't carry a musket—men do."

Andrew nodded again and stepped out onto the boardwalk, watchful as he mounted up and rode back to the doctor's office to relieve Joshua.

CHAPTER 30

Seven in the a.m. arrived quickly. Philip yawned and made his way up the steps to the doctor's door. He'd been alternating between pacing and sitting for the past six hours and was beyond fatigued, but the prospect of seeing Lara again erased away most of the tiredness.

The doctor answered his knock within a few minutes, a grin on his face, "My, my, but you are prompt, aren't you?"

"Indeed, but considering I've been standing guard outside for nearly the entirety of the night, punctuality was a rather simple affair." Philip smiled, removing his hat. "And how is your patient this morning, doctor?"

The doctor headed down the hallway, but instead of going to Lara's room, he headed for his study, "She's dressing," the doctor said, seeing the perplexed look on Philip's face.

"Ah."

"And to answer your question, Lara is just fine. Woke up with a healthy appetite and more than ready to be on her way."

Philip laughed, "Well, I certainly am glad to hear it. I must admit to being more than a little concerned."

"As were we all," the doctor said. The doctor sighed, pointing to a chair across from his desk, "I still have one small apprehension."

Philip quirked a brow, "And that is?"

"Well, Lara doesn't seem to recall you being her fiancé; doesn't recollect you at all, in fact. Do I have a reason to be apprehensive, young man?"

Philip smiled, "I can't fault you for it, but perhaps I can put you at ease somewhat. Did you ever read the advertisement that Lara placed in the newspaper?"

The doctor rolled his eyes and shook his head, "Nonsense, that was, but I'm sure she had her reasons."

"Well, that advertisement is why my brother and I traveled all the way from Virginia. Lara needs a husband and I was, just so happens, searching for a wife."

"And you couldn't find one in Virginia?"

"Apparently I was having as much trouble finding a suitable wife as Lara appears to have been in finding a suitable husband."

"So, what you're saying is, you haven't actually proposed to Lara. You've just been going about declaring her yours? Taking it a bit for granted that she'll have you, aren't you?"

Philip laughed again, "A bit, I guess. But just as Lara had her reasons for placing that ad, I have legitimate reasons for announcing our engagement ahead of actually becoming engaged."

"And I take it that reason isn't any of my business?"

"I think that if Lara wishes people to know the reasons, she'll tell them. It isn't my place to do so."

"Fair enough, but I do want you to know that if Lara has any qualms about leaving here with you, she won't be doing so."

"I completely understand. Hopefully that won't happen."

"It won't."

Both men stood quickly and turned to face the door as Lara walked into the room, "My Lord," she greeted Philip, curtseying. "Thank you again for coming to my aid yesterday."

Philip stood speechless. He wanted to tell her not to stand on formalities, but was having difficulty getting the words past his lips, mostly because he was shocked at how tall she truly was. Most women of his acquaintance barely reached his chest, while Lara was nearly to his chin. That realization made him laugh aloud. Both the doctor and Lara looked at him strangely. He cleared his throat to assist in regaining his composure, but couldn't wipe the grin from his face entirely.

"I must apologize, but when you walked in…well, I must confess that the first thought that popped into my head was that I wouldn't get a backache after kissing you repeatedly."

Lara's eyes widened and she lowered her head in embarrassment. The doctor sputtered a bit and then laughed shortly, "Aren't short on gumption, are you, young man?"

"If I were, I wouldn't have made the trip all this way to marry a woman sight unseen," Philip admitted and then moved to stand in front of Lara. That statement erased Lara's embarrassment and she looked up.

"Well, since you're being honest about your thoughts, then I'll be honest as well," she said, falling back on her professionalism to get past the feelings of insecurity welling within. "Most men would have excused themselves the moment I walked in the room, so for you to state your willingness to marry me even after seeing me is quite startling."

"Most men are fools."

"But not you?"

"I'd wager my intellect is on par with yours."

Lara smiled then, and Philip noticed the twinkle in her eye.

"I guess it'll take some time to prove that last statement, if your expression is any indicator."

Lara's smile faded, "I apologize. I guess that I haven't met many men who…well…"

"Like I said," Philip interjected, "most men are fools, but I can only assure you, my lady, that I am not most men."

"And I can assure you that I knew immediately upon entering the room that you were not most men."

Philip grinned widely. He liked this woman, and he knew that if any man prior had taken the time to engage in conversation with her, most would have fallen madly in love in no time at all. He knew that he himself was spiraling towards…well, like at least…at a rapid pace and he'd not conversed with her for more than a few minutes.

"You realize that we have much to discuss," he said, changing the subject before he disproved he was a fool and kissed her.

Lara nodded.

Philip smiled softly and then turned to face the doctor. He walked over and shook the elder man's hand, "Thank you again for taking such good care of Lara."

"Well, if you hadn't jumped in the river and rescued her, I wouldn't have had her to care for, so it's you who should be thanked."

Philip smiled, "I like you, but hopefully we won't require your services again for some time."

"As it should be," the doctor said.

Philip turned, "Shall we?"

Lara nodded again and allowed Philip to escort her from the house. When they reached the porch, Philip stopped, "Well this is embarrassing."

"What is?"

"I spent the night watching over you, so failed to realize that I only have the one horse," Philip explained.

Lara didn't comprehend his concern and it showed on her face.

"It's going to be a mildly uncomfortable ride with you seated in front of me, but that's the only way we're going to make it back to your home."

"Ah, I see." Lara's face revealed her discomfort over the idea, but Philip couldn't tell whether that discomfort stemmed from having to squeeze both on the back of his stallion, or whether she was discomfited over having to ride in such close proximity to his person. Of course, he knew if he asked her, she'd have no qualms in answering.

"I suppose the only alternative is for me to sit and wait for you to return with my buggy," Lara said thoughtfully, "which, in truth, I'd rather not do. I'm rather looking forward to getting home."

"Ah, she's brave *and* beautiful. Well then, after you my lady," Philip bowed, waving his hand toward his horse.

Lara laughed softly and curtsied, "Thank you, my Lord." She lifted her skirt and walked down the steps. She reached the side of the horse only just realizing that along with being the only ride home; there was lacking a mounting step for her also. "So, how do you propose for me to get upon his back?" She asked when Philip came alongside her.

Philip sighed, "Here I've declared myself a man of intelligence, yet I was sorely ill-prepared to escort you home this morning. If you will permit me?" He asked, placing his hands on either side of her waist, but stopped short of actually touching her. Lara looked down at his hands and felt her skin alight with emotions foreign. When she looked back up at Philip, all she could do was nod her consent.

He saw her widened eyes and fearful expression and realized that, because of the rejection she'd faced all of her youth, no man had ever touched her; had probably never offered such assistance either. He suddenly felt the urge to comfort her and, simultaneously, to challenge every man in Savannah to a fight for the pain they'd caused her.

He smiled encouragingly, then placed his hands upon her waist and hoisted her in front of his saddle. He shook his head when he realized that lifting her required more of his strength than would have been required of a woman several inches shorter. *A weaker man could never have married her,* he thought, *for they'd never have been able to carry her over the threshold. I guess God did know what He was doing.*

He pulled himself up onto the saddle, "Turn slightly and place your hands on the pommel. That will keep you from toppling off."

Lara nodded and did as he bade, "I would have had you upon my lap, but I think we'd both agree that wouldn't be fitting."

Lara nodded again, and glanced down at the ground. Her seating was precarious and she prayed silently that they arrived at her house without her becoming unseated.

"I'll keep this beast at a walk," Philip offered and Lara smiled nervously.

Twenty minutes later, Philip was pulling on the reins in front of Lara's home. He hopped down, reached up, and lifted her down. When she was standing before him, he smiled down at her, reluctant to release his grip, "See? Arrived uninjured."

Lara smiled up at him and was about to reply when shouting from the house distracted them both. Sasha was running from the house, calling her name, followed by Joshua.

"Oh Lara, thank God you're home safe," Sasha called. Lara stepped from Philip's arms, only to be pulled immediately into the embrace of her attendant.

Joshua walked up a bit slower and reached his hand out to Philip. Had it been anyone but Joshua, Philip would have shaken his head in amazement, and was still a little taken aback by the bond between master and servant in this household, but only a little. He'd met these two, conversed with them at length, and suffered their trauma at nearly losing the mistress of the house. These were no mere servants.

Realization dawned, as he gripped Joshua's hand, that if not for these two servants, Lara could very well have ended friendless her entire life. "Good to see you again," he said to Joshua, and sincerely meant it.

"Likewise," the elder man replied, and then turned toward Sasha and Lara, "Think you could let an old man have a hug?"

Lara laughed and pulled from Sasha's embrace, and then threw her arms around Joshua's neck. All Philip could think was that he looked forward to her greeting him like that one of these days.

"Oh Joshua, I should have heeded your warning, and allowed you to take the reins yesterday."

"That may have made no difference," Joshua said softly.

"Joshua's right," Philip interjected, "the person that caused your accident was determined, so Joshua may not have been able to prevent it happening. Either way, we can easily surmise that there will be some other attempt made since you're still alive. Is my brother here?" Lara heard what Philip was saying, but it didn't register through her joy at being home again, surrounded by familiar faces.

"He's sleeping, as was I, admittedly, until about fifteen minutes ago; however, now that you two are here, I'll see that breakfast is made. I take it you wish to have a discussion of sorts?"

Philip grinned, but it held no humor, "Of sorts," he concurred. "I'll go waken Andrew. We'll meet…" Philip stopped, uncertain it was his place to consult with Lara and her staff, and even if so, where such a meeting would take place. He looked at her, half expecting her to appear angry over his insertion into their lives, but she wasn't. She seemed pleased.

"If you want to talk to us, my study will suit," she said, as if his hesitation was only to do with where they could speak privately. She also incorrectly assumed that the conversation was going to be about their pending marriage.

"It will take the staff about an hour to prepare a decent meal, so we could meet and discuss things while we wait," Joshua offered.

"Sounds good. Say fifteen minutes, all?"

Joshua and Sasha immediately headed for the house, but Lara just stood, watching him. She had something to say, he could tell, but he waited until she determined the best way to convey that something.

"I think we'd both agree that this marriage is a likelihood?" She began, tentative. Philip nodded, and Lara continued, "Then you should consider yourself the master of this home, and should conduct our affairs accordingly, wouldn't you say?" Lara squared her shoulders and then concluded, "So, in future, we'll meet in *your* study."

Philip laughed softly and placed his hands on Lara's shoulders. He hadn't been certain of what she was going to say, but that certainly hadn't been on his thought list. Still, that which she did say, spoke volumes regarding her insecurities surrounding marital expectations. He didn't know all that was happening, but he did know he didn't want this lovely lady to feel displaced in her own home.

"*Our* study. I am not trying to usurp your place, Lara. I also know that you have a business to run, something I haven't a doubt you're adept at doing; however, I'd hoped that you would assist me in running our household also. I know ours wouldn't be considered a conventional arrangement, but you aren't exactly a usual sort, are you?"

Lara's cheeks tinted pink, "No, I'm not, I don't suppose."

"Does that appear to bother me in the least?" Philip asked when she lowered her gaze in apparent shame. "Lara look at me, please."

Lara lifted her gaze reluctantly and Philip smiled encouragingly, "I haven't had much time to engage in conversation with you at length, so the only information I have concerning you is from other sources. Joshua, for instance, speaks very highly of you and has relayed the hardships that you've faced in light of your certain…well, attributes, shall we say?"

The hue in Lara's cheeks deepened, but she held his gaze. Philip smiled and continued, "The fact that I am still here and willing to help you should—I hope—impart the sort of man *I* am. Wouldn't you agree?" Lara nodded again.

"Good," Philip said, and without thought, leaned down and placed a light kiss on her lips, "then let's go and discuss what's to be done with the rest of the family, shall we?"

"Thank you, Philip," Lara whispered, wrapping her arms in a

gentle hug around his waist, much as she'd do any member of her family. Relief flooded through her that perhaps, just perhaps, she'd get to keep her family's holdings; that no one was going to take away what was rightfully hers.

"It's been an adventure, to be sure," he laughed, giving her a firm hug, "but we're not out of the woods yet."

"I know, but whereas before, I felt all hope was lost; now, it's been restored."

He released the hug, "I'm grateful I could be of assistance. So what say we join the others, shall we? See about bringing these unusual affairs to an end?" He wrapped his arms around her shoulders and led her into the house. When they reached the study, three grinning faces greeted them.

"I saw that you and Miss Lara were busy conversing," Joshua said, "so I took the liberty of waking Master Andrew."

"Kept us waiting too," Andrew quipped.

"Lara, since you didn't recall *me* upon waking, I'm going to presume introductions are in order?"

"But I'm more memorable than you are, Brother," Andrew laughed and went over to place a kiss on Lara's cheek. "Hope you don't mind the presumption, but I do believe we're going to be related soon."

Lara smiled, "So everyone keeps telling me. It's a pleasure to meet you."

"Likewise," Andrew said, giving her a look of curiosity. "You'll forgive my impertinence, I hope, but you can only imagine our surprise at finding someone, not only normal, but extraordinarily comely also. Your advertisement had us concerned that we'd encounter a hideously deformed creature upon our arrival."

"Then what could possibly have prompted you to come?"

"Divine intervention, of course," Andrew quipped. "So Brother, what's our next course of action? Someone is going to get hurt far worse than a near-fatal swim in the river if we don't stop these men."

"People already have fared far worse, Andrew, as we all know."

"We do?" Lara asked, and the men in the room grew very still. "Did someone else get hurt yesterday? What am I missing?"

Philip looked at Joshua who gave him a barely perceptible shake of his head.

Philip drew in a deep breath and released it slowly, "Why don't we all take a seat. Apparently there is more that needs to be discussed than what we're going to do next."

Lara's eyes narrowed questioningly, but when no one responded to the silent query, she settled on a chair near the window; suddenly unable to relax.

"Lara," Philip began, "do you know why someone would cause your buggy to crash?"

"I assumed it had to do with the fog; that someone other than me lost control of his horse, but then you did say something odd about another attempt."

"You're aware that someone wants your property…"

"Oh, that, yes. But now that you've accepted my proposal, that is no longer an issue. As long as we make it to a preacher and say I do sooner rather than later at least," Lara quipped, attempting to lighten the suddenly heavy atmosphere. When no one smiled, she added, "Perhaps someone should explain what I'm overlooking. That will be a lot faster than a prolonged question and answer game. Joshua, do you know something that I don't?"

Joshua nodded, "What I do know…what *we* know…well, there is no proof of, mind you."

"Our theories are supposition based on highly suspicious, coincidental deaths that have taken place over the year," Andrew added.

Lara was quiet for a moment and then she looked at Joshua, "Are y'all talking about my parents?"

Joshua nodded, and Lara's brow knitted, "But the constable assured me that it was a buggy accident…oh, my God. A buggy accident—like mine." Lara slumped in her chair, but instead of falling apart as the men thought she would, Lara just sat in contemplative silence for a short bit, and then sat back up, "My Uncle and his family? Are those deaths suspicious also?"

Philip nodded, "As are the deaths of the previous constable and that of a Pinkerton agent I had sent ahead of my arrival to make some inquiries."

"There was also a suspicious death yesterday. The man that we think caused your buggy accident was murdered. At least we believe it to be the same man."

"But why? I mean, I knew that someone wished to get possession of my home, but what benefit does anyone gain by murdering so many people; my entire family? What is it about my home that makes murdering an option?"

"We were hoping you would know the answer to that," Andrew answered, "but apparently you're as much in the dark as we are."

"Thanks in large part to the law," Lara muttered.

"What do you mean, Lara?" Philip asked, moving to sit next to her.

"If there is anything of value related to this property, I wouldn't know it, because my lawyer, or rather my father's lawyer, refuses to disclose any information regarding my inheritance because I'm female."

Philip took a deep breath and released a long sigh. He picked up Lara's hand and held it on his leg, "Are you okay?"

"Better, now that I know that I will be getting answers soon, and that all of this nonsense over my property will be resolved. It's been a long exhausting year, to be sure."

"And knowing that your parents may have been murdered?"

"I mourned their deaths aplenty last year, and doing so again would be counter-productive. Besides, I'm too angry at it all to cry. What I want more than anything is to go pay a visit to the attorney again."

"Permit me to speak with him on your behalf?"

"Permit me to accompany you?" Lara asked in return.

Philip smiled, "Of course. This has more to do with you than anyone else."

"Oh, it hasn't to do as much with the information I'll obtain but rather, admittedly, to gloat when the lawyer finds he hasn't any option but to allow me to peruse my father's will and other paperwork. Childish, I know."

"Justifiable, if you ask me."

Lara smiled, "Thank you, Philip. Of course, he may deny you the right to view my father's papers also until we're wed."

"This brings me to my next point—our wedding. Would you be upset if I were to recommend a quick visit by the minister? We can always plan an elaborate wedding later…"

"A quick ceremony will be fine. I haven't any family left which to invite to a fancy celebration. Of course, you may have family you'd wish to invite?"

"All of my relations live abroad, other than Andrew there, so a simple ceremony would suit me also. Still, it wouldn't be very romantic."

Lara wanted to tell Philip just how little she believed in romance, that romantic nonsense was Sasha's favored topic, not hers, but the last thing she needed was to reveal how pessimistic she was about the topic. Instead, she just smiled and said, "I think that romance would be out of place with all that is happening."

"Of course you would think that," Sasha muttered.

"Hush, girl," Joshua scolded, and Lara laughed softly.

A knock sounded at the door, and Joshua stood, "I do believe that is to let us know that breakfast is served."

"Good, I'm famished," Andrew declared, jumping up from his chair.

"You're always famished," Philip snorted.

"Hey, I'm a growing boy."

"Andrew?" Philip said, halting his brother's departure from the room. "As soon as you eat, pay a visit to town…" He stopped and faced Lara again, "Do you have a permanent minister here? It wouldn't bode well if we had to wait a month for a traveling preacher."

"Yes, we have a minister. His name is Dougherty and he lives on Magnolia Lane."

"Very good. Andrew?"

"I'll go and locate the man right after I eat. This afternoon good for a marriage ceremony?"

"Yes, see if he's available to stop by after the noonday meal. Is that too soon for you Lara?"

"No, that should be suitable. Are we going into town after breakfast also?"

"Eager to speak with the attorney?" Philip grinned as they made their way down the corridor to the dining room.

"I'm not certain we'll get anywhere, but yes. I also need to stop in at the shop. Since I'll be busy today, perhaps I should see if Mrs. Harper will look after things for me. She's also heard what happened, no doubt, and I wouldn't want her worrying over my well-being."

"Sounds good. I'm interested in seeing this dress shop also. I hear it's a tremendously successful venture."

"It has enabled us to continue living comfortably since my parents' deaths, so for that I am grateful."

"Yes, but had it not been for your business acumen and your apparent care with money, it could easily have ended far differently."

"Sounds as if you speak from firsthand experience?" Lara asked as she settled down at the dining table. Something in Philip's tone bespoke of a past bitterness; however, it was Andrew who answered her query, as he settled next to her at the table.

"Our father was a poor steward of money, thus permitting the Crown to abscond with our family lands." While Andrew's tone held a flippant quality, he couldn't quite cover his own bitterness.

"Oh my. I'm sincerely sorry. Is there nothing to be done?"

"Yes, pay my father's debt," Andrew said and then regretted his outburst, for he suddenly realized that it sounded as if he and Philip were wedding Lara simply to abscond with her money, a topic they'd joked about only recently. He blanched as he looked at Philip and then at Lara.

"Perhaps that's something I can assist with," Lara said, finishing off her last bite of grits. "After all, you gentlemen have…"

"Proved to be our knights in shining armor?" Sasha interjected with a grin.

Lara laughed, "Okay, Sasha, I will bow to your assessment—this time. Goodness!"

"Lara, I don't want you to assume…" Philip started, but wasn't quite certain if he could finish. While he didn't want her to think that money was the only reason he was willing to marry her, it had been his sole purpose, at one time. He knew what had changed—that someone was trying to hurt this woman; a woman he'd only just met, but could sense was different in more ways than just physicality.

"I learned long ago not to assume much of anything, Philip. My offer to assist your family stems from your assistance in my time of need. After all, as my father always said, kindness begets kindness." She wiped her face on her napkin and pushed away from the table, "If you gentlemen will excuse me, I need to prepare to depart for town. Sasha?"

The men stood as the women departed the room, and then Philip turned to Joshua, "Is she always so business-like?"

"It's all she's ever known," Joshua admitted sadly.

"Well, perhaps I can do something to change that."

"I was certainly hoping that you might," Joshua said, and then stood and began clearing away the dishes.

CHAPTER 31

"My apologies, Miss Lara, and to you as well sir," the lawyer said with his ever-present smug countenance, "but without proof of marriage, circumstances haven't changed. This gentleman is no more legally authorized to view your father's paper than you are."

"I see what you meant," Philip said to Lara, "and I'm only sorry that we'll have to wait to wipe that smug look off of his face."

"I do beg pardon?" The attorney said, his face reddening in agitation.

"Quite simply, sir," Philip said, wondering how Lara had managed to maintain a lady-like decorum when speaking about this man, for he was the most unprofessional professional he'd encountered, "I am well-acquainted with others of your vocation, and never once has anyone required proof of marriage prior to conducting business. For you to demand proof bespeaks of ill intentions. There is information that you wish not to impart and are using the absence of a marriage license as an excuse to keep it hidden. Well, sir, I'm here to inform you that Lara and I will return this afternoon, marriage license in hand, at which time I expect you to have all of her father's papers ready for us to peruse; moreover, once we have concluded our business with you in ascertaining Lara's inheritance, your services will no longer be needed."

"You can't fire me! I'm Lara's family's attorney…"

"Of whom Lara is the final member, and she will be my wife presently," Philip stated, standing. "Until this afternoon. Lara, shall we?"

Moments after their departure, Alfred Garamond and Henry Wattlestone stepped from the back office.

"What are we to do now?"

"I've already taken care of it. They won't be back this afternoon. Still, keep an eye on them Henry, as you've been doing. If they devise another method for seeing this wedding take place; I want to know it before they have the opportunity to execute it."

"Why not just execute the suitor?"

"I'm working on it," Garamond replied, regretting his hasty removal of the scar-faced man.

* * * * * * * * * *

"I must admit that it felt good to see him get his just deserts[t]," Lara said the moment they stepped onto the boardwalk. "And it will be an exhilarating feeling when we can return this afternoon and really bring storm clouds to his day, as he did mine all those months ago. It would appear that you have been a tremendous assistance to me yet again, sir," Lara said with a wide grin and formal curtsey.

"My, my, had I but known it would be this simple to bring joy to your day and a smile to your lips," Philip said, offering her his arm when she righted again.

Lara blushed and she placed her hand in the crook of his arm, "I'm not all business, sir," she replied with a faux haughtiness.

"So I see, and it is a pleasant surprise, I must confess."

Lara smiled. She had not felt this contented since her parents' passing, and never had she felt this relaxed in the company of a man, except her father.

However, she would shortly discover how fleeting her joy was as Andrew sprinted up to meet them.

"Bad news, Brother," he said with only a slight nod in Lara's direction.

"What has happened now?" Philip asked, dread running along his spine.

"Apparently the minister was summoned to attend the funeral of his brother in Atlanta."

"Say again?" Philip asked, uncertain he'd heard correctly.

"I stopped by the minister's home and spoke to his wife. Apparently a gentleman came bearing news late last night that the pastor's brother had passed on and offered to pay for his coach fare to Atlanta, a stagecoach which left only a half hour past. Bloody convenient, if you ask me."

"Bloody Hell!" Philip closed his eyes and lifted his face heavenward. He drew in several deep breaths through his nostrils,

---

[t] "Just deserts" is often mistaken for 'just desserts'; however, both mean the same – to receive what is deserved, whether good or bad (Miriam-Webster Dictionary).

whispering curses. When he'd calmed himself sufficiently, he lowered his head, "Forgive my language, my lady. It's just that these mens' determination is unbelievably resolved, which makes me just as curious as you as to precisely why. What is it about your property that has men going to such great lengths to possess it? For you, I could understand, but a house?" Philip had spoken with little thought as to what he was saying, and Lara knew it, so she remained silent; although his comment made her feel prettier than even her mother used to make her feel. Fortunately, Andrew drew her thoughts back to the urgency of present matters.

"What's our next plan, Philip," Andrew asked, "as our former one seems to have been quashed?"

"We need to find out where the first staging area is for the coach."

"That would be Augusta. It's a two-day journey from here," Lara answered."

"Do you know the route, Lara?" Philip asked, his tone hopeful.

"For certain," Lara stated confidently. "The coach traverses the trail next to the Savannah River, just beyond Port Wentworth," she explained, pointing northwestward. "It's one of the easier trails to follow, as the Savannah River runs a path from Savannah to Augusta. Only a blind man could get lost."

"Very good. Andrew…"

"We need to get our horses," Andrew replied, anticipating Philip's intentions. He turned and raced toward where Philip left the buggy earlier that morning.

Philip turned back to Lara.

"Go, take the buggy. The house is on the way out of town. Secure your horses and be on your way," Lara said, perceiving the rush. "I'll remain at the shop. It would be best for me to stay preoccupied with work. Have Joshua bring the buggy back this evening before dinner."

"I will, and Andrew and I are going to return with the minister posthaste."

"Well, at least before the twenty-third. That's the deadline," Lara said, trying to lighten the tension.

"It will be supper time, but it will be today."

Lara looked past Philip to see Andrew racing along the avenue toward them. He pulled the team to a halt with such ferocity, that dirt kicked up as high as Lara is tall. Fortunately, it missed coating Lara and Philip with dust by a few inches.

"By suppertime," Philip reiterated in a fierce whisper. "I'll not let these men dictate the events of our lives even once more after this moment."

Lara nodded and was about to thank him again, when he clasped her shoulders, pulled her towards him, and kissed her as fiercely and briefly as his declaration of a moment earlier. He set her away, climbed aboard the buggy, and was racing away before Lara drew in her next breath.

The buggy disappeared around the corner of Main Street onto Maple Lane before Lara was able to move. She stood there with a bemused look, uncertain what to make of Philip's cursory demonstrations of affection. Twice now he'd kissed her briefly, once as a brother might his sister, but this second time it reminded her of how her father kissed her mother on occasion.

Is he trying to prove his commitment to our union? She wondered, as she walked along the street towards the dress shop. A few people greeted her along the way and she answered perfunctorily, her mind on her own existence presently. *Does he think that these displays are required so that I'll feel more a wife than a business partner? Should I disabuse him of the necessity?* The moment the last thought popped into her mind another, sharper reply stopped her in her tracks, *No!*

It was but a single word but held connotations far greater than might a lengthy monologue.

"Perhaps the next time I see him, I should kiss him too. Express my commitment as he's done," Lara said aloud.

"Pardon me?" A woman exclaimed, gawking at Lara.

"Mrs. Kendall, I didn't see you there," Lara said, only just realizing that she was standing at the door to her shop.

"I bid you a good day, Lara," Mrs. Kendall stated sharply, "only to have you offer a risqué reply."

"Oh, I do beg pardon, Mrs. Kendall," Lara said, opening the

door to her shop, "I was only thinking aloud. Are you picking up your purchase?"

"Indeed," Mrs. Kendall said snootily, following Lara into the shop.

"Very good. I'll send Mrs. Harper to assist you."

"And Lara," Mrs. Kendall called in a softer tone, "I am glad to see you suffered no ill effects from your accident yesterday. It would be a sad day were we to lose such an exemplary member of the community."

Lara smiled, "Thank you, Mrs. Kendall."

Lara made her way to the back room where Mrs. Harper and her daughter, Rebecca, were working on alterations.

"Hello," Lara greeted.

"Goodness, Lara, you startled a year off my life," Mrs. Harper declared, and then stood to wrap her employer in a tight embrace. "I'm glad to see you're okay," she sniffled, pulling away.

"I just took an unexpected swim, Mrs. Harper. Would you be kind enough to retrieve Mrs. Kendall's dresses? She waiting in the anterior room; and since I missed a day of work yesterday, I'll be in my office for today, so would you see to any customers? I'm certain that Rebecca can manage the alterations today."

"I can, Miss Lara," Rebecca said.

"Very good. If you need me, let me know," Lara said, and then moved to her office, closing the door behind her. The new month's circulars were there waiting for her to peruse, along with yesterdays' receipts and the bill of lading for the latest shipment of Parisian fashions. Before long, Lara was engrossed in her work, oblivious to anything other.

It wasn't until Joshua cleared his throat, rather loudly, that Lara realized the afternoon had raced away.

"Ah, Joshua," she said, stretching the kinks from her back and neck, "thank you for coming for me. Has Philip and Andrew returned from their undertaking?"

"No, what time were they expected back? All Master Philip said was to come retrieve you at suppertime."

"There wasn't an exact time; merely suggested. I'm certain they'll be back soon. In the meantime, Sasha can assist me in getting dressed. When they return, they'll be bringing the minister with them."

"You aren't the least bit nervous?" Joshua asked, wondering at her calm demeanor over getting married, and rather hastily at that.

"What's there to be nervous about? I've been anticipating this moment for nearly nine months, remember? As it was all my idea to find a husband in the first place…well, if anything, I'm rather elated that all of our trials will soon be over."

Joshua sighed, "Well, I'll leave it at that then. I guess that's better than butterflies in the stomach."

Lara finished tidying up her papers and then stood, stretching, "Well, let's head on home, shall we?" She stepped from the office, only to see that Mrs. Harper was still there, reading the paper.

"It's closing time, Mrs. Harper. Did you lose track of time?"

"Oh my, I guess I did," Mrs. Harper declared. "I'll close up, so you can go ahead and leave. And by the way, did you happen to read about the shooting that took place yesterday afternoon, not too long after your buggy accident?"

"Indeed, I do recall hearing of it," Lara said, tying her bonnet beneath her chin.

"It's a sad thing that the owner of the home died also."

"Pardon?"

"The owner of the home," Mrs. Harper reiterated, locating and scanning the contents of the article again. "It says here that the owner, a Mr. Arthur Middleton, was apparently so distraught over having accidentally killed a man that, in his grief, he consumed several bottles full of laudanum, inadvertently taking his own life. Wasn't he the gentleman who was patroning the store not two weeks past?"

"Indeed," Lara muttered, glancing at Joshua, who leaned in and whispered, "Another coincidental death." Lara nodded.

"Thank you for imparting the information, Mrs. Harper, and for closing the store. As it's Friday, I will see you on Monday. Do try to enjoy your days free."

"A pleasant evening to you, Miss Lara. Do go along safely."

Lara and Joshua left the store and climbed aboard the buggy. Joshua clucked his tongue and they headed for home.

"If any more people get killed because of your house…"

"… Savannah is going to suffer from population depletion," Lara concluded glibly.

"So, where did Master Philip and Master Andrew race off to in such a hurry earlier? If it's any of my concern."

Lara smiled, "To deal with another coincidence. It would seem someone wished to remove the only minister from Savannah in order to prevent my marrying. They've gone to retrieve him."

"Ah, I must say I do like the gentlemen. They are nothing like I expected them to be."

"Nor I. They are quite…well…normal."

"I was thinking more along the lines of extraordinary," Joshua laughed.

"Well, I guess they could be normal in an extraordinary way," Lara clarified. "All that I'm saying is that they don't appear to be…"

"Dastardly fiends in disguise?" Joshua concluded with a grin.

"Precisely," Lara smiled. "For which I'm extremely grateful."

"Well, let's just hope you learn to express that gratitude in a less business-like way," Joshua muttered and Lara's brow quirked.

"Are you saying that I've been overly conventional?"

"I just think you'll need to be revealing that sparkly personality of yours before too much longer. We do want to entice the man to stay, after all."

"I do get your point, but goodness, Joshua, you can be blunter than even Father used to be."

"I just have your best interest at heart, Miss Lara. I hope you know that."

"Of course I do, Joshua, and I quite agree that I need to be less formal in my manner. Now, why don't you see to dinner and I'll go prepare to get married; although I don't see the buggy has returned as yet." Lara's brow knitted.

"Try not to worry, Lara. After all, with all the heavy rains this time of year, the road along the river can get a might treacherous."

CHAPTER 32

"What do you propose we do, Philip?" Andrew said, ducking behind a shrub as another musket ball whizzed past his head.

"I haven't come to a decision on the matter yet. I'm still trying to ascertain whether the person or persons shooting are simply poor shots or are merely playing with us; attempting to prevent us going onward."

"If we take a chance to mount up again, we could get a musket ball in the back, or we'll have called the shooters' bluff."

"And this is what I'm trying to decide upon. Attempt to flee in the hopes the persons unknown aren't really attempting to murder us; or stay here in the hopes that they get bored and leave. Are you sure the horses are safe from harm?"

"They dashed behind that stand of trees behind us as soon we jumped off."

Philip glanced behind him and saw the two stallions munching on a small patch of grass, oblivious to the sporadic gunfire taking place."

"We are fair shots, Brother."

"One needs to see what one is shooting at, Brother, to be effective. As far as this standoff goes, our adversary has the advantage of better cover."

"You know, if we were to crawl along on our bellies, we might be able to make it to the horses without being seen. Grant it, the grass isn't overly tall, but it may provide a fair covering. What say you?"

"I say we don't have much of a choice. We must reach the stagecoach soon, and return to Savannah sooner. The longer we crouch here, cowering, the longer it will take to complete our goal and thwart the plans of those out to harm Lara. Of course, we may have to contend with the shooters again on our return trip."

"We should probably cross that river when we get to it."

* * * * * * * * *

"Are you certain that we didn't miss them?" Alfred Garamond asked, pacing his horse back and forth along the bank of the river.

"They would have come along the road from Port Wentworth,

whereas I know a shorter route. Wait, I hear someone coming now."

"Dismount and take cover." Garamond ordered. Each quickly tied his horse to a branch in the grove of trees near the bank and ducked behind one of the tall Georgia pines just as Philip and Andrew rode by.

"Remember, fire *at* them, not into them," Alfred whispered, aiming Middleton's musket.

"I told you once I'm not a murderer," Henry hissed, "so if you plan to change your mind about where to shoot, count me out." He squeezed the trigger on his musket and saw the two stallions rear up in fear. When the hoofs impacted the ground again, Philip and Andrew leapt from their horses and lunged behind some nearby bushes.

"Ah, excellent shot," Garamond complimented, firing just to the right of the bushes behind which their quarry hid, while Henry reloaded. "Now we just need to keep them pinned down." He ducked to reload while Henry stood and fired again.

* * * * * * * * *

"There's only two," Philip said.

"How can you tell?"

"The timing between shots. One fires while the other reloads. And they aren't aiming, just loading and shooting. It's a stall tactic."

"So, we make a move for the horses?"

"We make a move for the horses," Philip confirmed. "We've wasted too much time as it is."

Both men rolled over to their bellies and began scooting across the ground as quickly as was possible.

"Stay low," Phillip said when he noticed Andrew's rear begin to protrude from the grass, "unless you want a hole shot through your buttocks."

* * * * * * * * *

"Um, Arthur," Henry said, lowering his musket. "We may have a problem. I see them crawling toward their horses, so yet another of your plans failed."

Garamond jumped to his feet, "Damnation!" He hissed.

"So what do you propose to do now? We didn't keep them down long."

Garamond leapt from behind the tree and started running across the expanse.

"I'm not killing anyone, Garamond!" Henry called, and then muttering to himself about plans going awry, he mounted his horse, pulled on the reins, and headed back to Savannah.

* * * * * * * * *

Philip and Andrew looked at each other and immediately rolled onto their backs, pulling their Flintlock pistols simultaneously. Garamond skid to a halt, breathing heavily, his face red with both exertion and anger.

"All I want," Garamond screamed, "is for you to mount your horses and ride on. Forget about any plans you had with Lara Esterhaus! Is that so hard for you to do?"

"He's the man that was at Middleton's," Andrew whispered from the side of his mouth, keeping his eyes and pistol firmly planted on Garamond's face.

"He's a raving lunatic," Philip whispered back.

Garamond sighed heavily, threw his musket onto the ground, reached into his vest pocket, and pulled out a billfold. "This is all I have on me," he said, suddenly calm and very business-like. "Take it. Then send any man of your choosing back to Savannah in two weeks, and I'll ensure that you get ten times this amount. All you have to do is leave Savannah behind you and never return."

After contemplating the man's demeanor and offer, Philip said, "Think it might be possible for us to get up off the ground?"

"By all means," Garamond said, his tone irritatingly agreeable. "After all, business should be tended to on equal footing, wouldn't you say?"

Philip and Andrew stood up and returned their pistol's to the waistbands of their pants, and then Philip reached out and took the money that Garamond was holding out.

"Philip, what are you doing?" Andrew asked, his eyes bulging from his head.

"I'll take your offer…" Philip said.

"What do you mean you'll take his offer?" Andrew pulled on Philip's arm, reached out and snatched the money from his hand. "Have you forgotten Carl already?" He snapped, waving the money angrily in front of Philip's face. "Forgotten the misery…"

"That's precisely what I was contemplating when I saw this madman bearing down on us," He barked, snatching the money back from Andrew. "Do you know how close we came to joining Carl in the hereafter? All because we decided to shoulder someone else's burden? Like we're doing dad's burden right now? The only reason we're marrying into Lara's family is to pay off his debt, and don't try to say there's anything more to it, because there isn't. But there is something that's been gnawing on me…" he continued, turning to address Garamond again, "I'll take your offer, if you'll explain to us what makes Lara Esterhaus' house so valuable as for you to have murdered at least…" he paused to count off people on his fingers.

Before he concluded his own count, Andrew hissed, "Eight people—that we know of."

"Eight people murdered," Philip reiterated.

"I didn't murder anyone," Garamond contended.

"No, you just hired someone to do it for you," Andrew snarled. "But the death of the scar-faced man and Middleton was your doing."

"Middleton killed himself because he couldn't handle the pressures of guilt; and the scar-faced man wasn't murder, he was just the by-product of business. Still, if I was a ruthless killer as you claim, why didn't I just have you eliminated? No, I'm just a businessman whose business has been disrupted and I am simply desperate to get it back on the right path."

"So what business do you have with Lara's house and what is she supposed to do once you take it away from her?" Philip asked, trying to keep his temper in check and his fist out of the man's face.

"Lara has her business and can easily board there or at the boarding house down the street, so there will be no damage inflicted when her house is confiscated. But it isn't only her house, sir, rather her family's holdings that I'm interested in obtaining, all of which will be forfeit in less than two weeks when the bank takes possession.

You don't know who she is, do you?"

"You had our investigator murdered before he could report all he'd discovered," Philip replied angrily.

"Well, let me enlighten you. Lara Esterhaus is the great-great-granddaughter of Thomas Salter, a brilliant entrepreneur whose ingenuity can be seen in every corner of every building in Savannah; whose brick-making enterprise was solely responsible for the rise of our fair city. It's a business that was started back in the thirties and, up until last year, was owned and operated by Lara's Uncle, on her mother's side, Josiah Salter. As Lara doesn't know about the business, it has lain nonproducing, since her uncle's unfortunate demise, and that of his family. Additionally, the Salter's owned every square inch of land from Lara's house southward, including the land surrounding the current earthen fort. All of which hold tremendous potential in the hands of the right owner."

"So, once the bank forecloses—not only on Lara's house, but the brick business and the land also—you will buy it all up at auction and become affluent overnight," Philip concluded. "Knowing that there is the potential of all that wealth, why would I accept a laughable sum to forgo marrying her?"

"Because you've already deduced what happens to those who try to prevent my plans coming to fruition."

"It makes me wonder why no one has been willing to wed her, despite her obvious flaws. That much potential wealth generally has a way of blinding most men to a woman's imperfections," Andrew muttered, as if thinking aloud.

"Lara doesn't know who she's related to, nor do most people. Her mother and father kept her in the dark, since they didn't anticipate her ever becoming a part of the business anyway. Her mother married Travis Esterhaus who purchased that dress shop. That was to be Lara's legacy. Josiah Salter paid Ava annual stipends from the profits, but it was to be his side of the family that continued on with the business."

"Then how did you discover…"

"The lawyer," Philip answered.

"That's right," Garamond concurred. "The stipend was paid through the family's attorney, who, after years of watching the level of profit multiply year after year, decided it would be better for him to be a direct recipient of that money. Only he didn't have any idea on how to make that happen, so he conferred with his childhood friends, and over the last several years, we've worked to bring things to this point; and in less than two weeks, all of our planning will come to an end."

"A hundred thousand in gold. None of these new American notes, which will be useless to us back in Britain," Philip said suddenly. "That's what it will take for us to walk away."

"Philip?"

"We'd be able to pay off father's debt and reclaim our land, Andrew."

Andrew lowered his head, shaking it slowly in disbelief. Philip reached out a hand and he and Garamond shook hands to seal the deal.

"We'll send our man, François, to collect the money at the start of October."

"I'll have it ready."

"I want you think on what will happen if you try to double-cross us. We're amiable now, because all we really need is the money, but if you don't deliver, you'll know vengeance unlike any you've ever encountered before."

"Oh, I believe you. After all, I know what the greed of money will drive a man to do."

Philip nodded, "Let's go, Andrew. It's a long ride back to Virginia," Philip said, stuffing the money Garamond had given him into his vest pocket. "At least this time we'll be able to sleep in hotel rooms," he said, patting that pocket.

"*You're* the heir apparent," Andrew muttered as he mounted his horse, his tone full of bitter disdain.

"That I am, which means it falls to me to pay father's debts and reclaim our family lands," Philip snapped, his tone equally bitter.

"I don't want to discuss it further," Andrew snapped, slapping his reins so that his horse jumped into a gallop. Philip sighed heavily and slapped his own stallion's reins. As he rode away, he hoped that Lara would forgive him his broken promise to return by suppertime.

CHAPTER 33

"I only hope that nothing untoward has befallen them," Lara said softly. Suppertime had long come and gone and Lara, Sasha, and Joshua sat in the kitchen trying to maintain a positive disposition, discussing everything except Philip and Andrew's inexplicable tardiness. They'd successfully maintained a steady flow of diverting conversation until the sun sank completely below the horizon. "So many people have been killed…"

"Don't think that way, Lara," Joshua said sharply. "I don't know too awfully much about those two men, but I can't say they impressed me as easily overtaken. Besides being giants among men, they seem quite comfortable with a weapon."

"And, I would just prefer to believe," Sasha interjected, "that they were unable to catch up to the stagecoach as quickly as they thought they might. They aren't exactly familiar with the territory and may have veered off the main path."

"Precisely," Joshua said enthusiastically, "but if they just keep heading north and follow the river, they'll find themselves in Augusta, and then it will be just a matter of finding the minister and getting him back. Even if it takes five days, you will still have time to marry before the bank deadline the Tuesday after."

"You both sound so positive," Lara said with a disconsolate smile.

"I am positive that God wouldn't have sent those men only to have them killed by the devil's spawn," Joshua said passionately.

Lara laughed and settled back in her chair, "You're right, about it all. There isn't reason to fret until we have no further options but to fret."

"So, what are we going to do while we wait for them to come back?" Sasha asked, playing with her napkin.

"The same thing we do every day of every week."

"Joshua's right. It's better to maintain a routine. Keep preoccupied."

"You know what I'd do?" Sasha said thoughtfully, wrapping the napkin around her hand.

"Oh, I shudder to know," Joshua laughed, but Sasha just

ignored him.

"If I needed a man to get what was mine, but no man would have me, I'd dress up like a man and pretend to be an uncle or something."

Joshua and Lara burst out laughing, but Sasha glared at them, "I wasn't jesting," she snapped. "I think it's a good idea, and Lara is tall enough to be a man," she said, pouting.

Lara stopped laughing of a sudden and Joshua mistook her sudden quiet as disquiet, "Now see what you've done, Sasha, you've gone and upset Miss Lara *again*."

"I don't see why she'd be upset. I was just offering a suggestion on how she could get around…"

"Don't say another word, Sasha!" Joshua barked.

"No, it's okay, Joshua. I was actually thinking that Sasha had a thought-provoking idea. I'm just curious why she never mentioned it before."

"You must be jesting, Miss Lara. There is no possible way that you could ever pass for a man, even if you was to shorn your hair all gone, you're just too comely to be a man."

Lara sighed, "I know, Joshua, but if Philip doesn't return in time, I may not have any other choice but to give it a go."

"You'd cut off your hair?" Sasha gasped.

"If it meant keeping my property, I would. Shave it off, put on some of Philip's clothes, pay a visit to the attorney to sign the proper papers, and…" Lara sighed again. "Oh, I don't know. It seems too simplistic as to prove doable. I mean…well, if we really thought it viable, wouldn't we have done it rather than place the advertisement?"

"You didn't have men's clothes that would fit before now," Sasha said automatically.

"Ah, good point. Well, it's an option now, isn't it?"

"You're just muttering aloud now, aren't you?" Joshua said, sipping at his tea. "You don't really expect us to entertain such a ridiculous notion."

"Well now, Joshua, if I'm not mistaken," Lara said, pouring

more tea into her cup, "you said that about my advertising plan also. "Ridiculous", you said. "No possible way it would work", you proclaimed; and yet, for a brief moment, it nearly did work. Someone did answer and was ready to walk me down the aisle. What makes this solution any less possible?"

"I'll say it again, because there is no way you would pass for a man. Even if the lawyer was blind, he would still discover your deceit."

"I don't know whether it will work or not, so we'll just consider it an alternative for the last minute, not throw it away all together. After all, wasn't it Fawkes who said that desperate diseases require desperate remedies[u]?"

"Like we would know," Sasha replied sarcastically.

"Well, we'll just wait to see what transpires over the next couple of days. If Philip hasn't returned by Monday's end…well, I'll leave it to you to shave my hair off, Joshua. Until then, we should try to go on as usual, beginning with a good night's sleep," she concluded, standing from the table. "Come along, Sasha. Good night, Joshua."

Joshua stood from his chair with a heavy sigh, after the women departed, and began extinguishing the candles. He stopped in the foyer and his shoulders slumped, "I must admit to feeling very weary of late, God. A lot has been happening and, well…I thought You'd taken care of everything, but now I'm concerned again that perhaps our hope came too early because it was extinguished too quickly, much like these candle flames. I don't know what You have in mind, and I don't dare question whether or not You'll actually pull us out of this pit full of swords, but you know we'd all be really grateful if You'll just find Philip and send him back this way."

---

[u] Guy Fawkes is credited with the indirect origin of the phrase 'desperate times call for desperate measures' when he declared, 'A desperate disease requires a desperate remedy' in 1605 England after he attempted to blow up the House of Parliament and assassinate King James I.

CHAPTER 34

Monday arrived, all too quickly, and Joshua wondered whether his prayer made it through to God at all, because there was no sign of, or word from, Philip or Andrew, and if there wasn't any word by the time the sun set, Lara was going to have him shave her hair off.

"Well, if I'm going to be forced to do this, I'd better make certain that the blade is sharp."

He was sitting at the kitchen with his sharpening leather and his straight-edged razor when Sasha walked in.

"Good morning, Joshua," she said, stifling a yawn.

"I'm not certain I'm speaking to you, girl," Joshua muttered, sliding the blade back and forth along the leather strap.

"What did I do now?" Sasha snapped.

"See what I'm doing?" Joshua asked, waving the razor in the air for emphasis, "Well, if you hadn't put that fool notion in Miss Lara's head, I wouldn't be preparing to shave off her hair."

"What would you have me do, say nothing? Ever!?"

"That's a start," Joshua muttered.

"Well, I can't help it if I want Lara to keep her home and us too."

Joshua sighed, "I want the same thing, but if you hadn't noticed, we're back to where we started nine months ago, with a deadline and no smart solutions, and the bank is going to be coming to take our home in eight more days."

"I know," Sasha said quietly, sinking onto a nearby chair, "and I'm scared, Joshua, and if I'm scared, imagine how terrified Lara is right now. I mean, she went off to work like she used to do when we were waiting for a response to her advertisement. Remember how I would gripe that she wasn't taking it seriously because she was too calm?"

"I remember."

"Well, she had that same business-like air, that she wears all the time, when she stepped out of the door this morning, but then she turned and gave me a cheerful smile and said, "Don't worry Sasha, hair grows back." And I couldn't do anything but agree with her because I can't think of anything else to do."

"It's alright, Sasha. Don't concern yourself. God came through for us once…"

"Only partly through…sorry."

Joshua shook his head, "Well, we can't give up hope that He will come all the way through before it's too late."

"If you believe that, why are you sharpening your razor?"

Joshua sighed again, "I guess I'm at the point where I only have hope partly. I'm scared too, Sasha. All I can think about right now is what that Mr. Middleton said, about him buying me up at auction and…"

"Mr. Middleton's dead, remember?"

"Yeah, he is, but there are hundreds of hims out there that are just as likely to do me harm as would treat me good like Miss Lara does. You know that as much as I do, or you wouldn't have come up with this crazy notion of her shaving her head and trying to pass as a man. You don't really think she could, do you?"

"I don't know," Sasha shrugged, "I just really don't know what there is left to do."

"Me either," Joshua said, and returned to sharpening his razor. "That's why I'm doing this."

* * * * * * * * *

Suppertime arrived far too soon, but whereas the meal was generally accompanied by some form of conversation, tonight everyone ate in quiet contemplation, mulling over the ramifications of what would happen should they be forced to move forward with this latest scheme.

Joshua, particularly, was dreading the events following their after-meal dessert. He would have to collect the razor if Lara insisted he do so, but had serious doubts as to whether he would actually be able to use it.

Even Lara felt ill in her stomach at the prospect at having to proceed; so much so, that she wondered whether the chicken they'd eaten would remain in her belly. Of all the trials faced over the last nine months, none had created a feeling of nausea as the thought of shaving her head and attempting to pass for a male.

"I don't know if I can do it," she whispered.

"Oh thank the good Lord above," Joshua exclaimed, throwing himself against the back of his chair, his hands raised in praise.

"But what other choice do we have?" She asked.

Joshua sighed heavily and lowered his hands, "All of this worrying is making me feel real old," he muttered.

"We could just quit hoping," Sasha said, keeping her eyes downcast. When no one responded, she dared look up. At the looks of surprise on their faces, she shrugged her shoulders, "What's so bad about just moving into the store? It isn't as if we'd end up living on the street, or being sold to other households, right?"

Lara nodded, slid back her chair, and quietly departed the room.

"I said something wrong again, didn't I?"

Joshua shook his head, "Not this time, Sasha. This time you spoke true, but that don't make it any easier to accept."

Sasha nodded, but couldn't speak. Tears began falling down her cheeks and she just sat staring into her coffee cup.

That's how Lara found them half hour later when she returned downstairs—Joshua staring out the window and Sasha staring down into her coffee cup. She stood in the doorway for several minutes just watching them, her heart hurting for their circumstances. Sasha had been right, things could be far worse than having to move into the shop. At least they would have a roof over their heads and money to subsist. It just galled her that these men, whoever they were, were going to win; that she was going to lose her childhood home simply because…well, there wasn't anything simple about it all. It was an accumulation of so many things—that she was a woman and that someone wanted her home being the top two.

She'd fled to her room when Sasha voiced all of their thoughts, that to hope at this point was a futile effort. Much as they were doing now, she'd done in her room for the past half hour; just sitting and thinking about everything that had transpired and what was to come. Those thoughts had been bleak.

When she was all thought out, she stood and started back downstairs, determined to face their circumstances head on, and then she'd seen her friends, sitting so dejected and her resolve slipped.

They appeared to have accepted their fate, "so then why shouldn't I?" she whispered.

Joshua heard her and turned, standing to greet her, "Are you okay, Miss Lara?" he asked quietly.

"Quite," Lara nodded. "I just wanted to say that, since we've decided to allow the bank to take this house," she cleared her throat before continuing, "that we should just continue on with our daily routine until…well, let's just say I'm not moving our things out or selling off any servant one minute sooner than needs be." She lifted her chin a notch, her features stony. "We may not feel there's any hope, but as long as there is a glimmer, I'll not give up entirely."

"Well said, Miss Lara," Joshua said softly.

"Why not I sit and play the pianoforte for a while this evening? It may prove an entertaining diversion."

"Better than some of those novels you read to us on occasion," Sasha said, finally lifting her gaze and swiping the moisture from her eyes. Lara noticed her reddened eyes and nose, but to avoid commenting, she decided to focus on what Sasha said, instead.

"What's wrong with the books I read to you? I thought you enjoyed them? They certainly assisted in improving yours and Joshua's level of communication, wouldn't you say?"

"Oh, it's better than listening to the Diocese sermons that some owners read to their servants, to be sure, but can't you select books with more adventure and romance? Why must they all be about tragedy and death?" Sasha continued as they made their way from the kitchen to the music room.

"If I ever meet any of the authors, I will be certain to pass along your concerns," Lara responded sarcastically.

"Perhaps read another by that William Shakespeare. I'm not certain I understand everything he writes, but there are some parts that make me laugh."

"He did write a romance entitled *Romeo and Juliet*, but since both characters die in the end, it wouldn't exactly be uplifting. Well, when next I select a book, I will try to ensure it has sufficient comedy at least. Now, how about I play *Black is the Color of my True Love's Hair*? That has romantic undertones?"

"Sounds good, Miss Lara," Joshua said, but in his heart he felt as if nothing would be quite good again.

CHAPTER 35

"Do you really think it's necessary to keep those men out on the trail, Alfred? After all, it's been four days and there's been no sign of…"

"Yes," Garamond said, resuming his work.

"But don't you think they'd have come back by now, if they…"

Garamond sighed loudly, "With only eight days remaining, I am not going to take any more chances. There have been too many slip ups of late; too many things threatening everything we've worked for. If I felt it was safe to presume those men did as they said and left for Virginia, do you think I would have immediately hired two men to keep watch?"

"You think they'll come back?" Henry asked.

"I don't know, which is why I'm taking every precaution. In eight days, the bank will take possession of Lara Esterhaus' estate, and one week after that, we will purchase the entirety of it using the funds Middleton stashed aside for that purpose, and if the Governor does decide to replace that earthen fort with the genuine article…well, we'll own the rights to that land and make even more money."

"It's too bad Middleton let the strain get to him. I mean, all he had to do was wait a little longer and he'd have had more money than you or I combined."

"Yes, well, stupidity has destroyed many a man, but it isn't going to ruin me."

"Us." Henry amended.

"That's right—us."

"Um, Alfred, I'm a curious sort, as you know," Henry said, deftly changing the subject, "so I was wondering if you could shed some light on the fact that…well, shortly after Arthur "killed himself", the constable seemed to go missing as well."

"Really."

"Well, that appears to be the case, since no one's seen him since then. You don't happen to know where he's gone to, do you?"

"Maybe he was called away on business."

"Kind of like the minister was called away for a death in the family?"

"Kind of. Who is it?" Garamond called, when someone pounded at the door. The response came but was too muted to comprehend. Garamond shook his head, and then signaled Henry to open it.

The moment the door opened, one of the men that Garamond hired strolled in, "Mr. Garamond, I'm here to report."

"Well then, report already."

"My partner and I decided to ride toward Augusta instead of just sitting back and waiting for someone that might not show. I just got back. Rode hard to do so. Discovered something that may be of interest. There were four men headed toward Savannah…"

"How does that interest me?"

"Well, two matched the description you gave us.

* * * * * * * * * *

"How long do you estimate before we reach Savannah?" Andrew asked, dismounting and moving to where the minister was inspecting his horse's foot. "Has she come up lame?"

The minister shook his head, "I can't tell. I don't see any cuts. She probably just stepped on a stone and bruised her foot. I think she can keep going, but it will be a slower pace. We may have been in Savannah tomorrow, but it will be Wednesday, at the earliest."

"Still time?" Andrew asked Philip, who'd remained astride. Philip's horse snorted and side-stepped frequently; responding to the tension of the rider.

Philip nodded, "There is still time. Lara mentioned the twenty-third as being the deadline," he said, glancing toward the horizon, "but as desperate as these men are, any delay could give them yet another opportunity to plan; to attempt to prevent the wedding moving forward."

"They would have to know there's something to prevent. As far as they are concerned, we're out of the picture, thanks to your quick thinking."

"Even if they do happen to determine what we're up to, I will do what I can to help prevent any further interference. This writ," the constable said, patting his pocket, "grants me the authority to bring Alfred Garamond and his associates back to Augusta to stand before the judge."

"I'm just glad that you and the judge were sympathetic to our plight," Andrew said. When the worry remained etched on Philip's face, Andrew walked up to the side of Philip's horse. He reached out and stroked the stallion's cheek, attempting to calm the beast, "Your plan was sound, Philip," he said considerately. "If you hadn't deceived Garamond, we'd have had to contend with his gunmen again on our return trip. In which case, Garamond's desperation could have driven him to kill one of us."

"I know, but it's hard to imagine what Lara is thinking about now. She depended on me. I told her that I'd return at suppertime four days ago."

"You certainly wouldn't be the first man late to his own wedding," Andrew said lightly. "And I'm certain that she'll forgive you once she knows what we went through just to get the minister back to perform said wedding."

Philip nodded, but the worry lines creasing his forehead didn't straighten, "We have a few hours before sundown, do you think your horse can keep going until we make camp for tonight?" He asked the minister.

"If we move at a slower pace, but if we push it, this old mare could come up lame."

Philip nodded again, then pulled on his reins and pointed his stallion downriver. He forced his horse to remain at a walk, which was difficult, for what he wanted to do was gallop.

Andrew pulled up alongside Philip, "I've been thinking."

"About?"

"I was talking to the preacher man, and he said that the main route into town isn't the only one. It's the quickest, but in our case, it may not prove the safest."

"Think that Garamond will have it guarded, despite my little show about our leaving town?"

"If it were me, I would."

"Me too."

"I think that the constable and I should continue on the main road. That will put us in Savannah a few hours ahead of you and the minister. If we're there, we could suss out any shenanigans ahead of time. Maybe go ahead and take Garamond and company into custody."

"What if you encounter trouble?"

"We've encountered nothing but trouble, but Garamond has made too many mistakes."

"Yeah," the constable said, "like sending me on that wild goose chase. He certainly didn't anticipate that I'd meet up with you two gentlemen."

"True, but by trouble, I meant armed men," Philip amended.

"We'll deal with it," Andrew said firmly.

"And if you get shot?"

"I'd better not die. You know I'm a crack shot, Philip. If we get pinned down…"

"Make certain you see what you're shooting at, or you'll end up without ammunition," Philip cautioned.

"If we get pinned down, that will keep the bad guys attention on us so that you and the minister can get to Lara's house and get married. If we miss the ceremony, you can always backtrack after the wedding, and give us some assistance."

"I can't find any flaws in your suggestion," Philip admitted.

"Good. We should reach the turn off sometime late tomorrow afternoon."

* * * * * * * * *

"How far out of town would you place them?" Garamond asked.

"We crossed paths with them Sunday. If they continue on at their leisurely pace, they'll be here sometime late Tuesday."

"And you're sure it's the two men I sent you to watch out for?"

"Nothing is for certain, Mr. Garamond, but there were two men that stood well over six foot, both with dark brown hair, both riding equally impressive stallions."

"Then who are the other two men?" Garamond asked rhetorically.

"One may be the minister. If those brothers went all the way to Augusta to locate the minister, then it's likely all would have discovered the ruse about the dead family member. He would have had no reason not to return with them."

"And the fourth?"

Both Henry and the hired gun just shook their heads.

"What do you want me and Charlie to do?"

"You have qualms about killing a man?"

"If the incentive is good enough, I'd kill my dog."

"It's good enough, so if you head out now, you should be able to intercept them by tomorrow afternoon. When you do, make absolutely certain that the suitor doesn't make it here. Any doubts as to which man that is, eliminate them all; and be doubly certain that no one will ever be able to find their corpses."

* * * * * * * * *

"This is it," the minister said Tuesday afternoon, pulling on the reins gently until his mare stopped. She was still limping, but the fact that she was able to walk at all, with his weight atop her back, proved she'd done no more than bruise her foot. "This is the other route to town."

"That's a path?" Philip tried to see past the wild bushes, but it was difficult to do.

"It's overgrown a bit, but I'd say that's because it isn't traversed often."

"It looks as if it hasn't been traversed in years."

"Well, be that as it may, it's still another route and it will get us where we need to go; although the footing won't be as sure…"

"Switch horses with me, minister," Andrew said, dismounting. "Hercules is bigger and will be able to maneuver through the area safer than your nearly-lame horse."

"You able to ride that mare safely, Andrew?" Philip asked, eyeing the mare dubiously. "You stand two heads taller."

"We can't risk his horse traversing a more dangerous path. It steps on another stone, or into a rut, and your horse will be riding double."

"As weighty as you are, that mare may feel it is carrying double."

"Even if I have to walk along beside it, the idea is for us to create a diversion from you two entering town from a different route. So, if we don't happen to get there ahead of you, we'll still get there in time to prevent mischief taking place."

"Hopefully," Philip said, still eyeing the secondary route skeptically. Finally he sighed, "Do you feel comfortable about riding Hercules?" He asked the minister.

The minister cringed visibly at the stallion's size, "As long as his disposition isn't as fearsome as his size, I should be okay."

"He's a giant pussycat, preacher," Andrew smiled. "He and Zeus are best mates, so just let him tag along behind and he should have no difficulties."

"Very good then, but I'll need a hand up," the minister said, moving to stand beside Andrew's horse.

Andrew laughed, and then knelt beside Hercules, tenting his fingers. "Place your foot here and I'll hoist you up."

"Very good."

When the preacher was seated in the saddle, Andrew clasped hold of the lame mare's reins, "Hopefully this—our diversionary tactic—won't prove an exercise in futility."

"I'm more concerned about you becoming a target of Garamond, should he find out you're headed back to town," Philip said. "I know I agreed that this was the best idea, but doubt is nagging at the back of my brain."

"We haven't the luxury for doubts, Brother. Especially as we are determined to assist Lara whatever may come."

"A curious thing, that," the minister chimed in. "Whatever has possessed you gentlemen to aid someone at risk to your own lives? A noble gesture, to be sure, but a bit odd as you hardly know Lara at all."

Andrew and Philip looked at each other, and then Philip replied, "Let's just say that we've encountered these types of men before, men determined to acquire what isn't theirs, even if at great cost to the actual owners."

"And as we don't care for those types of men," Andrew continued, "it gives us great pleasure to thwart any plans they may have."

The minister smiled, "And it hasn't one whit to do with how beautiful and charming Miss Lara happens to be?"

"That does make the assistance all the more sweet," Philip grinned, and then pulled on his stallion's reins, facing the entrance to the secondary path. "Carry forward with extreme caution, Brother, and, God-willing, we'll meet up again by suppertime tomorrow."

"When next we see each other," Andrew quipped, tugging on the mare's reins, "I expect to have a sister-in-law."

Philip laughed and then ducked behind Zeus's head as he urged the massive steed through the overgrowth.

* * * * * * * * * *

"I could have sworn there were four men," Charlie said, Tuesday evening as Andrew and the constable came into view.

"There were," Raphael said, stroking the stubble lining his chin.

"Maybe the other two were just travelers riding alongside these two for a spell. Or these aren't two of the ones we saw the other day?"

"The one on the right is for sure. There aren't many men that size around these parts. The horse doesn't look right though. And the other man—the one just as tall—he's gone. I didn't pay enough attention to the other two to tell if he is one," Raphael said, nodding toward the constable.

"Didn't Garamond say that the two really tall men were brothers?"

"So why wouldn't they still be together?"

"Exactly," Charlie replied.

"The question now becomes, how are we to proceed?" Rafael asked. "Garamond was quite adamant that none of these men were to make it back to Savannah."

"There isn't much we can do about the missing two."

"For now."

Charlie nodded, "For now, we'll eliminate these two. Then we'll head back to Savannah and watch for the other two to show their faces. Ready?" He asked, pulling his musket from the holster on his saddle.

"Ready."

* * * * * * * * *

The constable jerked and slid sideways off his mount, clutching his chest above his heart. Andrew jerked as a musket ball slammed into his shoulder, throwing him backwards onto his rear. His horse reared and he rolled away as the hooves slammed back down to the ground, inches from where his head had been. Andrew released the reins and rolled over to where the constable lay, clutching at his shirt, cursing a blue streak.

"I think I've reached the…" he paused as pain speared his chest and he arched stiffly. After a moment of shallow breathing, his body dropped against the ground again, eyes squeezed tight against the searing heat penetrating every molecule of skin. "Raise…right…" he tilted his head toward Andrew's right hand. "Oath…" the constable hissed, determined to finalize this last act on earth. "Swear…uphold…law?"

Andrew nodded, wincing against his own pain.

"Badge," the constable whispered, and Andrew reached down and removed the silver five-pointed star, stained with the constable's blood.

"Writ," the constable whispered next.

Andrew reached inside the constable's left coat pocket and retrieved the warrant for Garamond and associates. When next he looked into the constable's eyes, the light of life had extinguished. Andrew wanted to do the man the honor of carrying his body into town for a proper burial, but he heard the assassins headed his way, most likely to ensure both men were dead.

With a very abbreviated prayer for the slain man's soul—a majority of which was said while scooting along the ground— Andrew managed to slip into the wooded area to the right of the road, just as the two men walked up.

It was dangerous to stay where he was, but it was also necessary. He needed to see these men to know who to take into custody when he got to Savannah and obtained the requisite backup. What he wanted to do was shoot them down where they stood, but to their fortune, the shot went through the shoulder of his firing arm so he couldn't shoot them even though he very much wanted to.

He etched their faces into his memory then quietly started toward the sound of the river. *All I need do*, he told himself, trying to overlook the searing pain in his shoulder, *is to continue south and try to make it the remainder of the way to Savannah before I bleed out, or those men discover which path I've taken.*

* * * * * * * * *

"Where the hell did the other one go?" Charlie asked. "I know I hit him?"

"Obviously not as good as I hit this one," Rafael said, kicking the constable's body toward the woods. "Let's get this one off the main road and then we'll search for the other one."

Charlie circled around the area, peering carefully into the brush to both sides of the road, cursing his inexact shot. He kicked at the ground when he didn't see anything, "Damn it! He has to be here somewhere. I know I hit him."

"We'll find him," Rafael grunted, pulling at the constable's rotund body, "We *have* to find him. He's the primary target."

Charlie huffed and stomped back toward his mount.

"Where in hell do you think you're going?" Rafael shouted. He looked down at the body, determined that it was hidden well enough, and took off after Charlie.

"We're not likely to find him now," Charlie explained when Rafael caught up to him. "Especially as it's getting dark. It's better that we go back to Savannah and finish what we started once he gets there. *If* he gets there. I know I hit him."

CHAPTER 36

Late the following afternoon, Philip spotted the lights of Savannah from atop a small crest. *Nearly there,* he thought and quickly thought of the hazards they could face if Garamond had men waiting their arrival. He could only hope that Andrew and the constable had drawn attention toward the main entrance into the eastern part of town and away from the northern sector, from where he and the minister were arriving.

"I don't see anyone milling about down there," Philip said as he spotted Hercules in his periphery, drawing alongside, "but we should continue on with caution, just in case." He saw the minister's head jerk up when he'd spoken and glanced over. "I know we're both exhausted," he said, noticing the minister's drooping eyes, "but we'll need to see this marriage tended to this evening if it's going to occur at all."

Minister Dougherty shook his head and then nodded, "It won't matter if you say your vows this evening. I'll need to get the license registered before its official...we'll take it one step at a time. As for performing the ceremony this evening, I'll be okay once I get a cup of coffee into me."

"I'm of the same mind," Philip smiled. "Let's keep moving, but keep alert. While I'm anxious to reach Lara's house, I'd rather we do so without the addition of holes riddling our body."

Philip clucked his tongue and Zeus started down the hill, followed closely by Hercules.

* * * * * * * * *

At the same moment, from the east, Charlie and Rafael entered town.

"There's no way that man you injured is going to make it here tonight, so let's consider grabbing a bite of dinner and a good night's sleep. We'll meet up here again tomorrow morning to resume watch. Finish what we started."

"What do we tell Garamond about the other two?" Charlie asked, as they made their way down Magnolia Lane toward Main Street.

"Let's hold off telling Garamond anything until our business is satisfactorily concluded. After all, the other two men may show themselves in town still, at which time we can finish what we're getting paid for. And as long as we do it quietly, Garamond need never know that we didn't terminate business outside of Savannah. He was very specific about nobody finding corpses, so he may not be willing to pay up if we wind up shedding blood on Main Street."

"Whoa," Charlie said suddenly, pulled on the reins and steered his mount between the hotel and the diner. Raphael instinctively followed, question knitting his brow.

"What gives?"

"You will never believe who I just saw coming down Main Street from the opposite end."

Raphael grinned, "The other two men?"

"Yeah, at least the one looked to be one of the two brothers. Being that tall sure doesn't give him an advantage of blending in, I'll say that."

"Now that we know he's in town as we suspected he might be eventually, we'll need to find a way to draw him out without drawing too much attention. And we'll to tend to it quickly so we'll be able to take care of his brother when he finally gets here."

"Have an idea on how to see that done?" Charlie asked. "Personally, I would like to ride out and shoot him off his horse. See this whole affair dealt with decisively."

"And see our money vanish just as quickly," Raphael replied. "Remember Garamond's dictate—all four men have to be eliminated and disposed of outside of Savannah so that no one will ever find their corpses. He doesn't want them coming back to haunt him. So, if we don't comply, he won't pay. And besides," he said with a baneful grin, "an idea just came to me."

* * * * * * * * *

Philip pulled on his reins, drawing Zeus to a stop, "Something's going on." He nodded toward the rider galloping down Main Street as if he'd disturbed a massive bee hive and the whole hive community was out for revenge.

The rider jumped from his mount in front of the sheriff's office and ran inside. After a moment, the same man, clearly agitated, exited, scanning up and down the nearly vacated street. When his gaze fell on Philip, the man started running down the boardwalk in his direction. By the time the men met up, the man was breathless.

"Has either of you seen the lawman?" The man huffed.

Philip shook his head, "We've only just arrived," was all he said, not willing to trust anyone with the knowledge that the constable was in his brother's company.

The man drew in a deep breath, "I got to find him. There was a shooting on the road out of town. A man is dead…"

Philip's blood began to freeze over as the man continued on about how he was traveling in from Augusta when he heard shots ring out, but by the time he'd reached the area, a man was lying at the side of the road with a hole in his chest. "I saw a man ride off through the brush, toward the river, but I don't have the gumption to go after him alone."

"Go back and mount up. We'll ride out together."

The man nodded and turned to run back toward the constable's office, where he'd left his horse tethered.

"Are you certain it's wise to head back that way?" The minister asked. "I mean we did just go to a lot of trouble to keep you away from the main road into town, remember?"

Philip shook his head, "I know, but it could be my brother lying on the road out there."

"Or it could be a ruse in order to put a musket ball in your back."

"Do you believe in divine providence, Reverend?" Philip asked spontaneously.

The minister arched a brow and gave Philip a look of wonder, "You do recollect that I'm a preacher, right?"

Philip smiled, "That's right. Well, until my brother brought me that advertisement from Lara, I didn't really believe in divine anything, but since coming here, I can't help thinking that God has a plan which includes marrying her."

"Maybe, but men have been bungling God's plans for millennia by going off half-baked and taking matters into their own hands."

The minister countered.

Philip laughed and shook his head, "I see your point."

"Do you? Because if you do, you'd know that if it *were* your brother lying out there dead, then you wouldn't be able to help him."

"Capturing his killer and bringing him in to face justice wouldn't help?"

The minister sighed heavily, "You're making an awful lot of assumptions, Philip, based on the word of a stranger."

"Something I wouldn't do ordinarily, I have to admit, but there may be a chance it's Andrew…" Philip shook the fatigue from his brain, sighed and fell silent, contemplative. After several minutes, Philip looked toward where the rider sat waiting and then back to the minister. "I've made a decision—whether it's a wise decision, only time will tell. Let's go."

* * * * * * * * *

Raphael sat on his steed in front of the constable's office, his smugness waning as he watched the two men deliberate. What they said, he didn't know, but the fact that they weren't responding to his urgency, albeit fake, the way he wanted was beginning to wear on his calm. Then he grinned when both riders started his way.

"We'll follow you," Philip said, as they approached.

"Thanks for helping," Raphael said graciously, and then turned his horse's muzzle back toward Magnolia Lane. "It's only a few hours ride," he added and then turned his horse in preparation to depart, until Philip stopped him with a doubting comment.

Philip looked at the minister, "It'll be dark in a few hours."

"If we ride quickly, we might be able to make it there and intercept the killer before it gets too dark," Raphael persisted.

Philip nodded thoughtfully which Raphael took as consent to his argument, so he turned and bolted down Main. Philip looked at the minister again, nodded, and then both men clucked their tongues instructing their mounts to follow, neither certain precisely what their decision would cost them.

CHAPTER 37

Andrew kept his head down, cursing up a blue streak inside his mind that he wasn't going to get into Savannah proper with this lone rider guarding the road. *If I weren't injured, perhaps I could simply knock him on his rear end like he, or his partner, did me. One shot, and I wouldn't just injure,* he thought grimly, but then something he thought registered and he grinned, "He's alone."

That thought should have had him worried; had him searching the surrounding brush for the other man, but it didn't. Instead he felt capable. Even injured, he felt a certitude creep into his mind that he could prove victorious in a battle against this one man. Of course, had reason been present, it may have tried to argue with him; but reason had fled many miles back and all that remained was fatigue and blood loss—neither of which made for sound strategic planning.

All he could do was hold on to the fact that fortune had favored him thus far, sending him a stray mount in his time of need. The fact that it had taken more energy than he could afford expend to wrangle and abscond with said horse, he quickly overlooked. He merely clasped hold to that small victory which enabled him to move speedily and provide a small amount of rest for his weary and injured body.

While he wasn't thrilled at having his progress halted, even if temporarily, he did feel as if fortune were favoring him yet again, by giving him only one man to fight.

"He's waiting for me, or for Philip," he whispered to himself. "Well, maybe it's time he found me."

* * * * * * * * *

"We're approaching," Philip said, leaning over so he wouldn't have to yell over the pounding hooves.

The minister merely nodded, and only hoped that Hercules would respond accordingly when the time came. So far, the minister had allowed the beast its head; allowed it to simply trail along behind Zeus, as instructed. Until now, he hadn't had to actually command the animal, and he was afraid of doing so, especially as Philip had instructed that he do so without yelling at the big brute.

The minister pulled on the reins gently and fell behind Philip, awaiting his signal, and then leaned down to whisper in Hercules's ear, "You just keep copying what Zeus does, okay?"

The signal came quickly, and both men tugged on their horses' reins as hard and as silently as possible, and then turned down the lane that led to Lara's house.

* * * * * * * * * *

Andrew was determining his best mode of attack when the sound of galloping hooves reached his ears. The man on horseback drew his pistol and took aim, but as the rider rounded the bend, he lowered his weapon.

Andrew started silently cursing up a blue streak again, as he recognized the second shooter from his attack. He'd missed his opportunity to eliminate the one threat and now two threats stood between him and Savannah.

The ache in his shoulder reminded him that, even though the flow of blood from his shoulder wound had long ago dwindled to a mere trickle, it was still bleeding, which meant that he was still in danger of bleeding out; and the lightness in his head made it clear that it wouldn't be days before he did.

With a sigh of resignation, he decided that he was going to have to ride past these two men, so he moved back along through the thistle and underbrush, wincing as briars ripped at his pant legs and the skin beneath. When he reached the area in which he'd left his stolen mount, he was pleased to see that the animal had remained, munching contentedly at the sprigs of grass along the river bank. He wasn't sure how he was going to get the horse to agree to return up the bank and through the tangled, prickly mass of brush that he'd just come from, but if he were going to get back to town, he was going to have to ride. That meant, the horse was going to have to comply with his commands, whether it wanted to or not.

"Just don't give me too much grief, will you?" He whispered, as he patted the mare's nose. "I promise I'll get you a goodly supply of oats, if you'll just get me back onto the main road, and to Miss Esterhaus' home in one piece."

When the horse whinnied, Andrew winced, "Probably isn't a good idea to agree with me out loud," he said, stroking at the horse's nose. After another minute of prayers, Andrew clasped hold of the mare's mane, and hoisted himself onto its bare back.

* * * * * * * * *

Charlie looked past Raphael and worry lined his brow, "Weren't you supposed to be bringing two men back with you? Wasn't your idea supposed to be foolproof?"

Raphael skid to a halt, "Well, now, apparently the two questioned the veracity of my claim, which they failed to let onto until we were well on our way out of town. Now, we can sit here criticizing what I thought was a well-thought out solution for eliminating our problem, or we can ride back the way I came and go finish this once and for all."

"What about your worry over killing inside Savannah? I don't want to lose what's coming to me."

"I don't plan to use my gun this time. No sir, I'm so riled at being made an ass, that…" Raphael fell silent when a horse and rider shot from the brush next to the road and galloped past Charlie and him.

"What the…" Charlie said as the wind from the horse whistled past his ear.

Raphael didn't hesitate or reply. He'd recognized the rider immediately, and even if he'd had a doubt, the blood staining his shirt was a dead giveaway, "Let's move!" He shouted, and turned his horse, galloping after Andrew; determination to strangle the life from him, his driving force.

CHAPTER 38

Zeus had barely slowed when Philip leapt from the saddle and headed straight up the front steps to Lara's house. He raised his fist, ready to pound the door down, when it opened.

"Saw you from the kitchen," Joshua said, a huge smile on his face. "Come on and get in here. We were a might worried at your delay, I must say."

Philip clasped Joshua's shoulder, "It's good see you, Joshua, but we have a situation brewing and need to prepare. Is Lara about?"

"Upstairs dressing for dinner. Sasha and she will be along presently. Come on into the kitchen and I'll rustle you up some victuals."

"Coffee come with that food, Joshua?" Pastor Dougherty asked, stifling a yawn.

"It does now."

"We do need to eat, Philip," the pastor interjected when Philip refused to stop pacing. "It's not as if something can happen at this point without our knowing."

"A quick bite," Philip acknowledged.

Philip and the reverend were finishing up a plate full of supper when Lara and Sasha came in. Both women stopped in the doorway in stunned disbelief at seeing Philip returned, but Lara's next actions stunned everyone in the room into speechlessness.

Philip stood when he noticed the women, wiped his mouth on his napkin, and headed over to where Lara stood. Instead of waiting on him to close the short distance, Lara met him halfway, threw her arms around his neck and planted a kiss on his lips.

When she stepped away, she looked at everyone who, in turn, stared at her astonished. It wasn't until her gaze landed on Joshua's amused one that she broke the silence, "Why are you so surprised, Joshua? I told you that I would make an effort to be more…well… appreciative."

Philip grinned. He wanted to pull her back into his embrace and express *his* appreciation over her efforts, but humiliating her or scaring her wouldn't sit right with him.

"I certainly appreciate your willingness, Lara," he said instead, with a slight bow, and then ran his finger along her cheek, "it certainly is a move in the right direction, especially if we're to wed."

"Speaking of which," the minister interjected. "We can hold the ceremony now, if you want, but I'll reiterate that it won't be official until we fill out the paperwork and get it registered."

"Which may prove a challenge with everyone and his brother attempting to put a stop to it," Philip added.

"Is that why you didn't come back when you said you would? And where's your brother?" Lara asked, settling at the dinner table.

Philip settled onto a chair next to her, nodding, "Apparently, the men who want your inheritance are as determined as we thought. We were ambushed on the road out of town, so it took us far longer to reach Augusta than we'd planned; however, it did afford us the opportunity to meet the man behind this whole affair. Do you know an Alfred Garamond?"

"Vaguely," Lara said, her brow knitted. "He's a very affluent businessman here, but you didn't say what happened to your brother. He wasn't injured in the ambush, was he?"

Philip explained their plan for returning to Savannah via different routes. "Unfortunately," he concluded, "the plan went off kilter when we got back into town this evening. At least the preacher convinced me to be wary when a stranger approached with news of a shooting on the road out of town. I certainly didn't need to walk into another ambush. Anyway, since I haven't seen Andrew since we parted ways, I'm taking the chance that it was a ruse and that he isn't dead. He was with the constable, so he wasn't traveling alone."

"The constable?"

"Long story, but to make it short, Garamond came up with a similar ruse to get the constable to Augusta as the one he used to get the minister out of town. We met up with him on our return trip."

"Goodness. Well, I do hope he's okay."

"He is," Joshua said, glancing out of the kitchen window. "Although, he does appear to be in a mighty big hurry, and I think I know why," he concluded, snatching up a musket nearby and heading for the front door. Philip quickly ran to the kitchen window, assessed the situation, and pulled the pistol from the waistband of his pants,

"Stay here, and stay away from the window," he commanded, sprinting from the kitchen. When he reached the front door, Joshua had already exited and was standing on the front porch with his musket aimed at the street.

"Let me, Joshua," Philip said, taking aim at the street, "We don't want a citizen claiming assault by a slave."

Joshua twisted his mouth into a sneer, but lowered his musket, "I know, but I sure do want to be shooting something."

"You and me both."

Andrew came galloping down the drive, followed by two men, who skid to a halt when a musket ball hit the ground a foot in front of them. Raphael sent a searing gaze at the two armed men standing on the porch.

"We ain't going nowhere. Y'all have to come out of that house sooner or later," Charlie called, and then backed his horse from the drive. He and Raphael moved to stand across the street, a look of confidence on their faces that they'd win in the end.

So focused was he on those men, that Philip didn't notice Andrew's difficulty in dismounting. Not until he stumbled and fell when walking up the steps, did Philip realize something was amiss. "Andrew?"

"Going to need some assistance, Brother," Andrew whispered, pushing himself to standing with his good arm. "I'm afraid I went and got myself shot."

* * * * * * * * * *

"Well, it looks as if we're going to have to move away from murder to just plain stalling," Garamond said, when Raphael walked into his offices a half hour later and announced their failure in eliminating three of the four threats to his plans.

"Not to sound impertinent, Mr. Garamond, but aren't you the least bit concerned that those people will go to the law and report that you're trying to murder them?"

"The law needs more than just somebody's word, otherwise men would hang every day; and since I am a fine, upstanding member of society, there would need to be substantiated corroboration before the law would take an accusation of attempted murder seriously."

"Um, okay. If you say so."

"Still," Garamond continued thoughtfully, pacing slowly about the room, "there do seem to be a few individuals who could corroborate any accusation given the right impetus; individuals who didn't quite eliminate the threat that they were hired to eliminate."

Garamond drove the meaning of his statement home by pulling his cravat from about his own neck and throwing it over Raphael's head, pulling it tight against his Adam's apple, tightening his grip when Raphael began slinging his body around in the chair. His arms flailed one more time as Henry walked in from the rear office, and then he was still.

"I'm not involved in this," he said immediately, "so don't ask me to get rid of the body."

"You just go and relieve Charlie at his post. Tell him I want to see him. I'll take care of him and get rid of him and Raphael. The only thing you need to ensure is that no one in that house gets out to register any marriage license before the bank forecloses this coming Tuesday. Anyone gets loose, you better hope you take some type of action to prevent them succeeding, or you'll never be able to sleep again wondering when I'll be paying you a visit to slit your throat."

"Oh, that's just lovely," Henry said, rolling his eyes. "Nothing like murder as an incentive to get the job done."

"I find it a most effective motivator."

"Well, just remember I'm not one of your hirelings. I'm your partner, which means I have more invested in seeing this plan succeed. And while I'm not willing to murder, I'm also not willing to let our plans fail, especially when we're this close to becoming millionaires."

"Glad to hear it."

CHAPTER 39

"How's he faring?" Philip asked as soon as Sasha exited the room.

"There isn't any reason you can't go in the room. Lara has removed the ball from his shoulder and is stitching him up now. He passed out some time back though, so he isn't going to be offering up any explanations as yet."

"No explanations are required, since we all know who did it and why," Philip said, trying to keep the anger from his tone when addressing the women in the house. He bowed slightly toward Sasha and then headed into the bedroom. He noticed immediately that Lara was as adept when tending the injured as he'd heard she was in running her business.

"Is there nothing that sets your nerves to flapping?" He asked. He saw the corner of her lip twitch upward, but it was the only sign he'd disturbed her concentration. Only when she'd made the last stitch and closed it off, did she flop back against the back of her chair with a loud whooshing sigh and speak to him.

"Unfortunately for your brother, I was never talented with a needle and thread, so he may find his stitches falling out before he's fully healed."

He would have laughed, but he didn't detect any humor in her statement. She was quite serious. He walked over, leaned down to look at her handiwork, and cringed dramatically. The stitches were in no way evenly spaced, and some *were* a little loose, but on the whole, the skin appeared to be pulled together properly, so he decided it should knit okay. If he doubted it, he'd redo the work himself. Still, it was obvious that Lara wouldn't be darning his socks.

"Oh my. So, does Sasha do a decent job at sewing, or will we need to hire on a seamstress?"

"I'm not at all certain that Sasha even knows what a needle and thread is," Lara replied with a smile, and for the first time since meeting her, Philip determined that she was actually transparent. If she was serious, she was serious; likewise, if she were joking, it was obvious she was joking.

"Well then, we might consider adding to our staff, madam, but you really must tell me how a woman who hasn't skill with sewing can own and operate a dress store."

"I added to my staff there," she grinned.

"Ah, a wise woman you are then."

"Oh, indeed I am."

Philip was quickly falling in like with this woman. With her, he suspected, he would always have a sense of emotional balance. There would be no silly prickly games such as his mother played with his father, like seeking retribution for a perceived slight. Nor would she deny him access to her body simply because she decided he needed to be punished for a wrong word spoken. No, he truly believed that if Lara were upset, she would simply have it out with him, and no doubt until it was resolved.

"I like you, Lara," he said impulsively.

Lara's eyes widened in surprise, "Really?"

Philip laughed, "Yes, really."

"Well, I guess I like you too."

"Guess?" Philip said, his brow arched in surprise.

"Can I have a moment to think over it?" Lara said in all seriousness. "After all, I've only had a few, abbreviated, conversations in which to form an opinion, but if I had to base my opinion of you on those short occurrences, then…yes, I can change it to a definite like."

"Well, I'm certainly glad for that, since we'll be getting married…oh, dear."

"What is it Philip?"

"Our deadline for marrying is fast approaching, and while we've agreed it should be a simple affair, I don't see how I can possibly wed when my brother is lying here with a musket wound in his shoulder. He would be quite unable to attend."

"I should think he'll be awake in a few hours, and there isn't any reason why we can't bring the ceremony to him. I do believe that tomorrow is soon enough."

"You'd wed me in a sick man's bedroom?"

"Am I making another societal faux pas?" Lara asked, her cheeks tinted with embarrassment.

"No, it's just that I'd only come to the conclusion that nothing you could do would surprise me, which is a good thing, but yet everything you say surprises me a great deal—in a good way. You're quite capable of turning me in circles without even trying."

Lara smiled, "Well, if it will help any, you can rest assured that I am definitely not attempting to set you on your toes. And as long as I haven't offended you with my suggestion about holding the wedding in here, I really meant that I was quite amenable to the idea."

Philip was moved by her offer, more so than he realized he would be; and again he wondered at why a man would be so focused on her obvious flaws, which weren't flaws in his opinion, as to be blinded by all of her beautiful traits. He suddenly felt as if he'd found a rare solitary jewel, and intended to treasure that find for a lifetime.

He didn't want to frighten her, but he felt compelled to thank her—in his own way. He reached down a hand, and was pleased that she took it without hesitation, although there was a question in her gaze. As soon as she stood, he placed his hands on her waist, lowered his face to hers and placed a soft kiss on her lips. Her inexperience was obvious, but so was her acquiescence. She didn't stiffen or attempt to pull away. Instead she leaned into him and tilted her head, in a manner which bespoke of mimicry. She was doing what she'd witnessed her parents do. He smiled, and kissed her again, this time testing the waters a bit more. Would she object if his kisses became more intimate? Or would she surprise him yet again?

She surprised him yet again, so much so that he forgot her innocence. His hands slid from her waist around to her back and he gently tugged, closing the already narrow gap between their bodies. Fingers splayed along her upper back, he gently caressed her, his mind imagining that his fingers stroked her bare skin. She sighed, and he invaded.

One of his hands slid upward and firmly, lovingly, clasped her neck, holding her head so that she could not turn away from his exploration. She sighed again, and his tongue delved into her mouth, slowly stroking her tongue, motionless with inexperience. He tightened his grip around her waist, arching her into him, hoping to convey that love-making was a two-way avenue; a give-and-take in all areas. As if she'd received his message loud and clear, Lara slid her arms up Philip's chest and wrapped them around his neck, tightening her own grip. Then, with a moan, she began her own experimentation; her first experience with intimacy.

"Oh my," Lara sighed when Philip finally broke the kiss, "no wonder my mother always looked so happy when dad would grab her and kiss her."

Philip laughed softly, "They loved each other."

"Imagine if they hadn't. It would have taken me a lot longer to figure out what your intentions were when you grabbed me," Lara teased.

"Grabbed, huh?"

Lara grinned, "Not exactly, no. I think I'm just remembering my parents. My dad was always sneaking up on mom. No matter what she was doing, he'd grab her, pull over a nearby stool or a chair, anything he could stand on, and then kiss her until she was nearly incapable of standing. I never understood her reaction—until now." She finished that last statement with a tinge of pink in her cheeks, but she didn't glance away, which is why she noticed Philip's perplexed expression. "What?"

"Something to stand on?" Philip asked, a slight memory tugging at the recess of his brain about something similar that Joshua had told him.

Lara laughed, "Yes. You see, my mother was like me—very, very tall. I get my height from her. But my father was not tall at all. So, if he wanted to kiss my mother, he needed to elevate himself." Lara laughed again at the memory, but then the laughter faded, "That's why mother and I were oftentimes confused."

"Lara?"

"My mother was tall, like me, yet she managed to find someone to love her, despite it, and did so before she reached sixteen. But here I've reached the ripe old age of twenty, and no man will even look my way for a second, let alone long enough to fall in love with me and marry me."

Philip placed his fingers on her chin and tilted her face to look at him again, "Are you already forgetting that I'm here?"

"Oh no, I'm not forgetting Philip, but you don't love me. You're only marrying me..."

Philip's mouth lowered and quickly cut off her statement. She was right—he hadn't fallen in love with her as yet; hadn't known her long enough, but he didn't want to hear her say it aloud. Mostly, he didn't want a reminder that her money was the primary reason why he decided to ride to Georgia for a meeting; and he wanted her to forget it also.

After a few minutes, he lifted his head and had to smile at the bemused look on her face, "You're right, Lara," he whispered, "we're not in love, but don't give up hope of that happening. You're an extraordinary woman, and I'm honored to be the man that marries you. That's a good place to begin, wouldn't you say?"

Lara nodded, but could no more than smile softly. Philip sighed and wrapped him into her embrace. "Don't give up on me," he whispered against her hair, and held her close.

CHAPTER 40

"Are you ready to do this, Brother?" Andrew asked the following afternoon, as they waited for Lara to finish readying herself for the wedding.

"Oddly enough, the fear of marriage isn't with me now as it has been in the past."

"You've not been engaged in the past."

"Precisely, because I've been too afraid of making the same mistake that…"

"…dad made with mom?" Andrew finished when Philip fell silent. Philip nodded. "They weren't exactly the best role models for a joyous union were they?" Andrew quipped.

Philip shook his head, "But you should have heard the way Lara spoke of her parents. Even though her mother was unusual, like Lara, her husband adored her, if what Lara says is an indication. Knowing that, makes me feel guilty."

"Guilty? Whatever for?"

"For marrying her without that same type of love being present. She has been shunned her entire life, and now the only reason she's even landed a husband is because of her money—money which we happen to need."

"And you're fooling yourself if you believe that we've put ourselves in harm's way for the sole purpose of acquiring the money needed to buy back our lands," Andrew reprimanded. "You may not be heels over head with the girl, but you are fond of her, and that is a decent basis for a marriage if there ever was one. And if I can see it, so can everyone else."

"She is a most unusual woman," Philip said softly. "I can't say as I've ever encountered the likes of her ever in my life."

"And I'd wager she feels the same about you—a man willing to overlook…well…everything about her? You're an even rarer find, if you ask me."

"Could you overlook her obvious flaws?"

"Of course, but I'm even more of a rare breed than you are," Andrew quipped.

"Oh, of course you are."

A light rap sounded on the door and Philip jumped nervously to his feet.

"Thought you weren't afraid," Andrew whispered and Philip scowled at him. Andrew laughed and then bid the visitor enter.

Joshua stuck his head in, "I just need to check on something, if that's alright."

"Of course, Joshua, come on in."

"Well, Miss Lara is outside ready to proceed, but…well…she needed to make certain that you wouldn't hold an objection to…well…"

"My goodness, Joshua, I can't recall ever hearing you this nervous before. What could possibly be so bad?" Philip asked. "And by the way, you look very dapper."

"Thank you, sir, and what I need to check on isn't bad, sir, just unusual."

"Ah, well, since I'm convinced that Lara is the most unusual woman I've ever met, then anything she needs would most likely be unusual also. So, let's hear it."

"Well, sir, Miss Lara, she wants me to escort her into the room, much like her daddy would have done down the aisle of a church."

"Oh my." Philip sank onto the chair behind him as if someone had thrust a sword into his gut, and he was just as breathless. Tears welled in his eyes and he lowered his head, allowing them to fall unchecked down his cheeks. Of course Joshua was more than a servant to Lara, he realized. This elderly man, who had probably been as much a mentor to Lara as her father had been, had, in fact, become her father when Travis Esterhaus was murdered. The fact that he'd overlooked that fact knocked him heels over head.

"Philip?"

Philip heard Andrew whisper his name, and sniffed loudly. He rubbed his hands across his eyes, wiping the tears away before looking up. When he did look at Andrew, he nearly started crying again, for Andrew sat against the headboard, tears of his own trickling down his cheeks, "I believe Joshua is awaiting a reply," he said softly, and then cleared his throat loudly.

Philip nodded, straightened his shoulders, and stood again. He walked over to where Joshua stood with his eyes widened in concern, and then placed his hands on the old man's shoulders, "She couldn't have chosen a finer man to do the honors," he said, his tone laced with emotion.

Joshua nodded and his lips twitched and puckered as he attempted to hold off his own tears. He nodded again, straightened his shoulders, and then turned and left the room.

Shortly thereafter, the minister entered, "We were beginning to wonder whether Joshua would make an acceptable alternate, for as long as he lingered in here."

Philip and Andrew smiled, and then Andrew explained, "I think we were just awed at the level of affection within this home. Something we're simply unused to."

"Well I certainly hope you can adjust, because I have yet to meet any family as close knit as this one."

"I…we…" Philip amended, "will strive unerringly to be worthy of this household."

"Then let's get to a wedding, shall we?"

CHAPTER 41

Andrew lifted his glass of whiskey in the air, "I'm going to make a toast," he said, but then laid the glass down onto the nightstand, "as soon as someone helps me get more comfortable, that is."

Everyone in the room laughed. Philip walked over and placed his hand beneath Andrew's good arm, tugging carefully as Andrew slid further against the headboard.

"Better?"

"Much," Andrew said, reaching for his drink, "and will definitely assist in making this go down smoother. Now, a toast." Everyone lifted his or her glass. "To my brother and his new lady. May they find love one day and live to a ripe old age in peace, and without anyone else trying to kill them. To your health!"

"Hear, hear!" The minister exclaimed, and then downed his whiskey. "Ah, that was refreshing," he said, settling onto a nearby chair. "And while I'm happy to see the smiles on so many faces, I'm afraid I'm going to have to remind one and all, that this," he said, waving his hands toward the newlywed couple, "was merely ceremonious. It cannot be declared legal until I get to my office, fill out the paperwork, and enter your names in the registry. So, without trying to cover these proceedings with too large a damp cloth— anyone have suggestions on how to see that done, when men are milling about with muskets determined that it doesn't get done?"

"I guess that means we'll be discussing honeymoon plans after this is resolved," Philip said to Lara, placing a quick kiss on her lips.

"It does appear as if that will be the case," she smiled, a bit sadly.

"Chin up, sweetheart. We haven't run this far only to fall on our faces at the finish line."

"Nice analogy, Brother," Andrew laughed, "but how are we to finish a race when the finish line is heavily guarded."

Philip thought for a few minutes and then smiled, "We cheat."

* * * * * * * * *

"Any movement?" Garamond asked, dismounting next to Henry.

"Other than some laughter every now and again, emanating from the end room, all's been quiet. As of half hour ago, the house lit up with candle light, so I expect they plan to be up for a while. What is it you think they find so amusing?"

"I don't know, and I don't particularly care. I just rode out to let you know that I've hired another man to keep an eye on the rear of the house."

"Well, there's another person who doesn't realize that his life on earth just shortened by about forty years," Henry snapped sarcastically.

"I don't need your…"

"How do you think they'll manage to finalize this marriage?" Henry interrupted.

Garamond shook his head and took a deep breath, "They won't."

"Well, they certainly aren't going to just quit trying because a couple of men are standing outside their house. If they weren't determined, the brothers would have stayed gone."

"Their determination in no way rivals ours."

"You'll have to excuse me if I disagree."

"Excuse me," Lara called from the porch, startling both men into drawing their pistols. Lara stiffened, but remained motionless, confident that they wouldn't shoot her, at least that's what everyone in the house, during myriad discussion, concluded.

"At this point," Pastor Dougherty had said, *"I'm the one in the greatest danger. They'll have likely surmised that we've held ourselves a wedding, so their focus will likely shift—to me."*

"They need to prevent you from registering our marital information," Philip replied.

"Precisely."

"And with the constable dead…"

"We'll rely on Andrew when he's recovered."

When the two men lowered their weapons, Lara sighed in relief. She lifted her chin and affected an air of haughtiness, "As you are aware, I have an injured man in here," her tone was accusatory and she saw both men flinch slightly, which made her smile smugly. "I am in need of supplies so that I may continue seeing to his needs. Do you have any justifiable reason, Mr. Garamond, for disallowing me a trip into town? Especially as we both are well aware that only the minister can finalize the paperwork, legalizing my marriage?"

"You may come and go at your leisure, Miss Lara," Garamond replied graciously. "As I am also aware that you have a business to tend to; however, rest assured that I will permit no one else in that house the same latitude."

"Very good, then I will inform you now, that I will depart in the next quarter hour. A good day to you, sir." Lara turned quickly and retreated into the house, slamming the front door behind her.

* * * * * * * * * *

Fifteen minutes later, Joshua exited with his hands raised, "Just going to fetch Miss Lara's buggy!" He called, when he noticed the two men across the street watching him like a hawk. He carefully made his way down the front steps and around to the side of the house, then set about harnessing the horses, making certain that his movements were deliberate and could not be mistaken for anything other.

When the horses were attached to the buggy, he led them around to the front of the house, threw the lead around the hitching post, and then went back inside. A few minutes later the two men across the street watched as Lara boarded the buggy.

"A might bit uppity, isn't she?" Henry said off-handedly when the buggy passed by them, and Lara rose her chin snobbishly and turned her face deliberately away. Garamond snorted.

"I suppose she has a legitimate reason," he said.

"You realize that if she hadn't placed that advertisement," Henry said, reflecting, "then the deadline would have come and gone without anyone even knowing we were interested in Lara's inheritance. No one need ever have been killed or injured—well, no one but her immediate family anyway. But the way things stand now, I have to keep round-the-clock watch until Tuesday, and I have to say, it's going to be a might inconvenient having to rely on you to bring me my meals and afford me time to take a piss. Unless you're willing to hire another disposable gunman to watch the front of the house too."

Garamond ignored his sarcastic request and simply responded to his reflections, "Well, she did place the advertisement, and I foolishly assumed it would be an effort in futility. You know, in a round-about way, Lara is responsible for all the deaths that occurred."

"Really?"

"Yes. After all, had she not be so insistent in holding on to this property, when she could have lived in comfort the remainder of her years at the boarding house, then the bank could have done their jobs, and we could have moved ahead with our plans—no muss, no fuss, no bother."

Henry shook his head in bemusement, "You know, for a savvy businessman that was a rather dim-witted remark." He scratched at his ear for a minute, and then tugged on the lobe, "You know, every person in that house knows we're responsible for all of the mayhem of late; that the deaths of all of those people are on our heads."

"What's your point?"

"You told Raphael, before you strangled him, that the law couldn't touch us, because there has never been any direct evidence of our involvement in any deaths."

Garamond sighed, "And?"

"We're directly involved now, and they all know it." Henry said, jerking his head toward the house.

"Maybe, but they can't prove anything," Garamond argued and Henry shook his head again. *The man is too cocky by far*, he thought, continuing to shake his head. To Garamond he said, "I could take a piss without permission if a lighted match somehow found its way into a few of those dried bushes around the house."

"I thought you weren't willing to murder anyone. In point of fact, you're the only one whose hands are truly clean in this whole affair."

"I know, and I plan to keep them pristine, but you did just happen to hire yet another man to help with this whole mess, and the way I figure it, he's a walking dead man anyway, so we may as well put him to better use than just standing guard."

Garamond looked at the house, rubbing the stubble along his chin, "That's a mighty fine house. I hadn't really thought about torching it."

"Well then, perhaps we can find another way for your hired man to eliminate the persons inside."

"Perhaps."

"Too many fingers in there can point a finger in our direction," Henry persisted.

"I'll go have a chat with…whatever his name is…suss out his willingness to eliminate threats."

* * * * * * * * *

"They really don't perceive me as a threat, do they?" Lara asked, moving away from her vantage point at the window.

"The only threat you pose, is that you are the heir-apparent to the fortune that they want. Other than that, you are no more than a woman in their eyes," Philip said, taking her by the elbow and guiding her to a nearby chair, "And while I understand that you wanted to ensure your counterpart left without being detained, you really should stay away from the windows. If they discover our deceit…well, we already know how Garamond handles deception."

"Violently," Andrew concluded, rubbing gently at the bandage covering his wound, "but if they wanted you dead, their chance to do it successfully and without implicating themselves, past long ago. Their only hope now is that they can prevent your marriage becoming legal, and we are already in the process of quashing that hope."

"But how will we know that our ruse is successful?" Lara asked, ringing her hands in her lap.

"Perhaps I'll go make some Chamomile tea," Joshua offered. "It's good for the nerves."

"Thanks Joshua," Philip said.

"Sasha, you can come give me a hand," Joshua said when he noticed the attendant hovering over Lara, "you're gonna make Miss Lara a nervous wreck."

Andrew laughed when Sasha pouted, but followed Joshua quietly from the room.

Philip moved his chair next to Lara's, "The plan is sound, and the fact that the minister managed to crawl into your clothes and get past Garamond undetected offers us a hope that we've all not felt in many a day, I'd wager."

"And as soon as he registers your marriage," Andrew continued, "he will come back here and announce it to all and sundry. That'll put an end to this whole affair."

"You're right," Lara smiled. "Everything is going to be just fine."

* * * * * * * * * *

"There's more blokes in there as I'm able to dispatch on my own," the hired gun informed Garamond, "but if you was willing to pay out a bit more coin, I know a few o' my friends that might just be willing to help out."

"I'm willing to pay what needs to be paid," Garamond said. "So, go collect your friends and be back here within the hour. It's time to put an end to this whole affair."

"Sure thing, Guv'nor."

CHAPTER 42

The minister dipped the feather into the ink well and scratched down the date, *September 17th, 1800,* followed by *His Lordship, Philip Bensley, Fifth Earl of Ripon,* beneath the column indicating the male in the marriage. He then dipped his quill in again, and beneath the column for the female party, he scratched—with an enormous smile on his face—*Lara Charlotte Esterhaus.* When that was concluded, he sat back with a sigh, and then reached into his desk and retrieved a blank marriage license. Within another ten minutes, he'd completed that form. He blew at the ink lightly until it was dry enough, and then headed back out to the street. It was time to put an end to all of the nonsense surrounding Lara and her family.

He boarded Lara's buggy, but although he was still wearing one of her dresses, he deliberately left her veil-covered hat on the seat beside him. There was no longer any need to conceal his identity. In fact, it was important that he let Alfred Garamond and company know that they'd lost. Lara's marriage was now legal. They could no longer hope that the bank would foreclose.

He clucked his tongue and headed back down the street, sighing when half-dozen men rode by at full gallop, their whooping and hollering causing the mares to shy and rear. He held tight to the reins until the mares calmed themselves, muttering words that he hoped God wouldn't take offense at. When the mares were ready to proceed, he continued on down Main Street, whistling a happy tune.

* * * * * * * * *

"Do you think it would be possible for them to signal their arrival any more loudly," Henry asked, watching the half-dozen men galloping toward them.

Garamond closed his eyes and breathed in deeply through his nostrils, "I guess I didn't add "quietly" to my instructions for returning with his friends."

"I guess not."

"I'm back Gov'nor, and it didn't take me no hour to find 'em neither." The Brit said cockily, jerking his head toward his five mates.

"I see that. Well, well done."

"Want we should go ahead an' take care of business?" The man asked, dismounting. He pulled two pistols from the waist of his pants, and waved them in the air, indicating his enthusiasm for seeing the deed done.

Garamond rolled his eyes and shook his head at his buffoonery, but then nodded his consent.

The man let out a whoop and a holler, and his men followed his lead, leaping from their horses. Each pulled two pistols from his pants and flailed them in the air, and then they all headed down the drive, more than willing to commit murder.

"There's no reason for us to remain here," Garamond said.

"You don't want to make certain that there aren't any more errs in your plans?" Henry asked, uncertain whether these clowns would indeed see the deed successfully done.

"I suppose we could wait."

* * * * * * * * *

"How many weapons do you have, Joshua?"

"Enough to see this lot tended to," he said, heading for the master's gun cabinet, "but it will be a short fight if we take too long to load 'em all."

"The women can take care of that," Philip said, but was disappointed when Joshua started shaking his head.

"No sir, they can't. Not either of them can load a musket."

"Well, that's something we'll have to rectify in future," Philip said, starting on prepping the first musket. "Not that I plan to engage in any more gunfights after this."

"I was thinking along those same lines not a month past," Joshua said, adeptly prepping a second musket.

"Well, I have two muskets ready, plus these two, will give us four shots," Philip said as footfalls hit the porch.

"That won't be enough to take out six men," Joshua said, aiming at the front portal, "not unless we gets lucky enough to take out two with one shot."

Philip tried not to think of the consequence should either remaining adversary manage to get in the house and get a shot off before he or Joshua could reload a weapon. He saw Lara's head peer from around the bedroom door, "Get back in there and shut the door," he yelled, as the front door splintered open, and men filed in, yelling exultantly.

* * * * * * * * * *

"What in the name of all that is holy, is going on in there!?" The minister yelled, pulling the mares to a halt and leaping from the buggy.

Alfred's eyes bulged from their sockets at seeing Pastor Dougherty stomping toward him in a lady's gown. When Henry turned at the exclamation, his eyes bulged also, and he started sputtering incomprehensibly.

"I'm here to tell you, Garamond, that their marriage is legal. It's time to put this nonsense to a stop."

Garamond's gaze went from astonishment to fury in less than a blink, "No!" He railed. "They'll both die in there, and when they do, the bank will seize all of Lara's property! Nothing has changed, except maybe that you're still alive." He pulled his weapon and aimed it at the minister's chest.

* * * * * * * * * *

Shots rang out through the foyer, hitting the first four men that entered the house, but with their weapons empty, Philip's concern was that the other two—content to hover on the porch for the time being—would regain their courage and storm them before they could get the muskets reloaded.

As it was, their fortune held, and the men hesitated just long enough, so that when they moved to enter, Philip and Joshua were ready.

A shot rang out, startling the two men, "Stay focused on the door," Philip commanded, "We'll find out where that shot came from soon enough."

Joshua nodded, breathing steadily through his nostrils, "Don't you worry none, Master Philip. I've been ready for this day, cause I knew I'd have to kill someone real soon."

* * * * * * * * * *

"I missed," Lara cried, as Alfred and Henry took shelter behind their horses.

"That's okay, Lara," Andrew said, leaning against the wall. "The important thing is that you gave Pastor Dougherty time to take cover too. Now, follow my instructions for reloading carefully, so that we can keep the men outside unbalanced until I can step out there with Philip and Joshua and arrest those sons of bitches. Excuse my language."

* * * * * * * * *

Twenty minutes later, the smoke cleared, and Andrew did as he said he would, wearing the constable's badge and waving the writ in the air—with his good arm.

Defeated, Alfred and Henry laid down their weapons and were shot dead, by Joshua and Philip, when they made a dash for their horses and attempted to escape.

The whole unpleasant affair had finally come to a close, which left only one task to tend to.

EPILOGUE

With a grin the size of Savannah, Lara strolled into the offices of Bingham, Barley, and Baxter early the next morning, on the arm of her husband, and tossed their marriage license on Mr. Bingham's desk.

Muttering curses beneath his breath, the lawyer collected all of the paperwork related to Lara's estate and within half hour, she and Philip strolled from the law offices wealthier than either had ever dreamed possible.

When they reached the boardwalk in front of her store, Lara threw her arms around Philip's neck and gave him a thorough kiss, for all of Savannah to see, scattering their papers all over the boardwalk.

"You know, my lady," Philip said, keeping his hands on her waist, "we can plan our honeymoon now."

Lara smiled, "Can we go anywhere?"

"Anywhere your heart desires. You do trust Mrs. Harper with the running of the store, correct?"

"Absolutely."

"Then where would my lady like to go?"

"I thought perhaps we could journey to England," Lara said shyly. "Maybe see about acquiring the land you lost?"

Philip opened his mouth to speak, but no words came forth. Instead he swept Lara into his embrace, hugging her tight. After a few moments, he returned her feet to the ground and whispered against her hair, "I think I'm falling in love with you."

"Really?" Lara whispered in return.

"Yes, really."

He leaned back and looked into her gaze, misting over with tears. She nodded, but couldn't speak. Instead, she leaned up and kissed him again, this time expressing not joy over their victory, but that she was falling in love with him also. When she finally moved away, she glanced into the window of her shop and saw the translucent images of her mother and father standing there with tears of joy in their eyes.

"I love you," she whispered, as the images slowly faded.

She wiped her eyes and laughed, bending to pick up their papers. Philip bent to assist, and the two chatted blissfully, ignoring the glances of passersby. It was their world now, and Lara intended to live happily ever after.